"Your fellow Jake is a real challenge."

"He's not mine," Dani replied with feeling.

"Really?" Evelyn arched her eyebrows. "That's good news. I've been puzzling over him a lot, especially after you told me about the notes your mother's been getting."

"What's that got to do with Jake?"

"Consider the facts. He's from L.A. and he arrived here soon after you did. He got a job where you work. He moved in next door. Is this all coincidence?"

A chill went down Dani's spine. Jake *was* conveniently around all the time.

Evelyn continued. "I have no proof. Jake may be perfectly harmless."

No, Dani thought, remembering last night, *the man is definitely not harmless.*

Dear Reader,

Evelyn A. Crowe's legion of fans will be delighted to learn that she has penned our Women Who Dare title for November. In *Reunited,* gutsy investigative reporter Sydney Tanner learns way more than she bargained for about rising young congressman J. D. Fowler. Generational family feuds, a long-ago murder and a touch of blackmail are only a few of the surprises in store for Sydney—and you—as the significance of the heroine's discoveries begins to shape this riveting tale.

Popular Superromance author Sharon Brondos has contributed our final Woman Who Dare title for 1993. In *Doc Wyoming,* taciturn sheriff Hal Blane wants nothing to do with a citified female doctor. But Dixie Sheldon becomes involved with Blane's infamous family in spite of herself, and her "sentence" in Wyoming is commuted to a romance of the American West.

More Women Who Dare titles will be coming your way in 1994. Patricia Chandler and Tracy Hughes have two great, daring stories lined up for you in the spring. And watch for titles by Vicki Lewis Thompson, Margaret Chittenden and Margot Dalton this month and next as we begin to draw the curtain on '93!

Marsha Zinberg,
Senior Editor

ONLY IN THE MOONLIGHT

Vicki Lewis Thompson

Harlequin Books

TORONTO • NEW YORK • LONDON
AMSTERDAM • PARIS • SYDNEY • HAMBURG
STOCKHOLM • ATHENS • TOKYO • MILAN
MADRID • WARSAW • BUDAPEST • AUCKLAND

ISBN 0-373-70572-7

ONLY IN THE MOONLIGHT

ABOUT THE AUTHOR

Vicki Lewis Thompson lives in Arizona and is particularly fascinated by the area around the small town of Tubac, which is where she's set this story. "There's a real contrast about the place," says Vicki. "The valley is so peaceful now, it's hard to imagine its violent frontier history."

Books by Vicki Lewis Thompson

HARLEQUIN SUPERROMANCE

211–BUTTERFLIES IN THE SUN
269–GOLDEN GIRL
326–SPARKS
389–CONNECTIONS
497–CRITICAL MOVES

HARLEQUIN TEMPTATION

444–YOUR PLACE OR MINE
474–IT HAPPENED ONE WEEKEND
496–ANYTHING GOES
539–FOOLS RUSH IN

Don't miss any of our special offers. Write to us at the following address for information on our newest releases.

Harlequin Reader Service
P.O. Box 1397, Buffalo, NY 14240
Canadian address: P.O. Box 603,
Fort Erie, Ont. L2A 5X3

For Margaret Falk, who has taught me
to cherish things that go bump in the night

Special thanks to Robert Tims
for valuable information on the
art of creating channel jewelry.

PROLOGUE

A scream sliced through Dani Goodwin's dreams like a wire through butter. She sat up in bed, her heart pounding. Then she remembered the peacocks. Her landlord had told her that they would cry at night. In fact, a former tenant had once pushed all the furniture against the front door because she thought a woman was being murdered nearby.

Fighting the urge to do likewise and barricade the door, Dani lay back, her eyes wide open. The eerie sound came again. Definitely peacocks. She took a deep breath and tried to think of something calming, but instead, she remembered the damn notes. When the sun was shining, she could laugh them off as a prank, but tonight, in the cool light from a crescent moon, laughter didn't come.

There had been two notes mailed to her mother—two sheets of white paper, neatly folded in thirds, containing quotes from Helen Goodwin's latest bestseller *The Unvanquished*. Dani knew the quotes by heart, though she'd tried to forget them. *Sarah contemplated her child, a miracle born of love. She would die if anything happened to this sweet innocent.* The second quote was more specific. *Sarah felt no fear for herself, but searched frantically for a way to protect her child, knowing it would be hopeless to try.*

Dani was Helen Goodwin's only child.

CHAPTER ONE

DANI WOKE in the early dawn to the sound of the peacocks, hungry for breakfast, stamping on the tin roof over her head. She swung her feet to the rag rug beside the bed and fumbled for the robe she'd tossed on a chair. The landlord had warned her that peacocks got up early, but damn, she could barely see.

"Coming!" she called, and stubbed her bare toe on the packing box holding her lapidary equipment. All you have to do is feed the peacocks, her landlord had said. The job had sounded fun and exotic yesterday when she'd rented the place.

She unlocked the front door and stepped out on the rough boards of the porch. The couple who occupied the other small house on the property weren't up, but the landlord had explained that the peacocks only stamped on her roof, not theirs. Lucky her. The peacocks flapped to the ground and pranced up the steps toward her, their iridescent heads bobbing, their tails sweeping behind them. She called them all peacocks, but actually two of the three were peahens.

She flipped the wooden lid off a barrel beside the door and scooped up handfuls of seed. "It's raining grain!" she called, throwing it over their heads to the yard beyond. They scrabbled back down the steps and began pecking at the ground like giant chickens. Dani threw out some more; the landlord had said several scoops.

As she dusted off her hands, a train whistle sounded in the distance. How pastoral, she thought, until the engine blasted across the tracks just down the road. She held her hands over her ears as the porch boards shook under her feet. The noise receded and the whistle shrilled again.

She made a megaphone of her hands. "That's okay! I was up!" She'd noticed the tracks yesterday but hadn't thought to ask about the train. In a lazy little town like Tubac, Arizona, she'd imagined it would be a weekly milk run. Middle of the day. Apparently not.

Quiet settled over the yard, except for the bubbling of the Santa Cruz River, burdened with March snow-melt and spring rain, that ran behind her house. Taking a deep breath of the cool morning air, which smelled of damp grass and new leaves, Dani thought that the air alone was worth the move from L.A.

The sky grew lighter, providing a luminescent background for the gnarled branches of the giant mesquite that grew next to Dani's porch. Besides the peacocks, she'd been fascinated by a climbing cactus that twined through the branches of the tree. According to the landlord, one of these spring nights the cactus would burst forth with white blooms, perhaps as many as two hundred, which would all fade with the dawn. Dani had decided that the cracked stucco exterior of the house and its ancient bathroom fixtures paled in importance next to the shimmering elegance of a peacock's tail and cactus flowers blooming under the light of the moon.

Stretching both arms over her head, she yawned in contentment. She didn't have to report for her waitressing job until eleven. Maybe she'd allow herself the luxury of going back to bed.

The sound of a telephone ringing in the other house broke the silence, and a light snapped on in her neighbors' kitchen. Someone was calling the young couple next door at six in the morning. Apparently nobody slept late around here.

She was about to turn and go inside when the door of the house opened and the husband's tousled head appeared. Dani had a sinking sensation in her stomach. Surely her mother wouldn't . . . Dani had emphasized that the number was for emergencies only.

"Dani?" the man called. "It's for you. Your mother."

Brittle stubs of dead grass bit into the bottoms of her feet as she hurried next door. She began her apology when she was within twenty feet of him. "I'm sorry, Ron. I didn't expect her to use your number."

"It's okay. I have to get ready for work, and with the baby almost due, Liane doesn't sleep much."

Dani gave him a nervous smile and picked up the phone. Maybe there really was an emergency. "Mom?"

"I had to hear your voice to convince myself you got through the night in one piece."

Dani's concern boiled over into anger. "It's six o'clock in the morning." She kept her voice low, but it vibrated with fury. "You got these poor people out of bed."

"You said he worked for the mines. Miners always get up early. And you have those peacocks. Don't you have to feed them or something? I thought everyone would be up."

"Mom, that's not the point. The point is—" She paused and rubbed her forehead. Just what was the point?

"The point is that someone is plotting to harm you and you're disregarding it. I read through those notes again last night and I didn't sleep a wink. I think you should come back here, where I can be sure you're well protected. Your father would have wanted you to do that."

Dani felt a headache coming on. "Mom, Daddy's gone, and we each have to get on with our lives." Days ago she'd faced the horrible possibility that her mother, saturated with loneliness, had concocted the threatening notes herself, just to manipulate Dani into moving back into the Malibu beach house with her.

"Dani, I'm so worried about you. These notes—"

"I'll be fine. Nobody except you knows I'm down here, so if there is any danger—"

"There *is*."

"Then I'm better off out of L.A. Listen, Mom, I'm standing in my neighbors' kitchen in my bathrobe with my hair not combed or anything. I'll have a phone hooked up today, and I'll call you with the number tonight after work, okay?"

"Maybe you should install an alarm in your little house. And program your phone so all you have to do is push one button to get 911, and—"

"Take care, Mom. I have to go."

"Dani—"

"I love you. Goodbye." Dani hung up the wall telephone and stood there for a minute, praying it wouldn't ring again. When it didn't, she sighed and turned to Ron, who was making coffee. "Thank you. This won't happen again."

"No problem." He gazed at her. "I didn't mean to eavesdrop, but what was that about your being in danger?"

Dani waved her hand dismissively. "My mother was widowed two years ago, and I'm all she has left. I'm afraid she's turned paranoid on me."

"Oh."

"Part of my reason for moving here from L.A. was to force her to get on with her life and quit clinging so tightly to mine. That may sound cold, but I—"

Ron shook his head. "Liane and I have had some experience along those lines. It's tough to know what to do. How about staying for coffee?"

"Please stay," Liane said, appearing in the kitchen doorway, a bathrobe barely meeting over her enormous stomach. "We can sit and talk about mothers."

Dani rolled her eyes.

"This is the first grandchild." Liane patted her stomach. "My mother is driving us nuts, insisting we should move to Tucson so we'll be closer to her."

Ron sighed. "And she has a point."

"So you're moving?" Dani had liked the idea of the couple nearby. Without them...

"Not for another month or so," Ron said. "We had to give the landlord notice or pay for an extra month. But we're packing, a little at a time."

"Well...I guess having your mom around when the baby's born would be a good idea, especially if you get along better than my mother and I do."

Liane chuckled. "We'll see. She's already picked out names."

"Oh." Dani gave her a sympathetic look.

"So stay for coffee and we'll commiserate about meddling mothers."

"Sure, why not."

An hour later, Dani picked her way across the yard to her own house. Over coffee and muffins she'd successfully avoided telling Ron and Liane anything specific about her mother. Dani had noticed the bookshelves lined with current novels, several of them by her mother. Embarrassment kept her from confessing to her new friends that bestselling-author Helen Goodwin might be losing her grip. She'd stopped writing, stopped seeing friends. And now these strange notes...

Her mother's hysteria had led Dani to decide that now was the time to make a change. And she'd always fantasized about setting up her jewelry-making business in an artistic community like Tubac.

SEVERAL HOURS after her early-morning phone call, Dani drove her 1965 Mustang convertible across the bridge spanning the Santa Cruz. She navigated the dirt roads through town and turned onto the paved driveway leading to the Canada Verde Country Club. Her mother had suggested that Dani apply for a job at its restaurant, and Dani had discovered the club was one of the few places in town hiring.

Much as it had galled her to act on her mother's suggestion, she'd needed the job. She couldn't expect jewelry-making to support her just yet, and the country club was a decent place to work. She remembered it from childhood vacations, when her parents had taken her there.

The country club hadn't changed much since she was a kid. Whitewashed buildings topped with red tile roofs rambled over several verdant acres of the Santa Cruz Valley. The river lay east of the country club, and beyond that the Santa Ritas towered ten thousand feet into the cobalt sky. The raw majesty of the mountain range served as a backdrop for the manicured landscape surrounding the whitewashed buildings. She recalled that there had always been something in bloom—bougainvillea, geraniums, roses, petunias . . .

The country club itself was a converted hacienda, and Dani had always loved the restaurant, which had once been the stable. The atmosphere remained, with booths designed to look like stalls, and saddles instead of stools ringing the curved mahogany bar.

Wearing her uniform of a Mexican peasant blouse and full red skirt over several petticoats, her long brunette hair tucked into a net at her nape, Dani fit right in. She could just imagine how her sophisticated L.A. friends and customers would laugh to see her dressed this way! If they recognized her that is. The pair of kachina earrings she wore were all that they'd find familiar.

Fashioned in a Zuni Indian style, they incorporated turquoise, coral and obsidian into a design separated by thin silver wires, or channels. The technique had become her trademark, and she'd earned quite a following in the Los Angeles area. But that business was now lost to her, because in deference to her mother's fears, she'd told everyone she was going on an extended trip around the country.

Dani parked the convertible in the employees' lot near the kitchen door. She could already smell chilies and onions simmering in tomato sauce. Being only thirty miles from the Mexican border, the restaurant specialized in Mexican food. With one last look at the purple slopes of the Santa Ritas, Dani walked through the kitchen door.

"Dani!" Paula Jordan hurried toward her. Her blond hair, cut in a Dutch-boy bob, flapped like a beagle's ears as she propelled her sturdy body across the kitchen. "Wait 'til you see him!"

Dani smiled. Paula was slow, mentally challenged, and on her first day Dani had noticed that the rest of the staff often ignored her. After Dani had suggested they spend their lunch break together, Paula had stuck to her like Velcro. Dani didn't mind; she found Paula's honesty and forthrightness refreshing. "See who?" she asked, hanging up her purse.

Jean, another waitress, whipped by with a stack of napkins. "I saw him first. He's mine," she said.

"You have a husband," Paula said indignantly. "Dani doesn't. Come on, Dani." She grabbed Dani's arm and tugged at her.

Dani hung back. "Hey, wait a minute."

The chef glanced at her and chuckled. "Better go peacefully."

"Paula." Dani laughed as the young woman dragged her through the kitchen. "I don't need a husband. Or even a boyfriend. In fact, that's probably the last thing I need right now."

"That's what you think."

Paula's grim determination made Dani laugh harder. "I think we should talk this over," she said, gasping and wiping tears from her eyes while Paula heaved her through the doorway into the bar. "I think—"

"Hee—rre's Dani!" Paula announced.

Dani hiccuped and tried to stifle her laughter as she glanced around with swimming eyes. And there, behind the bar enjoying the show, forearms braced against the dark wood, was the best-looking man she'd seen in a long time. The fabric of his salmon-colored western shirt stretched across wide shoulders and powerful-looking arms, which conjured up images of cozy evenings cuddling by a roaring fire. His dark hair was thick and full, not too long, with a slight curl at the nape, just right for twirling around a finger. Brown eyes bright with laughter, a strong nose and a sensuous mouth quirked in amusement—she couldn't have asked for more if she'd been handed a checklist.

"Jake." Paula clasped her hands together and rocked back and forth with a look of satisfaction on her round face.

Dani cleared her throat. "Where's...where's Bill?"

"Gone," Paula said with a wave of her hand. "Now we have Jake." She turned to him. "Dani made those earrings."

"It's nice to meet you, Dani, earrings and all." His eyes danced with merriment. "Paula's been telling me about—"

Jean's voice floated in from the dining room. "Dani, Paula. Elise and I need some help setting up in here."

Dani started guiltily. She couldn't afford to lose this job, and getting on the wrong side of Jean, the veteran of the staff, would be a good start in that direction. "We'd better go. Nice meeting you, Jake." She took Paula's arm and guided her toward the dining room.

Paula looked back over her shoulder. "Let's do lunch, Jake."

Dani laughed. "Do lunch? What is this 'do lunch' stuff? What are you now, a Hollywood producer or something?"

Paula gave her a smug smile. "Jake's from California. California people say that."

"California people had better get busy," Jean said, bustling around with a handful of silverware while Elise fanfolded turquoise napkins. "We open in five minutes."

Dani picked up a pile of place mats and handed them to Paula.

Paula didn't budge. "But Dani, isn't he cute?" she whispered.

Dani made a face and grabbed some napkins. "Okay, Paula, he's cute. Are you satisfied?"

"Not yet." Paula walked over to a round table and began laying place mats in a precise circle around its perimeter.

DANI FIGURED she might as well try to halt the changing of the seasons as sidetrack Paula's matchmaking plans. With stubborn patience, Paula insisted that Dani, Jake and Paula all take the same lunch break, and at two-thirty, Dani found herself across the table from Jake in one of the booths lining the walls of the bar area. Paula sat beside him and kept touching his arm with a proprietary air. Dani realized then why Paula had been so forceful about this rendezvous; Jake treated her the way Dani did, cordially and without condescension.

"So what *did* happen to Bill?" Dani asked as they ate steaming plates of enchiladas, refried beans and rice. "I didn't know he was leaving."

"It was kind of sudden, and lucky for me." Jake took a swallow of water. "He had a family situation in Oregon he had to take care of, and he's not sure when he'll be back. I was in the right place at the right time to be the transition bartender."

Dani nodded. "Paula says you're from California."

"L.A."

Paula bounced in her seat. "Tell her, Jake."

Jake smiled at Paula. "Maybe she's not a baseball fan."

"Sure she is." Paula turned to Dani. "He was on the Dodgers team. He *pitched.*"

"Oh, really?" That explained his strong shoulders and forearms. "What's your last name?"

"Clayborn."

Dani thought a minute and shook her head. "I really don't follow baseball that closely. I'm sorry, but I don't recognize—"

"No big deal. I wasn't on the team that long."

"He hurt his shoulder," Paula said. "He had to quit."

"And you've always dreamed of tending bar in Tubac?" Dani couldn't quite fit the pieces together.

Jake laughed. "The truth is, I didn't manage my money too well when I was playing ball, so I'm what you might call financially disadvantaged. Tubac appealed to me, and I've got this job, so I guess I'll stay around a while. You don't happen to know of a cheap place for rent, do you?"

"Jake's living in his camper," Paula volunteered.

"Not right now." Dani thought of Ron and Liane's place. "My neighbors will be leaving in a month."

"I'd really like something sooner."

"You might not be happy there, anyway. The peacocks woke me up at five-thirty this morning, and the train from hell came through at five forty-five. I won't be sleeping in, that's for sure."

"Peacocks?" Paula's eyes grew wide. "You have peacocks?"

"They belong to the landlord. He used to live there, but when he moved down the road, the peacocks didn't want to move with him, so he gives me a break on my rent in exchange for feeding them."

Paula's blue eyes shone. "Can I see them sometime?"

"Definitely."

Jake looked up from his enchilada. "I don't mind peacocks. Or trains. Is that why your neighbors are leaving?"

"No. Liane's about seven months pregnant and her mother wants her in Tucson. Besides, Ron and Liane don't have to feed the peacocks, because the stupid birds only stomp on my roof, I think, because it's tin and theirs isn't."

"I'd be willing to feed a rhinoceros if I could get out of that camper. Last time it rained, the darn thing leaked all over me."

"Jake, we don't have a rhinoceros in Tubac," Paula said. "But maybe you could stay in my room. It's pretty."

"Thanks, but I don't think your folks would go for that." Jake looked across the table at Dani. "Anyway, if you hear of anything else, will you let me know?"

"Sure." She liked his eyes. At first glance, they were warm and friendly, but as she looked deeper, she noticed a spark there that was more than friendly.

"So what brings you to Tubac?" he asked.

She'd rehearsed her story, not willing to share her real situation with strangers. "My parents and I vacationed here years ago, and I've always liked it. I wanted a change from L.A., so here I am."

He accepted her explanation with a slow nod. "Sounds like we're on a similar path."

"Perfect," Paula said softly.

Dani felt warmth suffuse her cheeks and she looked away from Jake. "I think we'd all better get back to work."

"You're right." Jake slid out of the booth. "I wouldn't want to get fired my first day."

Paula looked up at him. "Can we do lunch tomorrow?"

"You bet." He glanced at Dani. "Anytime."

You are not down here to find romance, she reminded herself sternly, yet she couldn't seem to stop looking into his eyes. Finally, she wrenched her gaze away and busied herself with their plates. "I'll take this to the kitchen for you."

"Thanks. And thanks for the company."

"Sure. Come on, Paula, back to the salt mines." Certain that he was watching her go, she hurried out of the room. This whole business belonged in one of her mother's books. Two people, each searching for a new beginning, meet in the romantic little town of Tubac and fall in love. Dani shook her head. Now who was losing her grip?

JAKE WATCHED HER until she disappeared through the kitchen door. So that was Dani Goodwin. The picture in his wallet didn't do justice to the sparkle in her hazel eyes, although he'd liked the way she'd worn her hair in that picture, cascading down her back. He had what he assumed was a typical male fantasy of running his fingers through a woman's long silky hair. Not that he would be touching Dani Goodwin that way.

The blouse and skirt she wore today emphasized the swell of her breasts and her slender waist more than the loose-fitting L.A. ensemble he remembered from the photograph. The earrings made a bold statement. He'd been told about her work, and he could see that she was a talented designer. Jake congratulated himself. Only his second day in Tubac, and he'd already made contact.

CHAPTER TWO

PAULA AND DANI got off at nine that night, but Jake had to stay on until eleven when the bar closed.

"Let's go say goodbye," Paula said, zipping her nylon jacket.

"Paula, he'll think we have a crush on him."

"I do. He's just right."

Dani took her purse down from the hook on the wall. "You know, Paula, these are the nineties. Women don't have to have a boyfriend or a husband anymore. Many women feel complete as they are."

"Do you?"

Dani looked into Paula's guileless blue eyes, which demanded the same kind of honesty she gave. "Most of the time. I've been engaged twice, and both times I decided I'd rather live alone."

"That's because they weren't Jake."

"How can you be so certain about Jake? He just walked in the door this morning."

Paula looked at Dani as if she were crazy to be questioning Jake's suitability. "So what?"

Dani laughed, but in three short days she had seen evidence that Paula's instincts about people were usually right on. She sized up customers as being "good" or "bad" in five minutes or less, even if she'd never seen them before. When Paula pronounced a customer "bad," Dani knew she could expect petty complaints and lousy tips; those Paula labeled "good" praised the service and were generous with their money.

"Let's say goodbye," Paula repeated, taking Dani's arm.

"Okay." Dani relented, feeling a curl of excitement at the thought of seeing Jake. She'd been aware of him all afternoon and evening, but they hadn't exchanged any conversation beyond what was necessary for Dani to fill her drink orders. Each time she'd come up to the bar, though, he'd smiled, and each time she'd left with a tray full of drinks, she'd walked away with the sensation of being watched.

She'd kept her observation of him equally covert. She'd enjoyed watching his hands when he mixed drinks, and she'd admired the easy way he joked with the customers sitting on the saddles around the bar. Bill had been a taciturn sort, and people seemed to appreciate Jake's easy affability. Dani couldn't deny that her own attitude about being here had altered dramatically. She was already looking forward to tomorrow's shift.

Two of the saddles were empty when Paula and Dani walked into the bar. Paula hoisted herself up. "Hi, Jake."

Dani rested one hip against the other saddle and basked in Jake's grin.

"Can I set you two up with a cold one, or are you heading home?" he asked, wiping the bar in front of them.

Paula sighed. "Going home."

Dani glanced at her in surprise. According to Jean, Paula lived with her parents in one of the country club's plush fairway homes. She didn't sound particularly happy to be going there.

"You, too?" Jake asked Dani.

"Yeah. Gotta give those peacocks a late-night snack."

"I want to see them," Paula said.

"You will. I'll have you over real soon." Dani figured she probably ought to meet Paula's parents first. Besides, she wasn't even properly moved in yet. The phone should be working when she got home, though. Liane had offered to let the phone installer in to hook up the service.

"Jake, too," Paula said.

Dani caught Jake's amused look and glanced away as a flush rose to her cheeks. Paula might have brought them together, but the young woman didn't understand all the nuances of a budding relationship. Paula was ready to throw the two of them together and let the chips fall where they may. Dani knew she and Jake would execute a more involved dance. If, that is, they decided to dance at all. Yet every time Dani looked into his eyes, she had the feeling they'd already taken the first tentative steps.

"I guess I'd better say good-night, then," Dani said.

"Sleep well," Jake said gently.

The words, almost an endearment, sent a delicious shiver running through her. "Thanks."

Paula climbed down from the saddle. "See you, Jake."

"Sure thing, Paula. Are we doing lunch tomorrow?"

Paula beamed at him. "You got it, dude."

Dani and Jake exchanged a look of enjoyment. Whatever else they might share in the future, Dani thought, they definitely had a mutual affection for Paula and her outspoken charm. Feeling warm all over, Dani gave Jake a last wave and walked back into the kitchen.

As she and Paula stepped outside, the chill night air cooled her heated skin.

"You like him," Paula said as she unlocked her mountain bike from the rack beside the back door.

"Yes, I like him," Dani admitted.

"Good." Paula mounted her bike and switched on the headlamp.

"That sure is a fancy rig, Paula." Dani admired the delicate designs in various colors swirling over the painted surfaces of the bike. "Did it come like that?"

In the light by the kitchen door, Paula's face glowed with pleasure. "Nope."

"Whoever did that has real talent."

Paula studied her quietly before opening her mouth as if to say something. Then she closed it again. "See you," she said, and pedaled into the night.

Dani gazed after her. What an independent little cuss, riding that bike to work and back every day. Dani decided she'd hustle her moving-in process so she could invite Paula over in a few days, thinking she might be interested in seeing the lapidary equipment and Dani's supply of stones and silver, as well as the peacocks.

Then, she mused, after she'd had Paula over, maybe she'd invite Jake. Or maybe Paula and Jake together, and then Jake by himself. Being alone with Jake was the most exciting prospect she'd had in months. She hopped into her Mustang, unpinned the net from her hair and drove home with the top down.

THE SIGHT OF the ivory-colored phone hanging from her kitchen wall reminded Dani she'd promised to call her mother with the number. If she didn't, Helen would probably roust Ron and Liane from their bed again at six. This day had turned out so well she dreaded talking to her mother and spoiling her ebullient mood, but it couldn't be avoided.

The phone had a new-plastic smell as she held the receiver and punched in her mother's number. Helen answered on the second ring.

"Hi, Mom."

"Dani, I thought you'd never call."

"I just got home from work."

"Such a waste of talent. Have you placed your jewelry anywhere yet?"

Dani fought down her annoyance by telling herself that loneliness made her mother testy. "I've contacted a couple of the shops and their inventory is high right now, but I'm sure something will break soon."

When that happened, she'd quit her job at the country club. The idea didn't sound as appealing as it had yesterday, before she'd met Jake, but she intended to keep the new bartender at Canada Verde as her little secret. All her mother needed was an excuse to start haranguing her about the dangers of strange men.

"I take it you have a phone number for me, then?"

"Yes." Dani read off the number written on her phone.

"I'm relieved. This being out of touch has been very hard on me."

Dani smiled at that. She'd called her mother every day since she'd been gone, albeit not from her own phone, yet Helen considered them to have been "out of touch." This move was more significant than Dani had ever dreamed. "Well, I'm pretty tired," she began, preparing her mother for an abbreviated conversation. "I'll check in again in a few days, and—"

A piercing scream tore through the stillness.

"Dani! What was that?"

"Nothing, Mom. It's just—"

The scream came again.

"Dani, for God's sake!"

"It's the peacock."

"Are you sure? That sounded very human to me."

"I'm sure. The peahens cry, too, but they're not so long and loud."

"It's a terrible sound. Just terrible."

"You get used to it." Dani didn't want to admit how the cry had spooked her the night before. Even now, the hairs stood up on the back of her neck each time the peacock shrieked. She needed to get off the phone, make herself a hot cup of tea and get back to her engaging fantasies about the new bartender at Canada Verde.

"I have half a mind to fly down there."

Dani panicked. "Mom, please don't. I need some space. I think this is good . . . for both of us."

Her mother heaved a mighty sigh. "I suppose you would think that."

"I do, Mom." Guilt pricked her. "I hope you can understand."

"I'm trying. Is your door locked?"

"Yes, it is. Good night. And sleep well," she added, repeating Jake's words to her in the bar. The memory set off a pleasant vibration in her body.

"I doubt if I'll sleep at all."

"Well, give it a try," Dani said. "Good night." She firmly replaced the receiver with deliberation. *Please don't come down here, Mom,* she thought. *Please.* If she did, it would cause a rift between them that might never heal.

HELEN GOODWIN HELD the cordless telephone in her lap.

"What in heaven's name was that all about?"

Helen started. She'd almost forgotten that her new friend, Evelyn Ross, was sitting on the deck with her. Both women wore heavy sweatshirts to ward off the chill ocean breeze. "That was my daughter," she said. "While she was talking to me, a peacock screamed in the background, and I thought—"

"She has a peacock in her apartment?"

"No, she's—oh, Evelyn, it's such a complicated story." Helen reached for her margarita and took a long, cooling drink. A half-empty pitcher of the tequila-and-lime-juice mixture sat between the two deck chairs. Among other things, the women had discovered a mutual fondness for margaritas. "I don't feel like going into it. Let's get back to your manuscript. Now, in your third chapter, I think you need a stronger hook at the end. Maybe if they've just happened upon the body, that would be a good place to break."

"Okay. I can see that. But Helen, if you're upset about your daughter, we don't have to do this now. I guessed when you brought the phone out here, you were expecting an important call. That must have been it. Why don't we skip the manuscript discussion until next time?''

Helen glanced at her visitor with gratitude. "Thanks. I am a little distracted." Evelyn was turning out to be very sensitive. She'd called about two months ago and introduced herself by saying that they'd once been in a manuscript critiquing group together.

Helen had remembered. With a pang of guilt, she'd recalled that she'd lost track of Evelyn and the rest of the group as the demands of her career had increased. So when Evelyn had proposed lunch, Helen had agreed. She usually refused such requests, but Evelyn had caught her at a low point, when she'd sensed Dani pulling away.

Once Helen had committed herself, she'd wanted out of the engagement but couldn't summon the courage to cancel. To her relief, Evelyn had proved to be an interesting woman with a sense of humor. One meeting led to another, and another. Widowed recently herself, Evelyn sympathized with Helen's debilitating loneliness. All Helen's other friends were married, and Helen found it painful to be around them for long. Evelyn was an undemanding yet always-available buddy for a meal or a few drinks.

All she'd asked in the past two months, and it was such a small thing, was a critique of her latest manuscript. Evelyn's work wasn't publishable, might never be, but Helen had decided to be gentle in her comments. She didn't want to lose this new friend, especially now that Dani wasn't around to chase the shadows away.

Evelyn sipped her margarita. "You really have my curiosity aroused with that screaming peacock. You should know better than to throw something like that out to a fellow writer and leave it dangling."

Helen grimaced. "I guess you're right." She hadn't confided her problems concerning Dani, maybe because Evelyn couldn't possibly know how she felt. Evelyn didn't have any children.

"So, are you going to tell me where she's hiding this peacock?"

"In Tubac."

"Arizona? Where you set *The Unvanquished?* What's she doing down there?"

"She's moved there. She read my book and decided it was where she wanted to go." Helen gazed at the lights of a freighter moving slowly along the faint demarcation between sky and ocean. "Too bad I wrote the damn thing!"

"She ran off and left you to adjust to widowhood by yourself?"

Helen took a gulp of her margarita. She would not cry. She would not. "I should be coping better by now."

"Who made up that rule? Grief has no time limit. I think it's a real shame she left you." Evelyn expressed the indignation and despair Helen held back. "I can understand why you're upset. I'm sure having her close was a comfort to you at this time in your life."

"It's not just that." Helen couldn't bear for this woman to think she was a total wimp. "I worry that something might happen to her."

"Well, of course that's natural, but didn't you say she was twenty-six? She's old enough to take care of herself in a sleepy little place like Tubac. How could anything happen to her down there?''

"The town's fine. It's these threatening messages I've been getting."

Evelyn sat up straighter in her chair. "What messages?"

As Helen described the notes she'd received, she began to shake. She put down the glass so Evelyn wouldn't notice.

"How twisted," Evelyn said when Helen was finished. "Have you contacted the police?"

"I talked to a detective, somebody I've used as a resource for my books. The notes are untraceable." The waves hissed against the shore, sounding more mocking than soothing tonight.

"Maybe it's a bad joke."

"Dani thinks so. I tried to get her to move in here, where I have excellent security, but instead, she waltzed off to Tubac with no guarantee she'll be able to sell her jewelry, no place to live, nothing. I put in a call to the manager of the Canada Verde Country Club Restaurant and he promised to give her a job. Waitressing." She grimaced. "It's all I could think of, and John's an old friend. He won't tell her he knows me."

"How upsetting. You should have told me about this, Helen."

"I didn't want to presume on our friendship. After all, we've—"

"Presume on our friendship? Didn't I give you my six-hundred-page mystery to read?"

"That's different."

"I don't see it that way." Evelyn sloshed the margarita mix around in the pitcher and poured another glass. "Listen, I have a great idea. Let's go visit. After reading your book, I'm dying to see Tubac. Maybe I'd even research a book of my own. What do you say?"

"I wouldn't dare go. Dani would kill me if I showed up there. She thinks I'm way too overprotective as it is."

Evelyn was silent for a moment. "But you want to know she's okay, don't you?"

"More than anything."

"There has to be a solution. I'll go home and sleep on it."

"I wish I could sleep at all."

"We'll manage, Helen." Evelyn reached over and patted her friend's hand. "Leave it to me."

THE NEXT MORNING, Evelyn called as Helen was eating breakfast.

"I have the most wonderful plan. Have you mentioned my name to your daughter?"

Helen searched her memory. "I'm not sure. Maybe, but lately we haven't been getting along so well, and she ... didn't seem to be as interested in what I was doing."

"That works out just right, then. An old business acquaintance of Benjamin's has a house in Tubac. He doesn't normally rent it out, but he will to me. I'll just go down there and report back to you."

Helen was taken aback. "You? Evelyn, I couldn't expect something like that of you. You're terrific, beyond terrific to offer, but—"

"Hold it right there. Have you any idea how much it's meant to me, rediscovering our friendship?"

"I'm flattered, but still, I wouldn't ask anyone to do this, let alone a friend I've been so delinquent about keeping track of."

"Constant contact isn't the only measure of a deep and abiding friendship. I felt a spiritual kinship with you years ago and it resurfaced when we had lunch two months ago. What's more, you're taking your valuable time to critique my work. Let me do this, as a very small payment for your help."

"If you go to Tubac and check on Dani for me, I'll critique twenty manuscripts."

Evelyn laughed. "Better watch out what sort of promises you make. I might hold you to them."

"I wouldn't care." Helen felt pounds lighter. "It would be buying me peace of mind. What will you do, pose as a typical tourist?"

"Heavens, no! If I'm going to do this, I'll do it right. I'll open up a jewelry shop and offer to take Dani's work on consignment."

Helen almost dropped her coffee mug. "You're kidding."

"Why? Benjamin left me tons of money, so that's no problem. When this blows over, I'll sell the shop, and by then I'll probably have helped create a market for Dani's work. What could be better?"

"I have no idea. You sound like a fairy godmother."

"I feel more like Inspector Clouseau. This will be great, Helen. Trust me. I'll become her friend and confidante, and make reports back to you. And I'll definitely research a new novel while I'm there, so this plan isn't as selfless as it sounds."

"I don't know what to say."

"Just say, 'Fine, Evelyn'."

Helen stared out at the ocean beyond her deck. "Fine, Evelyn." Then she grinned. This would be kind of fun. Evelyn might not know how to write a book, but she could certainly plan a real-life adventure. Helen felt like a very lucky woman.

BETWEEN NINE AND ELEVEN that night, Jake found himself with very few customers and time on his hands. He used the time to think about Dani. He liked her. For a short while, he indulged in some regret that they were meeting under these particular circumstances.

During his ball-playing days, he'd had his fill of sowing wild oats. Even if he'd stayed in the game, he would have ended the high times with women by now. He was facing thirty, and recently he'd begun to turn a more discerning eye on the women he met. Dani had been promising. Too bad.

He pictured her at home, tucked into bed in that little rental she'd conveniently described to him. A tin roof with the peacocks shouldn't be too hard to find.

Another house was right near hers, apparently, with a couple staying there, the wife expecting a baby. Couples like that could always use a little extra money. They were moving out in a month, Dani said. Or so they thought. Jake figured it would be earlier. Much earlier.

CHAPTER THREE

DANI LOOKED FORWARD to work eagerly each morning. Jake was the reason, and even though she cautioned herself to go slow, she couldn't find anything to dislike about the man. Paula adored him and expected Dani to follow suit. Dani figured it wouldn't take much encouragement from Paula.

The three of them ate lunch together every day. Jake had dubbed them the "Three Musketeers," and Paula loved it. Every afternoon when business slacked off, she'd nudge Dani and whisper "Lunch for the Three Musketeers." Then they'd pile into a booth in the bar and share stories about the customers or the latest proclamations from the management.

Dani continued to be impressed by the way Jake interacted with Paula. He always listened to the young woman as if what she had to say was profound. And sometimes, it was. Paula often saw things that others missed. When Paula said she thought the restaurant manager, John Slattery, was like a scared little boy, Dani had asked why, and Paula said "because he talks loud." Dani watched Slattery's behavior more closely after that, and decided Paula was right.

Paula offered opinions about the others on the staff, too, and seemed to love finding contradictions in people. Jean was "bossy but nice underneath," Elise was "nice on the outside but didn't always mean it," and Humberto, the chef, "said he was lazy but smiled the whole time he worked."

One lunch hour, Dani asked Paula to describe her.

"Okay." Paula finished chewing and gazed at Dani. "You smile a lot, but you're sad inside."

Discomfited by the assessment, Dani tried to pass it off with a chuckle. "What do I have to be sad about? I love Tubac, I have good friends, and by next fall when the tourist season picks up again, I should be able to start selling my jewelry." She glanced at Jake. "How about this guy? What would you say about him?"

"Same thing," Paula said, her gaze moving between Jake and Dani.

Jake winked at Dani. "I think there's a hidden agenda in all this."

"I think you're right. I stepped right into her trap, too."

Paula sighed. "Too bad we don't have movies."

"What?" Dani laughed.

"That's what the man does. Ask her to the movies. We don't have any."

His eyes glinting with amusement, Jake turned to Paula. "Do you think I should ask Dani out on a date?"

Paula bounced in her seat. "Yes! A date!" Then she frowned. "Except we don't have movies."

"But we have the staff picnic and softball game on our day off. I could ask her to be my date for that."

Excitement skittered up Dani's spine. Despite all the joking, he was taking the next step in their relationship.

Paula clapped her hands together. "Perfect!"

Jake glanced at Dani, his eyes alight with that special interest he seemed to reserve for her alone. "Would you do me the honor, Miss Goodwin?"

Dani held his gaze. So now it would start. She thought of the peacock spreading his tail and strutting around in front of his chosen lady. Of course, Jake was more subtle, the glow in his eyes hinting at the sensuous depths they might explore together, if she said yes.

"I'd love to," she said.

Paula clapped her hands again. "I knew it."

So did I, Dani acknowledged as a slow smile spread over Jake's face. *From the moment I saw him.* They lived in a civilized world, where instincts had supposedly been bred out of them, yet Dani's response to Jake felt exactly like an instinctual need to bond with this particular man. She'd never experienced an urge anything like it. She wondered if Jake felt it, too.

DAMN, Jake thought as unexpected yearnings coursed through him. He hadn't meant to ask her out. Move in next door to her, sure. He'd set up a meeting with Ron for Saturday morning after discovering Dani had been asked to work overtime on a breakfast shift that day. He'd convinced Ron and Liane that it was worth their while to clear out by Saturday afternoon, and by Sunday he'd be in place, ready to do the job he'd been assigned.

Working with her and living next door would serve his purpose admirably. Asking her out definitely wasn't part of the plan. He'd allowed himself the fun of flirting with her and kidded himself it couldn't hurt, might in fact help him gain her confidence. But now he'd opened his big mouth and asked her for a date.

Worse than that, he *wanted* the date, and all the attendant privileges, like holding hands and the possibility of a good-night kiss. Hell, he wanted a good deal more than a kiss. If he had any sense, he'd take himself off the job right now and leave Tubac. Except when he looked at Dani, all flushed and expectant, sense flew out the window and desire rushed in to take its place.

A devilish voice spoke to him, asking if what he was thinking was so terrible. This whole business was crazy, so what was one more bit of insanity? Anyway, he couldn't take back what he'd just said. Maybe he and Dani would have a miserable time together at the picnic and that would be that. Sure. That was about as likely as John Slattery giving him a raise. No, Jake knew he and Dani would have a good time. Maybe too good.

THE FIRST RAIN since Dani had arrived in Tubac came on Saturday afternoon, and she ran to the restaurant parking lot to put up her convertible top. Jake's truck with its dilapidated camper shell was parked next to her car. He still hadn't found a place to rent, and Dani didn't like to think of him sleeping in that thing when it rained. Still, she had no solution.

At the end of the dinner shift, she and Paula told Jake goodbye, as they did every night.

"I'm afraid it'll be a wet night for you," she said as rain drummed on the restaurant roof.

Jake shrugged and smiled. "Won't be the first time."

"You should come to my house," Paula insisted.

"Thanks, Paula, but I'll just be patient. Something will open up soon."

"Let's hope," Dani said. With a last glance and wave, she left the bar. Paula trailed behind, muttering that she didn't want Jake getting wet.

"Say, what about you?" Dani asked as she remembered the mountain bike Paula always rode home.

"I have this." Paula pulled on plastic rainpants and a jacket.

Dani frowned. "That's it?"

"Sure." Paula zipped up the jacket and pulled a hood over her short hair.

"I thought your parents would pick you up or something."

For the first time, Dani saw disapproval in Paula's gaze. "This is *my* job."

"Well, I know, but—"

"I do it myself."

Dani recognized Paula's need to be free of parental interference. She'd certainly felt it often enough in the past year. "You're right. I shouldn't have said that about your parents coming. I wasn't thinking straight."

Paula smiled, all animosity erased from her expression. "It's okay."

Dani took her purse from the hook. The rain was coming down so hard it sounded as if they were standing under a waterfall. Riding a bike would be difficult, if not impossible. "Paula, I do understand." Dani turned back to face her. "Independence, being your own boss...it's important to me, too. That's one reason I moved here, to get away from my mother."

Paula stopped tying her hood and stared at Dani. "You did?"

"Yes. She can't believe I've grown up."

A light glowed in Paula's eyes. "Mine, either."

"What I'm trying to say is, you don't have to prove anything to me. I know you're your own boss."

"Damn straight."

Dani fought not to laugh. She'd never heard Paula swear before, but obviously this topic was a charged one. "Okay, so neither one of us wants to depend on our parents any more than we absolutely have to, right?"

Paula nodded so hard her hood came off.

"But you and I are friends. Maybe it's okay to depend on each other, because we won't try to run each other's lives."

Paula squinted, as she always did when she was concentrating very hard.

"What I'm trying to say is, the rain out there is ridiculous. I wouldn't want to try to ride a bike through it, and I'm a pretty good rider. I know you don't want to call your parents, but what if I gave you a lift?"

Wonder spread over Paula's features. "In the Mustang?"

"Sure. We can put the bike in the trunk. I have a piece of rope in there we can use if it doesn't quite fit."

Wonder gave way to a worried expression on Paula's face. She chewed a fingernail, as Dani had seen her do when she couldn't figure something out.

"Look, friends do favors for each other. I'm offering this favor, and sometime you can do me a favor. That's how it works between friends. It's nothing like when parents do things for you to prove they're still in charge. You and I are equals, Paula. Friends."

Paula chewed on her nail some more. Then she stopped and stood very still. At last, she looked directly at Dani and beamed at her. "Okay."

"Okay?" Dani laughed and held up her hand.

"Okay!" Paula slapped it in a high five.

"Then let's go."

Dani got soaking wet while they tied the bike into the trunk, but she didn't care. She and Paula had passed a milestone in their relationship and she was elated. She was beginning to realize that Paula didn't have many friends because she was choosy, which put Dani and Jake in an elite group. Poor Jake. As Dani drove through the rain to Paula's house, she thought about the leaky camper and hoped Jake wouldn't catch pneumonia tonight.

She found Paula's house easily. Every light in the place seemed to be on, including four floodlights that illuminated the paved driveway and turned the rain into a glittering sheet. Dani guessed the house was one of the more expensive ones in the subdivision, judging from the leaded glass in the double entrance doors, the three-car garage and what she could see of the land-scaped grounds.

"This is very nice, Paula."

"I want you to see my room."

"Okay." She tried to imagine Paula's room. Would it be the room of a child, with stuffed animals and toys scattered around? Or would it be more institutional, with very little personality?

As she pulled into the circular driveway in front of the house, a woman opened the front door and stood watching them. Then she turned and motioned behind her. Soon a man ran out, a large umbrella over his head.

"He's coming," Paula said, a note of despair in her voice.

"They can't help it, Paula. Parents are parents." She exchanged a look with Paula.

"And friends are friends," Paula said, grinning.

"Damn straight."

That made Paula laugh, and together they got out to help her father unload the bike.

The air smelled of cedar smoke and tobacco from the pipe Paula's father gripped in his teeth. "Great of you to do this," he said around the stem of his pipe as he took over the operation. "I'm Ed Jordan, Paula's father. Why don't you two go in and get dry? Madge has some decaf coffee made."

"Well, thanks, Mr. Jordan." Dani gave Paula a nudge. "Maybe we will go in."

Paula nudged back. "Sure. Maybe we will."

They wiped their feet on a woven straw mat at the entryway and stepped through the door Paula's mother held open.

"Goodness, such a night!" she said, closing the door. "And I thought Chicago had crazy weather. You must be Dani. Paula's mentioned you. I'm Madge Jordan."

Dani smoothed her damp palm down her skirt and shook Madge's hand while she briefly assessed Paula's mother. "Nice to meet you." Madge's stylishly cut white hair and the brown age spots on the backs of her hands suggested she was in her mid-sixties. She'd obviously had Paula late in life. Dani recognized the design of Madge's burgundy leisure outfit; her mother had a similar one and Dani knew they didn't come cheap. Madge's trim figure did the outfit justice.

Madge smiled at Dani. "Nice to meet you, too, even if it took dreadful weather to bring you by." Her glance flicked to her daughter. "We would have gone after Paula ourselves, but last time we tried that, she threw a very embarrassing temper tantrum. Paula, go put on some dry clothes while I see about the coffee. Dani, come on into the kitchen and keep me company."

Pink daubed Paula's cheeks. "I want to show Dani my room."

Dani saw Madge open her mouth to protest and she rushed to ward off a battle. "Yes, I'd love that, Paula."

Madge closed her mouth and nodded. "I'll bring the coffee into the living room. You two girls come out whenever you're ready." She turned and headed for the kitchen.

You two girls. In the blink of an eye, Dani had been lumped into that juvenile category along with Paula. Now she really understood Paula's fierce hold on independence.

"She's bossy," Paula muttered.

"Yes." Dani glanced around the living room. "But I like the house, Paula. Very classy." The Jordans had embraced their new southwestern environment. Indian rugs lay scattered over a red Saltillo tile floor, and large clay pots topped with glass served as end tables. Two sofas upholstered in white linen were grouped in front of a beehive fireplace, and Charles Gorman paintings hung on either side of it. Dani thought they looked like originals, which meant the Jordans were loaded.

"It's okay." Paula dismissed the elegant surroundings with a glance. "My room's better."

Dani followed her down a tiled hallway to a door at the far end of the house.

Paula turned at the room's entrance and presented the interior with the same flourish she'd used when introducing Dani to Jake. "Hee—rre's my room!"

Dani stepped inside and gasped. It looked as if someone had gone wild with a giant Spirograph. Every surface—walls, furniture, even the ceiling—was covered with delicate lines and squiggles in a rainbow of colors that turned the interior into a fantasy chamber. Dani stepped closer to examine a section of wall. The designs were perfectly executed. Lines were ruler-straight and curves were symmetrically rounded.

"Like it?"

Dani turned to find Paula beaming, her whole face alight with pride. "It's beautiful. Was this your idea?"

"Yep."

"The same person who did your bike did this, I'll bet."

"Yep."

Dani thought she'd like to meet the artist who'd done the work. The creator of this room would be a great resource for design concepts. "Who was it, someone from around here?"

"Yes. Me."

Dani blinked. She knew Paula wasn't capable of lying, and yet . . .

"You don't believe me." The glow left Paula's eyes.

And then Dani did believe her. "Yes, yes I do!" She hurried forward and hugged Paula, hard. "Forgive me for even doubting for a minute. Of course you did this. Each of us has something special we can do, and now I know what your special thing is." She stepped back so she could look into Paula's face and convince her of her sincerity. "You have a wonderful gift."

The glow returned. "Pinstriping."

"Pinstriping? But isn't that what they do to cars, those little lines down the side?"

Paula nodded. "Pinstriping."

"But this is so much more."

"This is practice. My cousin Billy taught me. In Chicago."

Dani laughed. "I think you're beyond practice. You're an expert."

"Can I do your car?"

"My car? Why—"

"For free," Paula rushed on, her hands waving in excitement. "Like you said. We trade. You do something. I do something. Okay?"

Dani grinned at her. What a delightful idea. "Okay!"

Paula jiggled a little, as if she were about to dance. "Okay!"

"Paula, we have lots to talk about." Dani felt as if she'd just found a soul mate. "I want you to see some of my sketches for jewelry. I've decided to try a peacock feather design, and—"

Madge's voice drifted down the hall, calling their names.

Paula looked impatient. "We have to have coffee now."

"That's okay. There's lots of time. You'll be coming over to do my car, anyway, and I can show you my sketches then. Paula, I'm so excited to have found a fellow artist!" She hugged Paula again and got a bone-crushing squeeze in return.

"Me, too." Paula's expression was radiant.

Madge called again, louder this time.

"Let's go," Paula said, starting out of the room.

"Aren't you going to change clothes?"

"No."

Dani followed Paula down the hall. Before she entered the living room, she took a deep breath. Obviously, Paula was aligned against her parents. In order to be Paula's friend, Dani would have to take sides. That was fine with her. Paula needed someone on her side. All artists did.

They gathered on the linen sofas in front of a crackling fire. Ed and Madge took one sofa; Dani and Paula the other. They'd had barely a sip of coffee before Paula announced that she was going to pinstripe Dani's car. Dani could almost hear the blare of a battle trumpet in her friend's voice.

Madge glanced at Ed. "Oh, I don't think so, Paula," she said.

The pink spots returned to Paula's cheeks. "Dani said so."

Dani knew her role. "I certainly did, Mrs. Jordan. Paula's a real artist and I'd be thrilled to have her pinstripe my car."

"You don't understand." Her father took his pipe from his mouth and pointed the stem at Paula. "She's never done a car."

"I've done my bike!" Paula said. "And my room!"

So they hadn't even allowed Paula to decorate the family car, Dani thought. How sad. Well, she was in this now, and she wouldn't back out. "I'd be honored if mine is the first car she's ever pinstriped. It will probably become a collector's item."

Ed knocked his pipe against an ashtray, dumping out the burned tobacco. "No, it won't, because Paula's not going to pinstripe your car. You have a classic little buggy there, and I'm not taking a chance that Paula will screw up your paint job."

Dani glanced at Paula. She looked ready to cry. A bossy mother and an autocratic father. The two made a bad combination for an emerging creative personality like Paula's. "But I'm the one taking a chance," Dani said quietly.

"Not quite." Ed looked at her with what she imagined was a chairman-of-the-board glare. "Paula is our responsibility. Therefore, whatever she does is also our responsibility. If you're upset with the paint job, you couldn't very well complain to Paula, now could you?"

"Why not?"

He held her gaze, forcing the obvious meaning on her and all of them, including Paula. His daughter couldn't be held responsible because she was intellectually handicapped. Retarded. Dani wanted to punch him.

Madge spoke up. "I'm afraid it really is out of the question, Dani. It's sweet of you to offer, though."

She took a deep breath. "Mrs. Jordan, Mr. Jordan, I really want Paula to pinstripe my car. I'll sign some sort of release if you feel that's necessary, but I would like you to reconsider your position."

Ed shook his head. "No. I can't approve it."

Dani heard a sob and turned as Paula jumped to her feet and stumbled out of the room. "Paula!" She started after her, but Madge gripped her arm.

"She's tired, Dani. You understand. Let her get her rest."

Dani turned back and eased her arm away from that firm hold. "I think both of you are making a terrible mistake. Pinstriping my car would be a great experience for both Paula and me. She has a tremendous gift for design. After seeing her room, I'm not worried about her doing a bad job."

"But we are," her father said. "You've only known Paula a short while. You're not in a position to judge whether she'd ruin your car or not."

"But look at her room! That's a masterpiece!"

Madge nodded. "So it is, but she did that when she was alone, with no distractions. You can't predict how she'd be with your car, when she's so emotionally involved. You see Paula was born with an I.Q. of about seventy-five."

"For no apparent reason," Ed added. "Nobody in our family is that way. Nobody."

Dani struggled for patience.

"Tests have shown Paula has the emotional maturity of a ten-year-old," Madge continued in a patronizing tone. "Now, I doubt you'd let a ten-year-old paint your car."

"If the ten-year-old had a room like Paula's, I would."

Ed sighed and started toward the front door. "It's late. Perhaps we'd better say good-night."

Dani knew when she was beaten. These people did have legal control over Paula. She'd just have to think this through and see if there was a way around them. For Paula's sake, she hoped so. "Good night, then," she said. "And thank you for the coffee."

She drove home, her heart aching for Paula, who was no doubt sobbing alone in her room. Dani didn't think either of her parents would be comforting her; they were involved in a power struggle, and believed they'd just won another round. Dani wasn't so sure.

She got home around ten, and noticed a note stuck in her screen door, out of the rain. The note was from Liane, telling her that they'd wanted to stay and say goodbye, but the rain had forced them to pack up quickly and begin the drive to Tucson. The landlord had let them out of the lease early, Liane wrote, and she'd had a few pains recently, so they'd decided to go now. They promised to bring the baby back to see her.

The peacock, huddled with his miniharem under the shelter of the porch, gave a shrill cry. Dani shivered. Her little hideaway didn't seem quite as cozy when Ron and Liane weren't right next door. Then she thought of Jake. He would jump at the chance to live here. The idea gave her a jolt of excitement. Jake, right next door? Why not?

She glanced at her watch. It was a little late to call the landlord, but if she didn't call him now, Jake would sleep in a leaky camper tonight. She could contact the landlord, get the key. If she vouched for Jake, the landlord would go on her recommendation. He'd probably be delighted to have a tenant after softheartedly letting Ron and Liane out of their lease and losing a month's rent.

Jake would be living next door. Dani could hardly wait.

CHAPTER FOUR

DANI STOOD DRIPPING water on the tiled entry of her landlord's house while he went to get the key.

Soon he returned and peered at her over the reading glasses perched on his nose. "Won't have gas or electricity until Monday. Had 'em turned off when Ron brought me the key. Water's off, too, but you can turn that on. Valve's in back of the house, near the rosebush."

"Okay." Dani hadn't thought of that. But Jake would still be better off in a dry house for the night, whether he had lights and heat or not. "By the way, I think you were sweet to let Ron and Liane out of the lease early."

He blinked. "Didn't. They had the money for the last month's rent, so it was up to them when they wanted to move."

"They had the money?" Dani remembered how carefully Liane budgeted every cent. "I guess Liane's mother sent it, then."

"Didn't matter to me where it came from." He handed her the key. "But if you ask me, you're crazy to run out on a night like tonight to keep this fellow dry."

Dani was feeling a little foolish herself, but after coming so far, she decided she might as well complete her mission. "He's a nice guy. He'll be a good tenant."

"Bet he'd be just as good starting tomorrow as tonight."

Dani shrugged. "Maybe he'll decide that, too. But at least I'll have given him the option."

"Uh-huh."

Dani squirmed under the man's assessing gaze. "Well, thanks," she said, and opened the door. With a final wave, she escaped.

As she navigated the muddy roads from her landlord's house to the country club, she thought about this morning's call from her mother. There'd been another note. The highlighted sentence had read: *The quarry was in sight now, and vulnerable.* No matter that, in context, the line referred to an Apache in 1833 stalking a woman he planned to take captive; Helen was convinced it was another threat directed at Dani. Dani hated to admit the notes were scaring her, too, but they were. Spending a cold, rainy night alone on the property wasn't appealing.

The restaurant's kitchen door was always locked at this hour, so Dani parked in the front lot and hurried toward the main entrance. She stood just inside and shook the rain from her hair. The restaurant was deserted, but guitar music and laughter drifted from the candlelit bar. Canada Verde had musical entertainment on Friday and Saturday nights provided by guitarist Jesus Ramirez, who drove up from Nogales for the gig. He was very popular with Tubac residents, and the bar was usually packed whenever he played. Tonight, however, the rain had kept people away; Dani's car had been one of only half a dozen in the parking lot.

As she started toward the doorway of the bar, a loud curse was followed by the sound of splintering wood. The music and laughter stopped. She got to the door in time to see Jake vault the bar and land poised on the balls of his feet with his hands in a martial-arts position.

Ten feet from him, a cowboy stood with a chair raised over his head. His date cowered several feet away. A second chair lay smashed in the corner among shards of glass.

Jake's voice was calm. "Put it down."

"This ain't your concern," the cowboy said. "It's between me and her."

"You just destroyed Canada Verde property. That's my concern."

"You wanna be part of it? Okay." The cowboy heaved the chair at Jake.

Jake caught it and tossed it aside just as the cowboy lunged forward.

Dani wasn't quite sure what happened next, because within seconds, the cowboy was on the floor with both arms pinned behind his back. She'd never seen reflexes like the ones Jake had exhibited.

Jake glanced over at Cindy, the cocktail waitress. "Call the sheriff."

"I already did."

"Then I guess we have everything covered. Jesus, would you like to finish that number this jerk interrupted?"

The guitarist nodded and continued a spirited rendition of "El Rancho Grande."

Dani let out the breath she'd been holding.

Jake pulled the cowboy to his feet and propelled him toward the doorway with the bully's date trailing along behind. On the way, Jake spotted Dani and did a double take.

"I, um, found you a place to stay."

The cowboy leered. "Nice going, bartender."

Jake pulled up on the cowboy's arm until he yelped. Then he glanced at Dani. "I'll take care of this little chore and be right back. Tell Cindy to get you a glass of wine or something." A siren competed with the guitar music, and Jake pushed the cowboy toward the restaurant entrance.

Dani walked over to the bar and leaned against it. She was still trying to assimilate the picture of Jake leaping over the bar and subduing the drunk cowboy. His response had been crisp, efficient... almost professional.

Cindy brought a tray of empty glasses over and set them on the bar. "Did you see that?"

Dani nodded.

"I had no idea I was working with Rambo."

"Me, neither."

Cindy's gaze skimmed over Dani's wet raincoat and hair. "What brings you back out on a night like this?"

"My neighbors moved today. I knew Jake needed a place, and his camper leaks."

"That's pretty darn nice of you, Dani," Cindy said. "Coming out in this kind of weather." Her implication that Dani had overreacted was clear.

"It's for my benefit, too," Dani said. "The property's pretty isolated, and I'm not crazy about staying out there all alone."

"Well, you just had a demonstration that should make you feel safe as the Hope Diamond."

"I guess so."

Cindy tilted her head toward the restaurant, where Jake was talking with the deputies. "Makes him seem sexier than ever, doesn't it?"

Dani flushed. "Listen, I'm not— I don't intend this to be—"

"Never mind." Cindy leaned close and murmured in Dani's ear. "No explanation necessary. If I didn't have Steve, I'd be in there working the angles, too."

Jake walked back into the room and through the swinging gate that let him behind the bar.

Cindy stuck out her lower lip. "Gee, I wanted to see you vault over it again."

Jake grinned. "Going in this direction, I'd probably break every glass in the place. Got some orders for me?"

"Yeah. Violence makes people thirsty." Cindy gave him the orders and he began mixing drinks.

"What's this about finding me a place?" he asked Dani.

Dani told him the details and warned him about the lack of utilities.

"I don't care."

Cindy laughed. "I'll bet you don't. After what we just saw, Dani and I think you sleep on a bed of nails." She picked up the tray of drinks and walked away still chuckling.

"What was all that karate stuff, anyway?" Dani asked.

He started washing glasses. "Just a little something I picked up."

"It looked like something that resulted from years of training to me."

"I've always been fascinated with martial arts."

Dani had a feeling she wouldn't get any more explanation than that. She fished in her purse for the key and placed it on the bar. "Here's—"

"Another vodka tonic and a draft for table three," Cindy said, putting her tray down next to the key. She glanced over at Dani and winked.

"Coming up." Jake pocketed the key before he turned away and began mixing more drinks.

Dani felt uncomfortably warm. Her delivery of the key was taking on more significance than she'd intended. "Well, I guess I'll be going home," she said.

"Just a sec." Jake moved quickly to finish the order and placed the glasses on Cindy's tray.

Dani waited until he was finished.

He leaned on the bar again. "With the way the rain's been coming down, the roads must be a mess."

"They're pretty muddy."

"That's what I thought, and I'd feel lousy if you got stuck going home with no one around to help. Why don't you stay until I get off, and I'll follow you over there? That way, I'll know exactly where the place is and I can help you if you get mired in the mud."

Dani gazed at him. He had a point. The roads were becoming more treacherous by the minute. She'd skidded a couple of times on the way over.

"You never ordered that glass of wine. Let me buy you a drink to help pass the time."

Dani glanced at Cindy moving around the room checking orders. Jesus had returned to the mike and was plucking a few strings in preparation for his last set. If she stayed until Jake got off duty and then he followed her out of the parking lot, it would certainly look to anyone who noticed as if she'd come here to pick him up. But if she couldn't act on her own without worrying about other people's opinions, she wasn't very free, was she?

She took off her raincoat, laid it across one saddle and swung up to the other. "A glass of Chablis, bartender."

"Atta girl."

Jesus began with a rousing redition of "Tequila." Jake put the wine in front of her and smiled. Her heart thumping, she raised her glass to him. *No guts, no glory,* she thought, and drank.

JAKE HAD GRABBED the first excuse he could think of to keep Dani at the bar until he was ready to leave. Fortunately, it was a legitimate excuse; she shouldn't be driving around on a night like this by herself. And after the call he'd received that morning, he needed to make the most of any opportunity to be close to her. At least that was the logical explanation for his behavior.

There was another part of his brain cruising along on autopilot, however, making decisions independent of logic. He knew which part it was, too, and what part of his anatomy governed it. There was a rebel loose in his system, a rebel who wanted to pick up on all the signals Dani was throwing out.

He didn't believe her gesture tonight was entirely out of kindness, or even fear of being in a rural area all alone. When he'd seen her in the bar tonight, he'd about come unglued. He'd expected to get word on the empty rental tomorrow when she came to work. Instead, she'd driven through this godawful weather to bring him a key that would ensure him a dry night's sleep. Something beyond casual friendship was going on here, and he wanted to respond. Lord, he did want to respond.

He drew another draft for a guy seated at the far end of the bar, and lingered to exchange a couple of jokes. He was longing to get back to Dani, but decided he'd better cool it. For both their sakes, he needed to distance himself a bit more emotionally.

He helped Cindy clean up the mess in the corner and waited for last call on drinks before returning to the end of the bar where Dani sat, her slender fingers toying with the stem of her wineglass. He could tell she'd been watching him from the sudden dip of her head as she glanced down at her glass. Jesus had slowed his tempo to include a few love ballads as the night wound down to closing, and Jake wished he could ask Dani to dance, wished he could smooth her rain-tangled hair. He wished they could both move naturally into this romance that beckoned so insistently.

Instead, he concentrated on business matters. "I didn't even ask you what the rent was."

She told him. "You pay a little more than I do," she added, "because—"

"I don't have to feed the peacocks," he finished for her. "Paula sure was turned on by those peacocks, wasn't she?" He realized this was the first time he and Dani had talked without Paula being around.

"Yes." At the mention of Paula, Dani didn't smile as he'd expected. "I met her parents tonight, Jake. They're pretty hard on her."

He didn't like the sound of that. "Like how?" He listened as she described Paula's bedroom, her excitement at the idea of pinstriping Dani's car and her devastation when her parents had forbade it. "That's not right."

"No, it's not. And I don't know if they'll even approve of her coming over to visit me now. They're trying to control her, and they may see me as a threat to that control."

Jake smiled. "Which you are."

"But Paula doesn't deserve to be restricted like that!"

"I know." Jake longed to reach out and smooth the worried frown from between her eyes, while the mellow chords from Jesus' guitar suggested other things to him—slipping his hand under her hair to the tender nape of her neck, brushing his lips over hers. "I'd hate to see Paula's parents reject you. You're a good influence on her."

"She's a good influence on me. I love the way she looks at the world. Jake, she has an inborn feeling for design! You should see the way she blends color, the flow of the lines around the room."

She drew graceful pictures with her hands as she described the intricate designs Paula had created, and he found himself wondering how her long, slender fingers would feel tracing those same patterns on his skin.

"There were these undulating waves that curled around corners as if those edges didn't exist," Dani continued. "Standing in that room was sort of like traveling through space at warp speed. It was wonderful."

He'd never seen her carried away like this, and he was entranced. He knew about her plan to sell the jewelry she designed, but she'd always spoken of it from a practical standpoint—the mechanics of finding a shop to carry her work and the seasonal nature of Tubac's tourist trade. Now he glimpsed the emotion she put into her art and her excitement at finding a kindred spirit. "I'll bet you can work out something for Paula."

"I hope so. We can't let a talent like hers be wasted just because her parents are dictators."

We. A dangerous word. He liked it far too much.

"Quittin' time," Cindy sang out as she marched around the room collecting glasses. "You two can hang out here if you want, but I'm heading home soon as I clear these tables."

Jake glanced up in surprise. Everyone had left, including Jesus with his guitar, and he hadn't even noticed.

Dani slipped down from the saddle. "Can I do anything?"

Probably everything he needed done, Jake thought. Maybe, if he could hang around Dani long enough, he'd even find some direction for his own life. He'd love to be as excited about something again as she was about design. Once there'd been baseball. Now... nothing.

"There isn't much to do," he said. "I'll just clean up a little, close up the cash register and we can take off." And he'd follow her home to the little house with the peacocks and the train that rumbled by at dawn. *This is just a job, Clayborn,* he reminded himself, but he knew that was no longer true.

Maybe he should have let her go on home ahead of him after all, he thought as he followed the bouncing taillights of her Mustang over the muddy, silent roads of the town. The drive to her house seemed too much like a prelude to a lovers' tryst. The rain had stopped, and a sliver of moon played hide-and-seek through the dark branches of the trees. The incident with the drunken cowboy had left him with an adrenaline high. He wanted someone to hold . . . and he was following a beautiful woman through the night.

DANI LED HIM across the railroad tracks and over the bridge that spanned the rushing river, then flicked on her right-hand turn signal and eased down the driveway to the parking space beside her house. Jake pulled up behind her and left the truck engine running and the lights on.

Her heart pounding fast, she got out of the car and sidestepped the puddles as she walked back to his truck. She and Jake were just friends, she told herself. Bringing him back here tonight didn't change that. They still hadn't had a date, let alone physical contact with each other, but their drive together through the night had subtly lured them into a new intimacy she couldn't ignore.

He rolled down his window. One look into his eyes told her he felt the strengthening bond between them as much as she did. Dani decided she wanted more time to be sure about Jake before she was hurled headlong into passion. Because she knew there would be passion.

"Your place is over there," she said, gesturing to the house across the way. It was a white stucco, like hers, but she liked hers better, even if the peacocks came with it. The windows were smaller in the other house, and it had no front porch, only a small concrete stoop, so it looked boxier and less welcoming. At the moment, it seemed almost forbidding, sitting there in total darkness. "With no lights or heat, it won't be great. The rain's stopped. I may not have done you much of a favor, after all."

He put the truck back in neutral and revved the engine. "I have a flashlight. No problem. And I've taken cold showers before. Just tell me where the main water valve is and I'll be set."

"The landlord said in the back, by the rosebush." The instructions sounded cold and inhospitable. "Want some help finding it?"

"Sure." He leaned toward the passenger side of the truck and opened it. "Hop in."

She picked her way back around the front of the truck, and climbed into the cab with him. The interior smelled musty and the floor mat was damp. He hadn't been kidding about leaks.

He reached for the gearshift and brushed the outspread material of her peasant skirt that had escaped the confines of her raincoat.

"Sorry," she murmured, gathering the skirt closer to her legs. Once inside the truck, she became intensely aware of him. At the restaurant, they'd always had some physical barrier between them, either the mahogany bar or the table where they sat to eat lunch. Now there was nothing but a slender shaft of metal and a few inches of empty space.

She noticed the tensing of his thighs as he worked the trucks pedals and started down the narrow lane, the

movement of his hand on the shift knob, even the
sound of his breathing and the scent of cigarette smoke
he'd picked up from working in the bar all night.

Until this moment, Jake had been a fantasy man to
her. As she rode this short distance in his truck, he was
becoming real in a way that was far more exciting than
her vague illusions. She felt restless and jumpy, as if
she'd taken in too much caffeine.

"Why don't I just pull around and shine my lights
back there so we can see." He angled the truck so the
headlight beams slid down the back wall of the house.
A raccoon scuttled away as Jake got out of the truck.
"Aha! Wildlife. By the way, where were the peacocks
when we came in?"

"On the porch railing or up in the mesquite tree, no
doubt." Dani climbed down from the cab. "There's the
valve, right over there."

"I see it." He skirted the rosebush. "Looks like I
might have flowers this spring."

"If you water them. By the way, I should warn you
about something. Have you ever heard the cry of a
peacock?"

"I don't think so," he said, twisting the handle.
"There, that should do it." He turned and walked back
to her. "Why?"

"It sounds like a woman crying for help, as if she's
being killed." Goose bumps rose on her arms as she
spoke. "I just didn't want you to think I was being
murdered in my bed or something." She forced a
laugh, but the idea didn't seem so funny on this cold,
rainy night.

He gazed at her. "Thanks, but what if you *are* being murdered in your bed? How will I know the difference?"

She shivered. "That's a scary thought."

"Never mind. I'm pretty good at picking out false alarms."

"Really?" She made a mental note to discuss her mother with him sometime. She needed to talk to someone about her mother's behavior, but she couldn't burden Paula with it, and she hadn't felt close enough to anyone else she'd met in Tubac. "Anyway, it's a moot point," she said, shrugging. "Tubac's not exactly the crime capital of the country, so if you hear anything alarming, it's bound to be peacocks."

"I'll keep that in mind."

She glanced up at him. They were so completely alone right now. She felt a delicious and dangerous thrill at the awareness in his eyes.

"Thanks, Dani."

She was afraid he'd kiss her, wished he'd kiss her. "You can thank me after you hear the train in the morning. That hot-rodding engineer will be through here in about five hours."

"I won't mind it. I like early morning."

And I like you. A lot. "I used to like sleeping in," she said, unsure of the wisdom of this bed-talk, "but I'm learning to appreciate mornings. The air is so fresh then, and except for that train and, of course, the peacocks, it's quiet."

"It's quiet now."

"I guess it is."

He gazed at her for a moment. "Go home, Dani," he said softly.

She sucked in her breath.

"That's not a rejection," he added, his voice low and restrained. "That's a suggestion."

Dani's face burned. "I hope you don't think that I brought you here because I had some idea that we'd—"

He groaned. "No." He stepped forward and cupped her face in his hands.

She trembled under his touch. "Then again, maybe I did."

He stroked her cheek with his thumb and gazed down at her. "I wish you hadn't admitted that," he murmured, and covered her mouth with his.

CHAPTER FIVE

SHE SHOULDN'T HAVE let him kiss her. Not after he'd just told her to go home, as if she were a child. Yet he wasn't kissing her as if she were a child.

He outlined her lips with the tip of his tongue and she held perfectly still, as if moving would spoil the work of art he was creating. And this kiss was a work of art. By the time he finally slipped his tongue into her mouth, her heart was racing with anticipation and she moaned softly.

His slow, deliberate exploration sent desire sluicing through her and she balled her hands into fists, as if she could maintain her balance that way.

But her balance was precarious. He tilted her head and deepened the kiss. Her heartbeat pounded in her ears, the sound mingling with the bubbling rush of the river. The earth smelled moist and fertile, and something primitive awoke in Dani, an urge more powerful than anything she'd ever felt before.

Frightened at the surge of need that left her trembling, she pushed away from him and held her hand to her lips. "I...think I'll go home." Yet her body wouldn't obey her and she stayed where she was, breathing hard. She couldn't look away from the untamed fire in his eyes.

Then his eyes closed, and he shook his head. "That was a mistake."

She wouldn't have called it a mistake, exactly. It was more like a warning, the kind posted on the back of tanker trucks carrying explosives. "I'll, ah, see you tomorrow, then."

"Sure. Right."

Praying her trembling legs would carry her, she turned and started around the house. She didn't want it to look as if she were running away, but she had to get out of there and give herself time to sort through her reactions to him.

Then she remembered he'd have no way to make so much as a cup of coffee in the morning. She glanced over her shoulder. He hadn't moved. "If you'd like coffee in the morning, I always make too much for myself. You're welcome to a cup." That was better. A homey detail of everyday life to normalize this encounter.

He seemed relieved that she'd lessened the tension. "Coffee would be nice."

"Any time after the train." She hurried away and stepped in several puddles as she crossed the yard to her house. Light glowed from the window, a beacon guiding her back to a safe world where she was completely in control.

WATCHING HER GO, Jake cursed himself. He should have known what would happen—should have known and stayed the hell away from those full lips. Except he hadn't known. Not really. How could he have realized that he'd drown in her the moment they touched?

Whoever had said that a kiss was just a kiss hadn't tried it with Dani Goodwin.

She'd been sizzling like a pan full of bacon, yet she hadn't moved an inch. Holding herself still like that, taking in everything he offered, had been the most sensual experience of his life. He wanted it again. Now. But he wasn't going to have it. He was a professional, with orders to follow, promises to keep. He couldn't allow himself to forget that again.

PAULA ALMOST ALWAYS did what people told her. Almost always. Except tonight, when her mother had said go to sleep, Paula hadn't. She'd stayed awake for the whole night.

Dani had said she could pinstripe the car. All night long, Paula thought about how it would look, what colors she would use. She had to paint that car. She had to.

Just before the sun came up, she decided. She put on her favorite blue sweat suit and filled her fanny-pack with paints and brushes. Then she moved silently down the dim hall. At the door to her parents' room, she stopped and listened to her father snoring. Good. But she had to hurry. He got up early.

He didn't think she knew how to turn off the burglar alarm. She knew. In the garage she looked at the big car her father loved so much. Paula thought it was ugly. She'd wanted to fix it up but he wouldn't let her. Dani was different. Dani was her friend.

Paula pushed a button and the garage door rattled up, making lots of noise. She held her breath, but nobody came running out. Good. She unhooked her bike from its holders on the side of the garage and rolled it out into the gray morning. A few stars were still out, and the air smelled like rain. She put up the hood on her sweatshirt and tied the string under her chin.

"Hi-ho, Silver," she said, and shoved off.

Dani's house was across the river. Paula knew where the river was. Dani had peacocks. Paula would find her. And pinstripe her car. Damn straight.

DANI WOKE UP before the peacocks had a chance to get started. The restlessness that had disturbed her all night—the aftermath of Jake's kiss, the promise of seeing him again this morning—propelled her out of bed. Pulling on a robe, she went out to the porch.

The peacock and his hens drowsed on the porch railing. "Wake up, sleepyheads." When she reached for the barrel lid, they came to life, erupting from the railing in a flurry of feathers.

She tossed out their bird seed and gazed across the clearing toward the white house where Jake was sleeping. The train would wake him up; Dani had no doubt about that. Then before long he'd tap on her door and ask for the coffee she'd promised him.

And then what?

They were just as alone as they'd been the night before. If Jake had spent the hours since they'd kissed thinking or dreaming about the same things she had... Dani wrapped her arms around herself and went inside. First things first. She'd brew some coffee.

JAKE DIDN'T WAKE UP until the house began to shake. Naked, he leaped out of bed in a crouch, ready for whatever monster was bent on his destruction. Then he remembered the train and began to chuckle.

He stood and stretched, wincing only slightly at the pain in his right shoulder. He'd pretty much gotten used to that little souvenir from his pitching days. The doctors had said it would never be completely sound, but if he didn't throw any more baseballs, he wouldn't have a permanently disabling injury. In the Canada Verde employees' softball game scheduled for Monday, he'd agreed to be a first baseman and team captain. That much he could do if he played it safe.

The train rumbled away and the sound of the whistle reached backward in an acoustic farewell. The train had come and gone. Dani would be awake.

Residual emotion from last night's kiss warmed him, pushing away the chill of the unheated house. He ran his tongue over his lips as if to taste her presence, and desire moved within him. So last night hadn't been temporary insanity, an urge that disappeared with the cold logic morning usually brought. No, he still wanted her. And that was a problem.

She'd be expecting him for coffee, and he needed to be there if he was going to do his job. A cold shower beforehand would help. Maybe he just wouldn't turn on the hot water heater while he was living here, and everything would be fine.

Fifteen minutes later, he'd shaved, showered in icy water and dressed in a clean pair of jeans and a blue T-shirt. He combed his damp hair and glanced out the window at the lightening sky. The peacocks, looking less than magnificent with their tails dragging in the dirt, pecked at the ground in front of Dani's porch. Apparently she'd already been up to feed them, which meant he might as well go over now. Maybe he'd discover that she was ugly in the morning. Maybe she'd be grouchy. Maybe—

He leaned closer to the window. A chunky shadow moved around the corner of the house. It definitely wasn't Dani.

He watched a moment longer to make sure he wasn't imagining things, then quietly let himself out. Keeping to the shadows, he made his way quickly across the yard. The person hesitated on the steps leading to Dani's porch. Jake did not.

He launched himself at the intruder's feet, toppling both of them away from the steps and into the dirt. The peacocks flapped and squawked as they scurried out of the way. Jake grabbed the intruder's flailing arms and flipped his prisoner over.

His mouth dropped open as he gazed at Paula's flushed face. "Paula?"

"Jake!"

"What the hell is going on?" Dani yelled, charging down the steps with a bag of coffee in one hand.

Paula glanced her way. "Dani, Jake's here," she gasped.

"Hey, I'm really sorry." Jake released her and helped her to her feet. "Nobody told me you were coming over. I thought—"

"*I* didn't know she was coming over." Dani glanced around the yard. "How did you get here, Paula?"

"My bike." Paula started brushing the dirt from her sweat suit.

Jake brushed at the places she couldn't reach. "Isn't it a little early for a visit?"

"It's not a visit. It's pinstriping."

Jake stopped brushing and exchanged a glance with Dani.

She walked over and laid a hand on Paula's arm. "Did your parents say it was okay?"

"Nope." Paula looked proudly defiant. "I sneaked out."

Dani groaned. "I think we're in trouble."

"They won't find me."

The sound of a powerful V-8 engine and tires crunching on stones in the unpaved road made all three of them turn.

"I think they already have," Jake said as a white Lincoln Continental pulled into the yard. A man and woman dressed in matching navy jogging suits got out of the car. He would have judged them an attractive older couple except for the scowls on their faces.

The man he assumed was Paula's father marched up and grabbed her arm. "What sort of stunt are you pulling, young lady?"

"How did you find me?"

"We called the restaurant manager," her mother said. "Paula, sweetie, you worried us half to death, wondering if you were okay. You know your father has a bad heart."

Paula lifted her round chin and looked at them with a coolness that amazed Jake. "I'm going to pinstripe Dani's car."

"Absolutely not," her father said. "We're going home." He started to pull Paula away, and although she was struggling, she was no match for him.

Dani hurried around in front of them. "Mr. and Mrs. Jordan, please reconsider. This would mean so much to both Paula and me. She's a fine artist."

"She's an embarrassment!" her father blurted out. Then his face reddened. "What I mean is, it's embarrassing for us to have to chase around after her and—"

"Mr. Jordan." Jake surprised himself. He hadn't meant to get into this. It sure wasn't part of his job description. He strode forward and stuck out his hand. "I'm Jake Clayborn."

Jordan hesitated. He was holding Paula with his right hand. In order to be polite, he had to release her, which he did. Paula scurried over to stand next to Dani.

"The baseball player," Jordan said, grasping Jake's hand with a firm grip. "Rookie of the Year, as I recall."

"Yeah."

"I'm Ed Jordan." He released Jake's hand. "Been meaning to get over to the bar and meet you. Saw you pitch against the Cubs. Damned impressive. That shoulder injury ended a promising career."

"So the sportswriters said."

"Surprised to hear you're tending bar for a living. Did the ball club screw you financially?"

"I take full credit for being broke. Several people told me to invest my money, but—" He shrugged.

"Ah." Jordan winked and pulled a pipe from his back pocket. "Wine, women and song, eh?"

"Something like that."

Jordan filled the pipe from a tobacco pouch he pulled out of his jacket pocket, then gave Jake a sly wink. "I guess that explains what you're doing here so early this morning."

"What?" Dani started forward.

"I must have misunderstood you, Jordan." Jake said, flexing his fingers. "At least I hope I did."

Paula's father paused with the flaming match halfway to the bowl of his pipe and gazed uneasily at Jake. "Sure, sure. Just a misunderstanding. Didn't mean anything by it."

"Ed." His wife tugged at his arm. "Maybe we should go. Nice to have met you, Mr. Clayborn."

"Yeah," Ed Jordan shook out the match and clamped the unlit pipe between his back teeth. "Same here. Come on, Paula."

"I'm staying."

"No, I'm afraid you're not."

"Staying," Paula repeated.

Jake took a deep breath. "I have a proposal. Paula can start with my camper." He gestured across the yard to the dilapidated truck. "As you can see, it won't win any beauty contests. Anything Paula does to it will be an improvement."

Ed glanced at the truck. "You weren't kidding about being broke." He took the pipe out of his mouth and pointed across the yard with the stem. "That's the sorriest piece of transportation I've seen in a long while."

"I could make it pretty," Paula said.

Ed paused and seemed to gauge the situation. Finally, he shrugged. "Well, why not? Would make a good story. My daughter painted Jake Clayborn's truck."

"And when she's done that satisfactorily, she can move on to Dani's Mustang."

Ed studied Jake. "I still don't like it, but okay. Just remember, if either of you think you can sue me, I have the toughest lawyer in Arizona."

"I have no doubt of that," Jake said.

"Well, Madge, let's go have some breakfast. Didn't even get my coffee this morning." Ed stalked off with Madge trailing after him.

Dani spoke softly. "Nice going."

Jake grinned at her. "Thanks."

Paula's eyes were wider than usual as she stared at Jake. "I can pinstripe your truck?"

"You bet. I wouldn't lie to a man who has the toughest lawyer in Arizona."

"Hurray!" She lunged at Jake and almost knocked him to the ground as she gave him a bear hug. "I'll start now! I have paints. I can—"

"Whoa," Jake said, laughing. "We'd better wash it first."

"Where's the hose?" Paula asked, rolling up the sleeves of her sweatshirt.

"Tell you what." Jake looked over at Dani, who was watching them with a smile on her face. She didn't look ugly in the morning. Dressed in jeans and a soft pink sweater, she looked...perfect. Her hair was down. He hadn't taken time to admire the soft ripple of it down her back, but he admired it now. "I think we could all use some coffee before we get started."

Dani held up the bag in her hand. "I was in the middle of making it. Shouldn't take long."

Jake thought fast. "I have a loaf of bread in the camper that can only be saved by toasting it. Why don't I get that while you two set us up with some coffee?"

"Awesome," Paula said, beaming.

Jake sighed with relief as Dani and Paula headed up the steps into Dani's house. He kept a .38 Special in the camper as a backup, though he didn't much like the idea of using it. Other methods were usually more effective. He didn't want either Dani or Paula to stumble across it. Eventually, he might have to start carrying it. Maybe it would be the only way to accomplish what he had to do, but he hoped not. For now, he'd just move it into the house.

CHAPTER SIX

PAULA'S PRESENCE answered the question of whether Dani and Jake would pick up where they'd left off the night before. Paula made the perfect chaperon.

After the showdown with Paula's parents, breakfast was a jubilant meal, and then the sun came out in full force to warm the clearing where Paula and Dani helped Jake wash the truck. Work soon turned to play as they sprayed each other with the hose and joked about the disreputable state of Jake's vehicle.

When the truck was as clean as they could make it, Paula grew serious and turned to sorting through her paints and brushes.

Dani watched Paula pick up and discard a color. The action reminded her of the indecision she always faced at the beginning of a jewelry project. "It'll be great, Paula," she said.

"I know." Paula chewed on her fingernail and gazed at the truck.

Dani recognized the signs of a preoccupied artist concentrating on her work. Paula needed to be alone while she pinstriped the truck. Dani tapped Jake on the shoulder. "How about another cup of coffee?"

He caught her look. "Sure. Sounds good."

She led the way into her kitchen, which had a view of the clearing.

"Do you think it's too much pressure for her?" Jake asked, glancing out the window. The window was open a few inches to let in fresh air, so he kept his voice low.

"She'll be fine. Especially if we don't hang over her shoulder." She measured coffee into the basket. "Not this first time, at least."

Jake sat at the table. "Can you make jewelry with people watching you?"

"Now I can. I had a little shop in Hollywood, and I was the only one in it, so I had to make jewelry and wait on customers at the same time. People love to watch. Often they'll buy what you're working on, because they saw it being created." She switched on the coffeemaker and sat across the table from Jake. "If Paula wants to turn this into a business some day, she'll probably have to work under all sorts of conditions. But that's an evolutionary thing."

"A business?" Jake lowered his voice another notch. "You think those parents of hers are going to allow that?"

"I was counting on you to help me convince them." She smiled. "Mr. Rookie of the Year."

He made a face. "I hate that kind of thing. People liking you because of some past accomplishment, instead of for who you are now. But it comes in handy sometimes."

"It sure did this morning." The coffeemaker stopped growling and she got up to pour them each a cup. "And another thing I've wanted a chance to say..." She replaced the carafe on the hot plate and rejoined him at the table. "Thanks for defending my honor out there."

"I wanted to deck the son of a bitch."

Dani gazed at him. "But if you had, everything would have been ruined."

"Yep."

"I admire that kind of control."

He grinned. "Baseball."

"What?"

"Baseball taught me that. If you lose your temper on the mound, you're out of the game, both mentally and physically."

The sun through the window burnished the hair on his forearms, drawing Dani's attention to the way his muscles flexed as he picked up his coffee mug. She wished she'd seen him play ball. He must have been magnificent to watch. "It's too bad about your shoulder."

"I gave up feeling sorry about that. It's counterproductive. Besides, if I were still playing, I—" He stopped abruptly and glanced away.

She wanted him to finish the sentence. Why was he being so hesitant about his attraction to her? "You what?" she prompted.

"I wouldn't have been able to help Paula this morning," he finished, giving her a steady look.

Dani sighed softly in frustration. Last night might have been too soon for both of them, but she'd noticed the way he studied her when he thought she wasn't aware of it. He seemed to take the same delight in her that she found in him.

Perhaps she needed to open up a little more, herself. Maybe now was the time to tell him about her mother. "I also appreciate your coming to my rescue when you thought someone was lurking around, even if it did turn out to be Paula."

Jake looked out the window to where Paula was kneeling next to his truck applying a thin line of black along the rusted fender. "I feel bad about tackling her like that, but I couldn't imagine a legitimate reason for someone to be sneaking up on your porch at dawn."

"She probably would have scared me to death, too, if I'd seen her out there. Fortunately, I was working in the kitchen and didn't realize she was here until I heard all the noise." Dani sipped her coffee. "You see, I'm a little jumpy these days. My mother's convinced I'm in some sort of danger down here."

His gaze sharpened. "Like what?"

"It's stupid. She's probably making it up. After all, she writes fiction and she's desperately lonely. I think she's trying to scare me enough to move home and stay with her."

"What does she say is going on?"

Dani filled him in on the notes, explained who her mother was and that her father had died two years ago. Confiding in someone, especially someone like Jake who had such empathy, felt good. She'd kept her concerns bottled up too long.

"And you think your mother is making all of this up?" Jake asked when she'd finished.

Dani laughed nervously and toyed with the handle of her coffee mug. "Let's hope she is. Otherwise, some weirdo really is on my trail."

"It's hard to believe someone would dream up such an elaborate hoax."

"You don't know my mother. When my father died, it seemed as if she'd lost her whole reason to live. She stopped going out with her friends because they all had husbands and she didn't. She pestered me constantly to move back in with her and keep her company. And she does have an incredible imagination."

Jake got up and refilled their cups. Dani accepted the gesture as a nurturing one and was pleased that Jake felt comfortable enough to do it. He sat down and stared into the black liquid in front of him. "I can believe a lonely widow would lay a guilt trip on you and try to rope you back into her life. That happens all the time. But I've never heard of anyone trumping up a conspiracy against her child to scare her into moving back home."

"But what motive would someone have for harming me? If they wanted money, they'd have snatched me by now and asked for ransom. These have been vague threats, all quotes from my mother's book, printed on a machine exactly like one she has in her office. They seem pointless, unless she wrote them herself to bring me home. And as I said, she writes fiction. She has a fertile brain."

Jake gazed at her for a long time. "I don't know what to make of it."

"Neither do I, but thanks for listening."

"Any time." He glanced out at his truck. "She's got red, white and black so far. Think we should wander out there yet?"

"Depends on how many colors you want on your truck."

Jake consulted his watch. "And whether I'll be able to drive it to work in an hour."

Dani jumped up. "It's that late? I totally forgot about the time."

Jake tipped his head toward where Paula labored on the red stripe's swirling tail. "I'll bet she has, too."

"If she's anything like me when I'm on a project, she's totally engrossed. I hate to break in on her, but she has to go home, change clothes, and get back to the restaurant. We'll have to postpone the rest of this for another day."

"Let's go tell her how great it looks."

Dani studied the truck from the window. "It does, doesn't it?" She turned back to him with a smile. "I told you so."

"We'll make sure she keeps up with it. Maybe she could go into business, after all."

"And you'll help convince her parents?"

He nodded. "I'll help."

DANI ENDED UP driving Jake to work to make certain the paint on his truck had plenty of time to dry. On Sunday nights, she and Jake got off at the same time, so it would be no trouble for her to drive him home again.

No trouble, Dani thought as she dressed for work, but filled with possibilities. They were growing closer every minute. She could feel it, but she kept running into that strange resistance in him. Maybe tonight she'd find out what that resistance was all about. Or maybe tonight it would disappear.

She and Jake had pried Paula from her painting with great difficulty, especially after Paula realized the next day's softball game would mean postponing the rest of her pinstriping until Tuesday. But Jake reminded her she'd be playing right field on his team, which seemed to make up for the forced interruption. Paula was whistling as she rode away to change into her work clothes.

The rain appeared to be over for a while, so Dani put the Mustang's top down for the trip with Jake to the country club. As they wound through the streets of Tubac, Dani chatted with him about Paula and her amazing ability. Jake commented on the beauty of the mountains, the clarity of the air. But underneath their casual conversation flowed a current of awareness. Tonight they would be alone again.

The knowledge teased Dani as she waited tables. Getting orders from the bar became a charged encounter, and lunch with Paula and Jake became an exercise in thinking about something else besides his lips, his strong arms, his gentle eyes.

Paula was so excited about her pinstriping and the coming softball game that she didn't seem to notice Dani's preoccupation. Sometimes Dani caught Jake looking at her, and his gaze telegraphed frustrated longing. Or was she imagining his carefully bridled response to her? She didn't think so.

During dinner, she served her customers automatically, paying scant attention to the small talk that usually accompanied the job. When a sophisticated-looking brunette dining alone complimented Dani on her cactus-flower earrings, she thanked her absently. She wasn't much in the mood for conversation.

"Did you buy them in Tubac?" the woman persisted.

Dani became more attentive. She couldn't afford to be uncommunicative where her jewelry was concerned. "I made them." She set down the plate of *flautas* and rice. "Be careful. The plate's hot."

"You *made* those? You do channel settings?"

"Yes."

"Oh, let me look at one."

Dani slipped the French hook from her earlobe and handed the piece of jewelry to the woman.

She smoothed her finger over the design. "Exquisite. The silver and stones mesh perfectly."

"Thank you."

"I suppose you found this pattern in a book."

"No, I design my own."

"You're joking."

"Each of my designs is an original. No two are alike."

The woman clapped her hands together. "I can't believe my good fortune! I've been in Tubac exactly three days and I believe I've found just the designer I've been looking for. It must be fate."

Dani stared at her. "Excuse me?"

"Let me give you my card." The woman dug in her purse, produced an elegant embossed card and handed it to Dani.

She read the inscription aloud. "'The Silver Coyote, Evelyn Ross, Owner.'" Then she glanced at the address on Tubac Road. "I don't remember seeing a shop by that name."

Evelyn smiled. "That's because there's no sign yet. I'm renovating the property. I closed the deal on Friday and put a rush on those cards. I picked them up today in Tucson and came here for dinner to celebrate."

Dani's head buzzed with excitement. "You'll carry jewelry?"

"Primarily. I picked up some inventory from a gift shop going out of business in Tucson, so I have a few pots and baskets, and some mediocre jewelry. I was

hoping to find a local source for some better designs."
She held up Dani's earring to the light. "I hadn't expected anything as magnificent as this to drop in my lap, though."

Dani wanted to shout with joy. Here was exactly the kind of break she'd been hoping for! As she started to ask Evelyn for more information, Jean brushed past her.

"One of your orders is getting cold in the kitchen," she murmured.

Dani started in surprise. She'd completely forgotten she was supposed to be waiting tables. Tucking the business card in the pocket of her skirt, she glanced apologetically at Evelyn. "I have to get back to work. I'll make sure there's some time to come back and talk to you before you leave."

"Please do." Evelyn handed back the earring. "And don't fret about this job. I have a feeling you won't be waiting tables much longer."

Dani replaced her earring and hurried back to the kitchen. As she served her next order, her attention kept wandering over to Evelyn's table. The woman obviously had money. Her pale gray pantsuit looked like raw silk, and the heavy gold jewelry she wore with it gleamed with a twenty-four-carat patina. Dani wondered why a woman who preferred traditional gold pieces had admired Dani's earrings, which were southwestern, like most of Dani's designs.

But now wasn't the time to look a gift horse in the mouth. Evelyn liked Dani's earrings, and they were representative of what she had packed carefully away in her little house, just waiting for this opportunity.

The next time she had an order from the bar, she leaned toward Jake. "There's a woman in there who's opening a jewelry shop, and she wants to see the rest of my designs."

"Yeah? Hey, that's great." Jake smiled. "Must be a lucky day for both you and Paula."

"Must be." She savored the warmth in his eyes. She felt like celebrating, and she couldn't think of anyone she'd rather celebrate with than Jake. She had a bottle of wine in the refrigerator at home. Maybe she'd ask him in for a glass. She realized how he might interpret that. She didn't care. "See you later," she said, and picked up her tray.

"You bet."

As Dani carried the drinks back to the dining room, she hummed a Spanish love song under her breath.

The dining room bustled with activity, and Dani didn't have another moment to talk to Evelyn Ross until she was taking care of the woman's bill. Along with her change, Dani handed Evelyn a piece of paper with her address and telephone number written on it. "Here's how you can reach me," she said.

"That's fine." Evelyn glanced up from the paper. "But why don't we make plans to get together in the morning around ten? I noticed the restaurant's closed tomorrow, and I'll be working in the shop, getting it ready. You could come by with some of your inventory. Maybe we could have a little lunch, and talk about the possibilities."

"Tomorrow? Oh, I..." The softball game started at ten, and then there'd be a picnic. She'd agreed to play second base for Jean's team. Paula, too, was counting on her to be there. And then there was Jake.

Dani hesitated, then made her decision. "Could we possibly make it the next morning? I don't have to be at work until noon, so if I came by at ten on Tuesday, I'd have plenty of—"

"Of course." Evelyn looked irritated. "If that's what you'd prefer."

The change in her tone worried Dani. She didn't want to blow this. "You see, there's a company picnic tomorrow, and I have a friend who's counting on me to—"

"I understand completely."

Dani didn't think she did, but Paula would be devastated if Dani missed tomorrow's activities. And Dani didn't want to miss them, either. What difference did a day make? If Evelyn Ross was inflexible, perhaps Dani didn't want to work with her, after all. "Then I guess I'll see you at ten on Tuesday," she said, keeping her tone pleasant.

"Make it nine." Evelyn reached for her purse and stood. "I don't like to rush through things."

"All right. And thank you for the opportunity."

Her manner was chilly. "Certainly. I respect exceptional talent." Then, without another word, she left the restaurant.

Dani shook her head. Strange lady. Maybe she'd reconsider her offer because Dani hadn't been willing to change her plans. Whatever, Dani wouldn't find out until Tuesday.

On the way home, Jake was full of questions about Evelyn. "So she just blew into town a few days ago?"

"I guess." Cool night air brushed Dani's warm skin. She wasn't thinking about Evelyn anymore.

"No family or friends?"

"She didn't mention any, but I didn't have a long time to talk to her." She cast a brief glance in Jake's direction. Moonlight splashing into the open car silvered his hair and picked up the metal studs of his tan western shirt. Just the sound of his breathing made her heart beat faster.

"Seems funny that she just waltzed into town to start up a gift shop."

"I don't know. I just waltzed into town to sell my jewelry, and you just waltzed into town and became a bartender. Tubac is like that, I think. People are drawn to the place, so they just pack up and move here."

"Maybe you're right. An artist came into the bar tonight who said he'd lived all over the country, and Tubac had the clearest light."

"There, you see?" She pulled into the driveway leading to their houses.

"Yeah, I do."

She felt he was looking at her, and when she turned off the engine and glanced in his direction, he was. She took a deep breath. "Would you like to... come in for a glass of wine?"

"I don't think so, Dani."

His refusal came like a slap. She stared out through the windshield, her heart thumping. Dammit, she might as well get to the bottom of this puzzle. "Why not?"

His voice grew softer. "I can't."

"Can't or won't?"

"All right. Won't."

"There's my answer, then. Have a nice life, Mr. Clayborn." She was halfway out of the car when he grasped her arm.

"Dani."

"Let me go! I'm tired of this game. All day long you send me these signals, but you—"

"I didn't mean to make you angry."

"Well, I'm furious! And hurt." She struggled, but he was stronger. He captured her other arm and drew her partway across the seat until his face was inches from hers. "I don't understand you," she whispered.

"I know." His gaze roved her face. "I know, and I'm sorry."

"Are you married, or something?"

"No."

"Then what's going on?"

"More than I counted on." His grip relaxed but she didn't pull away. "I can't come in for wine, because then I'd never leave."

Her skin tingled where he touched her. His words reverberated in the stillness of the night and left her aching. "Does that matter?"

"Yes. For now. I need a little more time, Dani. Things are . . . complicated."

"What things? Why can't you tell me?"

"I will. Soon. But first I have to— Dani, don't look at me like that."

She closed her eyes.

Jake groaned. "That's worse."

A movement of air warned her of his intent. His kiss was greedy, and she responded with heat of her own. She didn't know what his problems were, and she didn't care. She needed the warmth of his mouth on hers—taking, giving, seducing. She shoved her fingers up through his hair and pressed his head closer. He groaned again and wrenched himself away.

Slowly she opened her eyes.

He gazed down at her, his eyes shadowed, his breathing heavy. "Believe me when I tell you this is the toughest thing I've ever had to do." Then he released her and opened the car door. "I hope some day you'll forgive me," he said, and climbed out.

Forgive him, she thought as she hugged herself against the sudden chill of the night. For what? He refused to do anything to be forgiven for! She turned and watched him walk across the yard. When she was sure he wouldn't be back, she got out of the car and went into her lonely little house. *Some celebration.*

JAKE FELT LIKE slamming the door behind him, but he shut it carefully. Dammit! He stood in the darkened house fighting his desire and wondering what the hell to do. Finally, he grabbed the keys to his truck and went back outside. A light was on in her kitchen. All he had to do was walk over there. She wouldn't ask for explanations. She was trusting her heart, and he knew she'd let him make love to her without knowing a single other thing about him.

He took a step in her direction, cursed and walked back to his truck. The paint would be dry by now. In a few moments he drove away from the house, away from temptation. He knew there was a pay phone on Tubac Road. He'd already used it countless times.

He pulled up to the curb and fumbled in the glove compartment for his phone card. He was going to get some straight answers this time. He wasn't at all sure he'd gotten them before. It hadn't really mattered until now. He was getting paid, and that had been enough for the time being. No more. The phone rang twice before a woman answered.

"Okay," he said without identifying himself. "Who the hell is Evelyn Ross?"

CHAPTER SEVEN

HELEN GOODWIN sighed into the phone. "I didn't think she'd be a problem."

Jake swore under his breath. So his hunch had been right about the mysterious appearance of this gift shop owner. "Who is she?"

"A friend of mine."

Jake rolled his eyes upward to the star-sprinkled Arizona sky. "And you sent her down here to keep track of Dani."

"She offered to go, Jake. I know you can't watch Dani every minute, so I thought it wouldn't hurt anything if Evelyn came down to keep an eye on her, too."

"She's got Dani all worked up about selling her jewelry through this bogus shop."

"It's not bogus. That was part of the plan. Evelyn will give Dani a boost. I hate the idea that she's down there waiting tables."

And he was tending bar. So what? Jake clenched his teeth. He hated this kind of interference on a job. "I thought nobody but John Slattery and I were supposed to know where and who Dani is."

"This is just one more person, and she means well."

"You should have told me."

"I . . . I didn't think you'd figure it out."

After absorbing the insult to his intelligence, Jake wondered what else she didn't think he'd figure out. That she was faking this whole thing? That the threatening notes had backfired and driven Dani away, so Helen had to hire a bodyguard to make reports on Dani? Jake thought over his alternatives. If he was only a paid baby-sitter, Evelyn Ross could do the job. And if he resigned as Dani's bodyguard, he wouldn't have to rein in every impulse toward her. The idea warmed him considerably.

"Jake, are you still there? Listen, I'm sorry about this. I should have told you."

"I'm here. Listen, Helen, maybe you don't need my services, now that Evelyn's in Tubac. After all, her services are free, and mine aren't. We can cancel—"

"No! Absolutely not. Evelyn's just sort of a backup. She's no use against this crazy person who's threatening Dani."

"*Is* someone threatening her?"

"Yes!" There was a pause. "She told you I made all this up, didn't she?"

"That was the gist of it."

"All right." Helen's voice grew hard. "I'll say this once. The notes are real, and you'd better guard that daughter of mine with your life."

Jake sensed her fear and desperation even across the telephone line. It was the same emotion he'd responded to when he'd taken the job. One of his strengths in baseball had been an instinct for knowing when opponents were bluffing. A chill ran down his spine. He wanted Helen to be bluffing. Despite all the evidence to support that, he couldn't convince himself she was.

"Then it's time to tell her the truth about who I am." That would solve many of his problems.

"No!"

"You're tying my hands, Helen! I can't set up surveillance equipment. I can't even stay close to her all the time without seeming suspicious myself."

"If you tell her, she'll run away."

Jake thought about that. Helen had a point.

"Besides, telling her will destroy what little relationship I have left with her. She's everything to me. I can't lose her."

"She'll find out eventually. Then what?"

"Why will she? Why can't you be a convenient friend who just happens to be there to protect her at a critical moment?"

"I think she's smarter than that."

"You're smart, too. You can convince her."

Jake clenched the receiver. "So she's never to know? I don't seem to recall your mentioning that."

"I didn't know it was important to you. Come to think of it, why is it important?"

Jake didn't answer, and the silence lengthened between them.

Finally, Helen gasped. "I should have guessed. Forget it, Jake. You so much as lay a hand on her, other than to keep her from harm, and your career is finished. Is that clear?"

"Perfectly clear." His head ached something fierce. "And now that we have that straight, you tell Evelyn Ross to stay the hell out of my way."

"I can't do that."

He leaned his pounding head against the cool glass of the phone booth. "Why not?"

"I didn't tell her I hired you. I was afraid if she knew that she wouldn't go down there, after all."

"Son of a bitch." He hung up the phone and left the booth as rockets exploded behind his eyes. Hell, maybe it was better if Evelyn didn't know who he was. She might interfere with him less that way.

As he drove back over the river, his head pounding, he thought about the path his life had taken since leaving baseball. If he hadn't met the rock singer who had an ex-football player for a bodyguard, he'd never even have thought about this line of work. He certainly hadn't needed the money. Contrary to what he'd told people in Tubac, he'd invested his money well. But he'd needed the sense of purpose.

The training had been enjoyable, and his years of karate gave him an advantage over others in the program. He'd always liked adventure movies, and the training lured him into believing he'd have one long adventure after another. He'd learned early, though, that a good bodyguard anticipated adventure and did everything he could to avoid it. If he did his job well, it was pretty boring. Still, it was better than sitting home watching television.

Lots of well-known people in L.A. hired bodyguards, but this was the first time he'd been asked to remain anonymous. And the first time he'd been attracted to the person he was guarding. It would also be the last. He should have resigned from this job the first day, when she walked into the bar and his heart kicked into high gear. But he hadn't resigned, and now he was too committed to leave.

His head was pounding. Could he stay close enough to protect Dani and not respond to the invitation in those gray eyes? And he'd thought Major League Baseball took nerves of steel.

"STRIKE TWO!"

Dani gritted her teeth and brought the bat up over her shoulder. She was swinging wildly, but she'd decided to pretend the softball was Jake's head and gotten carried away by the idea of clobbering him into the middle of next week.

They were playing fast-pitch, although nobody threw really fast in this game. Jake's team was ahead of Jean's. Paula had managed a bunt that surprised everyone, and both Jake and the cook had hit home runs. Dani was glad Paula was having a good time, but she dearly wanted to see Jake go down in defeat.

Sometime during the night, her hurt feelings had disappeared, leaving only anger. Why couldn't he tell her what the complications were? Did he have a social disease? A history of mental disorders? What? A gentleman would have confessed by now, or else stopped kissing her. She couldn't bear to look at him, standing there so smugly on first base. The worm.

The pitcher, one of the guys who worked in the golf course pro shop, wound up for another throw. Dani concentrated. She'd struck out the last time she'd been at bat. This time, she not only imagined that the ball was Jake's head, but that his face was stitched right on it.

Here it came. She adjusted her stance, lifted her bat and watched Jake's face come flying at her. There. Right there. Right on the nose. *Bam!* The bat connected with a solid thud and Jake's head sailed over the shortstop into the outfield. From the sidelines, Jean and the rest of the team cheered as Dani tossed down the bat and took off for first base, her hair flying out behind her after she lost her cap.

From the corner of her eye, she saw the left fielder scoop up the ball and rear back to throw it to Jake. She'd have to slide.

She sailed in, dust billowing around her, one foot connecting with Jake's leg. The force of the impact made her teeth click together, but Jake stayed solidly upright and caught the ball. Choking on the dust, she heard the verdict.

"Safe!"

She scrambled to her feet and punched both fists in the air. "Yes!"

"Nice going," he said, tossing the ball back to the pitcher.

"It was no contest," she boasted, dusting herself off and wincing at a sore spot on her hip.

"Are you okay?"

She glanced up into his brown eyes. "Fine." Someone brought her hat over and she pulled her hair back and put it on. "Just fine." She gave the brim another tug to bring it down over her eyes.

Jake chuckled.

"What's so funny?"

"It's almost worth having you mad at me to see the other side of sweet Dani Goodwin."

She glared up at him. Her next goal was to steal second so she could be the tying run. She edged off first.

"Gonna steal second?" Jake crouched, ready to catch the ball and tag her out.

She didn't answer.

"The catcher's got a good arm. Better wait and see what the batter does."

She focused on the pitcher. He wound up. The moment he released the ball toward home plate, she sprinted toward second. Too late she saw that Jake had been right. The catcher caught the ball and fired it toward second. She'd never make it.

She turned and headed back toward Jake, who was watching with a big grin. Damn him for being right! The ball swished past her and Jake caught it. He jogged toward her. She ran back toward second, but the second baseman was coming toward her, too. Jake tossed the ball to him. She was caught in the middle.

She charged toward Jake, knowing he'd have the ball any second. "Your fly's open," she said.

"So what?" He caught the ball neatly and tagged her out.

She growled in frustration while he laughed and tossed the ball back to the pitcher. At that moment, she thought he was the most irritating man she'd ever met...and the sexiest. Watching him move around the softball diamond gave her goose bumps. She was a sucker for excellence, and when it came to this game, Jake had it.

She'd also noticed how patiently he encouraged his team. When someone dropped a fly ball, he told them they'd get it next time. A strikeout was met with "Good swing!" Later she saw him working with the batter on stance and timing. Best of all, his acceptance of Paula as a valuable member of the team was changing the way the rest of the Canada Verde staff treated the young woman. Dani couldn't remember ever being so attracted to a man—a man who kept putting her at arm's length.

After the softball game, which Jake's team won easily, everyone gathered for a self-serve picnic of barbecued chicken, beans and fresh fruit salad. Paula motioned Dani and Jake to stand in line with her and then herded them toward a picnic table under a large mesquite just leafing out in tender green. The setting was idyllic. Dani would have preferred not to eat with Jake, but she couldn't bear to hurt Paula's feelings.

Paula was having the time of her life. Taking Jake's lead, several people came by to congratulate her on how well she'd played, and she was smiling so broadly she could barely eat. They'd arranged themselves by habit with Dani on one side of the table, Paula and Jake on the other.

The dappled shade of the mesquite felt good after the exertion of the game. Dani lifted her hair off the back of her neck to catch the breeze blowing through the grove. The breeze smelled of warm grass and barbecue sauce. She decided that life could be pretty wonderful right now, if only she understood what was going on with Jake.

"Did you see my bunt?" Paula asked for the third time.

Dani didn't mind the question. Paula was too excited to avoid repeating herself. "I saw it. You laid down a beauty, all right."

"Laid down a beauty," Paula murmured, taking a forkful of beans. "Yep." Then she glanced up. "Too bad you didn't win."

Jake looked at Dani over the rim of his paper cupful of ice tea. "She had a good hit."

"You made her get out," Paula said, looking accusing.

"That's part of the game. If I hadn't tagged her out, we might have lost."

"Oh."

Dani picked up a chicken leg. "Fat chance of that."

"You had a good chance," Jake said mildly. "If you hadn't tried to steal second, you would have been able to score when Jean hit that double. Then maybe the momentum would have turned in your team's favor."

"So I lost the game for us, is that it?"

Paula put down her piece of chicken and frowned. "You sound mad."

"She sure does," Jake agreed.

"Dani, don't be mad. Jake's nice. He just had to make you get out."

Dani was ashamed of herself. Her ill temper had nothing to do with the game, but Paula couldn't know that. Her ego was bruised because this was such a beautiful day, such a romantic setting, and Jake wasn't throwing himself at her feet. On top of that, she was acting like a poor sport in front of Paula.

"You're right," she said, smiling at Paula. "Jake played well and I took a chance that maybe I shouldn't have. We all played well. It was a good game."

"Good game." Paula's forehead cleared and she grinned.

"In fact, I was impressed with how well you motivated your team," Dani said, glancing at Jake. As long as she was being magnanimous, she might as well do it up right.

"Thanks."

"You'd make an outstanding coach."

Jake shook his head. "I thought of that, but I don't know if I could be happy watching other guys do the job I want to do. Coaching's okay if you've had a full career to look back on. I haven't."

"It seems a shame to waste that kind of talent. You're so good at sports, and with people."

He gazed at her. "Some people."

There it was again, that look that vividly reminded her of warm lips, an erotic touch and the promise of paradise. Maybe he'd perfected that look to give him power over women. She didn't want to believe that about Jake, but he was giving her no choice.

She swung her legs from under the picnic table. "Think I'll get some more ice tea. Anyone else want some?"

"Me," Paula said, holding out her cup.

"No, thanks." Jake's refusal seemed to carry more meaning than warranted by an offer of ice tea.

Dani took Paula's cup and headed toward the serving tables. She couldn't figure him out. His expression, his tone of voice, even his body language signaled regret. It was as if he wanted her as much as she wanted him, and for some reason he was denying himself. Maybe he'd taken a vow of celibacy. But, no, somehow that didn't seem likely with a man as sensuous as Jake. She wondered how long they could live in such proximity before he'd crack.

TORTURE. Jake had never experienced anything like this before. When Dani had stepped up to the plate and waggled her butt to get in position, he'd nearly lost it. The determination on her face was so endearing, he'd longed to run down the baseline and take her in his arms. It was a longing that came over him regularly, an urge he was finding more and more difficult to resist.

Obviously, she was furious with him about last night and he couldn't blame her. He'd known she'd decided to give him the cold shoulder when she'd refused his offer of a lift to the picnic. So they'd driven two vehicles, which he'd decided was just as well, and they'd managed to avoid each other for most of the game. Then she'd hit that single and ended up standing next to him on first base. Breathing hard.

It didn't take much imagination for Jake to picture another activity that would have her breathing hard. Her perfume, warmed by the sun and her own perspiration, wafted around him. He fought the desire rising in him and tried to concentrate on the game, even giving her some advice about base running.

Of course she'd done the opposite of what he'd suggested. And that remark about his fly had knocked him out. She was the sort of spirited woman he'd always dreamed about. He'd wanted to tackle her right there on the baseline. It was a tribute to his rigorous training in curbing emotions that he'd kept his composure and tagged her out.

After a performance like that, she probably thought of him as impervious to temptation. If only he were, he thought.

He noticed his team's pitcher, the guy from the pro shop, talking to her at the serving table, and had a chilling thought. What if someone asked her out? How could he protect her then? Of course, if he monopolized her time, he wouldn't have to worry about it. His heart beat faster at the thought.

He could follow her on a date, too. *Sure.* Follow her as some guy made the moves on her, kissed her, maybe even . . . no. There were limits to what he could endure.

As he watched Dani smile, Jake knew he'd have to prevent her from dating someone else. And not all of his reasons were noble.

CHAPTER EIGHT

DANI MAINTAINED her equilibrium with Jake throughout the afternoon. Someone had brought a volleyball and net, and Jake supervised setting up a makeshift court by stringing the net between two trees.

He's good with games, Dani thought with a trace of bitterness. For Paula's sake, she didn't allow that bitterness to creep into her speech or actions again. She spent time talking with Larry Perrine, who worked in the pro shop. After the first few minutes of conversation, Dani learned that Larry liked to talk about himself. A lot.

She tried to be charitable and believe he was nervous and trying to impress her. She wasn't impressed, which was too bad, because he seemed ready to ask her out, and a date with someone else would take her mind off Jake. Instead, as Larry talked, her attention kept veering toward the broad-shouldered man organizing the volleyball game. She tried to focus on what Larry was saying, but then Jake's laugh would drift across the clearing and she'd have to ask Larry to repeat himself. He didn't seem to mind.

Paula tried to rope Dani into being on Jake's volleyball team, but Dani said she'd promised Larry she'd be on the other side. Paula looked disapproving, but Dani decided there were limits to appeasing Paula. No point in taking the risk of jostling up against Jake during the game and having all her longings shoved back to the surface.

She played volleyball until sweat dampened her T-shirt and she was out of breath. The effort felt good, and her team actually pulled off a victory. When the game was over, she found a napkin to blot the perspiration from her face.

Larry, his blond hair damp with sweat, came up and offered her a paper cupful of water. "You're a good athlete."

"Thanks." She swallowed the water in several quick gulps.

"Ever played golf?"

"I took it in college." Dani laughed. "I don't think it's my game. On my final round of nine holes, my score was a hundred and eighty-two strokes. Not counting whiffs."

"I'll bet you had a bad coach. How about coming out first thing in the morning and I'll give you a lesson? Free of charge."

"Thanks, but I have an appointment." Dani was grateful for the excuse. Unlike Jake, she wasn't the type to confuse members of the opposite sex about her intentions.

"The next morning, then."

Dani smiled to soften her refusal. "I really don't want to learn golf, Larry."

He looked disappointed but not defeated. "Okay, then how about dinner tonight? We could each go home and change and maybe drive into—"

"I really don't think so."

"I see." He glanced over to where Jake was talking with Paula and Jean. "I'd heard you were spending a lot of time with our new bartender, but I didn't realize it had turned into an exclusive thing."

"It hasn't," Dani said. "Jake has nothing to do with this." Which wasn't exactly true. Jake had given her a yardstick. A month ago, she might have accepted Larry's invitation, but after knowing Jake, Dani had raised her sights. "I just don't want to waste your time and money on something that will never be more than friendship."

"How can you be so sure?"

"Trust me on this."

Larry shrugged. "Well, I tried. If you have a change of heart, I'll be around."

"Thanks." Dani waited until he left before making her way over. She couldn't go home without telling Paula goodbye.

"Here comes that vicious spiker now," Cindy said as Dani approached.

"You guys gave a good accounting of yourselves. It was close," Dani said.

Paula's face was pink from the sun and the exercise. "I want to play some more."

"We *should* do this more often," Cindy said, glancing up at Jake. "Especially now that we have a jock in the group."

Jake grinned. "This group is full of jocks and jockettes. I played my heart out just to keep up with you."

Dani steeled herself against his charming modesty and Cindy's irritating fawning. She had to adjust her attitude. She couldn't afford to care about Jake. Her best bet, she decided, was to get out of there. "I don't know about anyone else, but this jockette is bushed," she said. "I'm heading home for a shower and an early bedtime."

"Stay longer, Dani," Paula begged. "Please make her stay, Jake."

"Dani doesn't like it when people make her do things, Paula."

"That's right." She didn't look at Jake as she moved to give Paula a hug. "Gotta go, toots. You were great today."

"You, too. Tomorrow is pinstriping."

"Sure is. Come as early as you like. You can help me feed the peacocks."

"I will! If Jake won't knock me down."

"I won't," he promised.

Cindy looked puzzled. "What's all this about pinstriping and knocking people down?"

Paula started explaining as Dani waved and walked away. She hadn't been bluffing about being tired, and she suspected she might even be stiff tomorrow after so much exercise. But at least tonight she should sleep like a baby.

She didn't notice until halfway home that Jake's truck was following not far behind her. "Damn." She'd been an idiot to suggest he move in next door to her. She'd have been better off buying a large dog if she'd wanted protection. Of course, with the peacocks in residence, that probably wasn't an option, but still, there had to have been other alternatives. Now that Jake was here, it looked as if she'd have a hard time keeping away from him.

After parking the car, she tried to get into the house before he left his truck. She was on the porch when he called her name. She turned.

"I've been meaning to ask you about this thing climbing the mesquite tree. I've never seen anything like it."

He could have asked the landlord himself when he paid the rent, she thought. He was just looking for an excuse to talk to her, Lord knew why. "It's a vining type of cactus—a night-blooming cereus."

"It wound up that tree by itself?"

"No, the landlord trained it that way when he lived here." She turned and started back inside.

"It blooms at night?"

She glanced over her shoulder. "Yes. Apparently around the full moon. Judging from the buds, it should bloom soon." She reached for the handle of the screen door.

"I saw you talking to Larry Perrine today."

She clenched the door handle. Did he actually have the nerve to question her about that?

"Are you, um, going out with him?"

She spun around. "That is none of your damn business."

"I only asked a—"

"A simple question? Is that what you were about to say?" At her tone of voice, the peacocks looked up sleepily from their roost on the porch railing. "Because that is not a simple question! *Nothing* is simple with you, Jake. You are the most complicated, maddening male I have ever had the misfortune to meet, and that includes the peacock!" She thrust open her door, stalked inside and started to slam it, then she remembered the drowsing birds and closed it with a soft click.

JAKE STOOD in the yard rubbing the back of his neck. She was really ticked. He'd had enough experience to know she wouldn't get that upset if she didn't already have strong feelings for him. The knowledge made him more frustrated than ever.

He couldn't imagine her with someone like Larry, but then a woman in her frame of mind could end up doing all sorts of dumb things. He'd have to ask Larry and hope he'd get a straight answer.

None of this was working out for the best. But then, Helen Goodwin couldn't have known what an explosive combination he and Dani would make. He should have had a clue, though, as soon as he'd seen her picture. Obviously he hadn't examined the possible complications carefully enough before taking this job. That first meeting with Helen, he'd reacted like Sir Lancelot riding to the rescue of a damsel in distress.

Jake sighed. He'd had a few assignments that involved protecting someone from a jealous lover, and a few where celebrities were threatened by crazed fans. The jobs had been straightforward, the enemy known. He didn't much care for this shadowboxing. That reminded him that he owed the woman directing the shadow play a call, she was paying for the privilege of knowing his new telephone number.

The phone had been hooked up early that morning, but he'd postponed the call to his employer. He couldn't stall any longer. He sighed again as he headed toward his house.

As he started into the house, he heard the growl of an engine and paused. The sound came nearer; somebody was coming down the driveway. He moved quickly, slipping around the side of the house where he could observe unnoticed and move quickly if the need arose.

A delivery van pulled into the clearing. It bore the logo of a flower shop in nearby Green Valley. Either that creep Perrine was sending her flowers, or the van was bogus and the driver was a threat to Dani. Jake studied the driver as he got out with an elaborate bouquet of what looked like orchids. The driver was young, no more than eighteen, and he had no suspicious bulges under his clothing that could indicate a gun. Of course, something could be hidden in the bouquet.

Jake wished he had his own gun, but it was in the house. No time to get it. After the driver rounded the front of the van and started for Dani's porch, Jake bolted across the yard. He used the van as cover while the driver knocked on the door. Jake looked for any suspicious movement, but there was nothing. Probably flowers from Perrine, after all. The guy was a fast worker. Jake didn't like the idea of Perrine making that sort of gesture, but it was better than a killer in delivery boy's clothing.

Dani came to the door and exclaimed in surprise over the flowers. She took the bouquet and closed the door. Jake had five seconds to disappear, and he managed to duck behind a bush at the edge of the yard. When the van was gone, he crept over to the kitchen window, and keeping to the shadows, glanced in.

She'd set the bouquet on the kitchen table. It had to have cost Perrine a small fortune. Jake grimaced as she read the card and smiled. Dammit. He'd have a little talk with Perrine tomorrow. Not that he wanted to stand in the way of young love, but Perrine was one complication he didn't need.

He kept out of Dani's line of sight as he returned to his house. If she saw him, he could always say he'd gone for a walk by the river, but he preferred not to have to make up little lies to tell her. One big lie was enough.

Once in the house, he went into the kitchen and dialed Helen Goodwin's number. She answered quickly, and he wondered if she'd been pacing by the phone.

"At last!" she said. "I thought you'd never call."

"I'm here. And my number is—"

"Never mind that now. I got another note."

"Okay." Even though he was half-convinced this wasn't legit, the thought of another note still gave him a sick feeling of dread. "What does this one say?"

"It's another quote from my book, and Jake, they know she's in Tubac."

"I see." He was fast running out of patience. "How do you suppose that happened? Does your friend Evelyn have a big mouth, by chance?"

"No, it couldn't have been Evelyn. Maybe one of Dani's friends, although she wasn't going to tell anyone, but there are a couple of people she's close to. You know how it is. These things can get out."

"So I've noticed. Are you sure you can trust Slattery?"

"Certainly. I'm convinced Dani's told someone."

"Then I suggest you have her friends checked out. This note writer could be a disappointed lover."

"I'll put someone on it."

"Good. What does the note say, exactly?"

"It's from chapter fifteen of *The Unvanquished*. It says 'Sarah always considered Tubac a haven from danger, but now she had to face the fact that her daughter was not safe there.' You see? They know she's there. They could be in Tubac this very minute!"

"Maybe I'd better read your book." He was only half-serious, but it might not be a bad idea. Maybe he'd pick up some clues.

"You're right. I should have given you a copy. Buy one down there and add it to my bill."

"All right. Anything else?"

"Yes. I was...a little harsh last time we spoke. I should realize that you're too much of a professional to allow yourself to become involved with Dani. After all, I checked and rechecked your references."

"And nobody complained that I hit on them?"

"Jake, no need to be nasty. We need to maintain a cordial relationship."

"I guess we do."

"How are things going? Anything out of the ordinary?"

Jake thought of the peacocks, a cactus that blooms at night and a mentally handicapped woman who was expert at pinstriping. "Not really. We had a softball game and picnic for the country club employees today. I didn't notice anybody acting strange around Dani, but then I've checked on all the hired help. Everybody's worked there longer than she has, so they're not suspects." But one guy is becoming a pain in the rear, sending flowers and who knew what else.

"I don't know why," Helen said, "but I don't think they'll strike in daylight. I worry about after dark."

Jake thought that sounded like a theory straight out of a suspense novel, but he didn't risk saying so and ruining their uneasy truce. "I sleep with my window open, and I'm a light sleeper." He glanced through the kitchen into the living room. He could see through his front window across to Dani's house. She'd just switched on a light in her kitchen. It gleamed softly in the gathering dusk. "I suppose she's told you about my moving in next door here."

"No."

"No?" He felt hurt, diminished. "But she's told you about the bartender at the country club."

"No. I've been wondering if she would, but she hasn't. Just that young woman who has the problem."

"Paula." Jake flicked on his own kitchen light. Now that he had the electricity turned on, he didn't want Dani to think he was sitting and brooding in the dark. "I can't believe she hasn't mentioned me. We eat lunch together every day, and of course she was the one who suggested I move in, and she even came over in a rainstorm to tell me the place was empty."

Helen was silent for a moment. "I guess that's why she hasn't said anything, then."

"What?"

"She's attracted to you, and she doesn't want me to know she's interested in someone. For fear I'll disapprove or give her advice."

"I see." Jake squeezed his eyes shut in frustration. "Look, this is all getting too crazy for me. How about if you find somebody else for this job? I can supply some names. I'll stay on until you send someone down."

"Absolutely not. I know what you're made of, Jake, and you're exactly the person I need to watch over Dani. This attraction of hers will pass. She's probably just lonely down there without her usual friends."

Just like that, Helen had dismissed the subject of Dani's interest in him. He felt his headache returning.

"Jake?"

"I'm here."

"You had a phone number for me?"

"Right." He read her the number typed above the push-button dial. "Call if you get any more notes. Good night, Helen." He hung up the phone and swore eloquently and long, but it didn't help. Only one thing would help, but he was much too professional to indulge himself in such activities, now wasn't he? He smashed his fist against the doorjamb. That didn't help, either.

DANI WAS OUTSIDE feeding the peacocks in the pussy-willow gray light of dawn when Paula rode up on her bike.

"Hi, Dani!" she called.

"Hi, yourself. Any trouble with your parents this morning?"

"They're asleep."

Dani groaned. "They're not going to come looking for you again, are they?"

"Nope. I left a note."

"Oh, good." Dani was glad to know Paula was exhibiting such responsible behavior, although the mention of a note reminded her of her mother's call the night before. The threatening person, if there was such a person, seemed to know Dani was in Tubac. Despite Dani's anger at Jake, she was glad he'd moved in and that he slept only yards away from her front door. Maybe she should just think of him as a guard dog. No more, no less.

"Can I throw them some?"

Dani looked down at the handful of seed she held for the peacocks. "Sure thing." She transferred the seed to Paula's pudgy hand and stood back while Paula heaved it into the yard.

"Here, peacocks. Chow time!" Paula watched with rapt attention as the birds pecked at the ground. "Over there," she directed, pointing to some they missed.

To Dani's amazement, the birds moved in that direction. "I guess you speak their language."

"I wanted a kitty," Paula said. "Mom and Dad said too much hair."

"That's too bad." Dani chalked up another point against Madge and Ed.

Paula shrugged. "That's life." Then she smiled and glanced over at Dani's Mustang, as if painting that would make up for many past disappointments. "Ready to wash it?"

"Let's have a little breakfast first," Dani suggested. "We'll wait for it to warm up some. Your paints will work better then, too."

"You know about that?"

"I worked with oils for a while, but it wasn't my medium. When I got my hands on some silver, and saw how it could be shaped into beautiful things to wear, I was hooked.''

''That's me and pinstriping.''

Dani nodded as they exchanged a look of understanding. The moment was shattered as the train roared across the tracks and Paula stood as if frozen to the spot. When it had passed, Dani spoke. ''Pretty loud, huh?''

Paula nodded and stared after the departing train.

''Did it scare you?''

She shook her head.

''Come on inside. I have a blueberry muffin mix going to waste.''

''Where does it go?''

It took Dani a few seconds to realize she was talking about the train. ''I'm not sure. Maybe California.''

''Wish I could go, too.''

''You've never been there?''

Paula shook her head. ''I've gone two places. One's Chicago. One's Tubac.''

Dani longed to promise she'd take Paula other places. Knew she had no right to promise her that. Paula's parents would have to agree first, and Dani didn't see much hope for that. ''Let's go make those muffins,'' she said, instead.

Paula followed her into the kitchen and stopped dead when she saw the bouquet of baby orchids. ''Ooh!''

''Pretty, huh?''

Paula surveyed the bouquet. ''From Jake?''

''No.'' *If only they were from him.* ''The woman I told you about, the one who's opening the jewelry shop.''

''Wow. How come?''

"I'm not sure. On Sunday at the restaurant, she was a little abrupt with me. Her note says she hopes she didn't hurt my feelings and she really is looking forward to working with me."

Paula touched the small lavender blooms. "Nice flowers."

"Expensive flowers." Dani turned on the oven and took a bowl from the cupboard. "The woman obviously has lots of money. Which is good, because you need lots of money to start a business, even in Tubac. Anyway, I'll find out what the shop looks like this morning."

"This morning?"

"Yes, I—" Dani turned and looked at Paula's stricken face. "Oh. That's right. You'll be pinstriping the car."

Paula's lower lip trembled. "Want me to...wait?"

"No, of course I don't."

"Jake! Jake could take you."

"That's okay. I can walk. It's not so—"

"I'll ask him." Paula bolted from the kitchen and out of the house before Dani could stop her.

In despair, Dani watched her run across the clearing and bang on Jake's door. With Paula around, there seemed to be no way on earth to avoid the man who was driving her crazy.

CHAPTER NINE

JAKE WAS UP, shaved and dressed. He'd made coffee, but an inspection of his food supply turned up a stale heel of bread, some moldy cheese and a can of chili. He was trying to decide if he could stomach any of it for breakfast when there was a knock on his door.

"Good morning, Paula," he said when he saw her on the steps. "Want some breakfast? I have some coffee if you'd like that, but otherwise the pickings are slim."

"Dani has muffins." Paula grabbed at his arm.

"Wait a minute. Did Dani send you over here to invite me for muffins?"

Paula hesitated. "She needs a ride."

Jake remembered Dani had an appointment this morning and figured she must have forgotten she wouldn't be able to drive her car if Paula was pinstriping it today. Maybe the muffins were a bribe, so he'd take her to Evelyn Ross's shop. He was willing to be bribed.

He disengaged his arm from Paula's grip. "Let me get a jacket."

"Okay." Paula stepped inside to wait. "Nice place," she called out as he went into the bedroom.

He returned, pulling on a faded denim jacket. "You're just being polite." He glanced around at the white walls and the tan Naugahyde furniture. "It's pretty plain, don't you think?"

"Yes."

"Too bad I can't let you do a little pinstriping in here. It would help a lot. But I doubt the landlord would go for it."

"You could get flowers."

"Mm." He ushered her out the door and closed it behind them. The thought of flowers left a sour taste in his mouth.

"Dani has flowers."

Don't I know it. That meddling Perrine. "Is that right?"

"I thought you did it."

"Not me." He slowed his stride to match her shorter one as they crossed the yard.

"Why not?"

He glanced at Paula. "It's a long story."

"That's okay. Tell me."

He put his arm around her shoulders. "You know, Paula, I wish I could. But I can't just now. Maybe one of these days."

"But you like her, don't you?"

"Yes."

"She seems angry, sort of."

"I know."

Paula gave him a wise look. "Send flowers."

"I'll consider it." If only he could simply empty a florist shop to make things right with Dani.

As they approached her door, he could smell muffins baking and his memory shot back twenty years, to Sunday mornings in a midwestern split-level. Blueberry muffins had been a staple of breakfast feasts on

Sunday mornings, when his whole family gathered around the table. His dad had been a high school coach, so weekday and Saturday mealtimes were always interrupted by practices and games. Smelling the sweetness of the muffins baking, Jake felt nostalgic for the coziness of his family.

His dad must have been happy in his job or he wouldn't have whistled getting ready for school each day. Jake had always considered coaching a second-hand life—grooming others to do what you hadn't been capable of doing. His mother worked in the school library, and together, she and his father had made a decent living, though it was nothing compared to what Jake could have earned if he'd stayed in the pros. It was nothing compared to his potential earnings as a bodyguard for the celebrity set of Los Angeles.

Jake had never thought he wanted the life his parents lived, and yet . . .

"Come on, Jake." Paula tugged him up the porch steps. "Come have muffins."

Dani didn't smile when she saw him. "Hello, Jake."

"Paula invited me to breakfast. I hope that's okay."

"Sure. Want some eggs?"

In point of fact, he was starving. Maybe suppressed desire heightened a person's appetite. "I'd love some." He glanced at the obnoxious bouquet sitting on the kitchen table. He wanted to read what that nerd Perrine had written on the card. "Why don't I just move these flowers?"

"I think there's space in the living room for them," Dani said. "Paula, will you set the table?"

He hoisted the silver vase and bore it into the living room where he pushed aside the latest *Rock and Gem* magazines on the coffee table and set it down. Baby orchids. Talk about major ostentation. The guy must be planning on a big score with Dani. Well, Jake would see about that.

"Jake?" Dani's voice floated in from the kitchen. "Sunny-side up or over easy?"

"Over easy, please," he called back while he searched through the flowers for the card. No card. Damn. She probably already had it in some scrapbook. He'd put a stop to this today. After he took her to Evelyn Ross's shop he'd drive over to the golf course. He'd tell Perrine . . . something. But one thing was sure. The guy was not dating Dani. No way. Even if she liked him. *Especially* if she liked him. The very thought made his stomach churn.

DANI TRIED TO dismiss the enjoyment she felt at serving Jake a meal. Warm pleasure rushed through her as he praised everything extravagantly and ate four muffins. He looked so darned good sitting there at her table, his eyes alight and his grin flashing often as the three of them talked about yesterday's picnic.

Jake told Paula about Dani's comment when she'd tried to steal second base.

"Dani!" Paula giggled and covered her mouth.

Dani laughed. "I didn't count on the fact he didn't care about such things."

"Oh, I care. But that's one of the oldest bluffs in the book."

Dani couldn't resist. "So you wouldn't believe me if I said it right now."

"Nope."

"Okay. It's your problem if you walk around like that this morning."

Jake stared at her and she stared right back, never cracking a smile. Finally, he frowned and looked down at his lap, where his denim fly was securely buttoned. Dani and Paula both burst out laughing.

"Okay, you got me," he said. "Remind me not to play poker with you."

"Or be so smug," Dani added. It was good to know Jake could be fooled once in a while. It made him seem more human.

"That, too." He cradled his mug in both hands and settled back in the chair. "I understand you need a ride to Evelyn Ross's shop this morning?"

"If you don't mind. Otherwise, Paula can't start on my car."

"Can't have that." He set down his cup and stood. "Let's get that baby washed and ready for the artist. Paula, did I tell you that two people at the picnic asked me who did the pinstriping on my truck?"

Paula's eyes widened. "They did?"

"I told them you were the artist, but you were tied up with another job at the moment. I said maybe we could arrange something later on. Both people were definitely interested in hiring you."

"For money?"

"Absolutely. And wait until they see the job you do on Dani's Mustang. If she drives it to work every day, plenty of people will notice, believe me. What do you think? Want to try someone else's car after this?"

"I...I..." Paula looked scared to death.

"Hey." He walked over to her and put his hands on her shoulders. "You're good. Very good. These people would be lucky to have you work for them. But it's your decision, and you don't have to make it now. You can think about whether or not you want to turn this into a money-making proposition. You can think a long time. No rush."

Dani's heart swelled with affection for Jake. He could do so much for Paula, and he was obviously planning to make the effort. Maybe he'd never open his heart to Dani, but that didn't make him a bad person. He was a very good person, in fact.

Paula gazed up at him in adoration. "Thanks, Jake."

"You're welcome. Now let's go wash that car."

DANI SHOWERED and dressed in an outfit from her L.A. days—a pair of wide-legged ivory-colored slacks, a gray-and-white-striped blouse and an unstructured ivory linen jacket. She chose abstract earrings inlaid with tigereye and mother-of-pearl, with a matching choker of the same design. Evelyn might have more money, but Dani had always prided herself on her sense of style.

She'd picked two of her six wooden jewelry cases to take with her. The rest were stacked with her boxes of equipment and supplies in a corner of the living room. Because she'd had no outlet for her work, she hadn't made anything new since she'd arrived in Tubac. She had a sketchbook full of ideas, though, and on an impulse, she scooped that up, too.

Jake appeared on the other side of the screen door. "About ready?"

"Ready." Dani picked up her cases, stacked her sketchbook on top and slung her purse over her shoulder.

"Here, let me help." Jake opened the door and came in.

"It's okay. I—"

"Nonsense. No use rumpling that nice outfit." He took the cases and stood back to admire her. "Very classy."

"I want Evelyn Ross to know I'm not some hick from the sticks."

"Dani, you couldn't look like a hick if you tried. You wear jeans and a T-shirt like no other woman I've known."

She absorbed the compliment. Jake was back on his game and she needed to watch out for her heart. She gave him a cool look. "Thanks."

On the porch she stopped and gazed at the peacock strutting around the yard, his gleaming tail spread like a gem-studded fan in the sun. The peahens clucked nearby, both of them clearly entranced. Dani could understand. She was a sucker for a beautiful male, too.

Spotting Paula crouched next to the Mustang, Dani walked down the steps and over to her. Paula, who almost seemed to have stopped breathing, finished a slim swirl of black near the taillights. "It looks fantastic, Paula," Dani said.

Paula glanced up. "Oh, hi, Dani. I didn't know you were there."

"That's the way I am sometimes when I work."

"Are you going?"

Dani nodded as Jake came up beside her holding the jewelry cases. "Just go ahead and work. We'll be back in plenty of time for you to go home and change into your restaurant clothes."

"Okay."

"The house is open if you need a drink of something. I think there's a muffin left, too."

"Okay." Paula looked proud of the responsibility Dani was handing her. "Should I feed the peacocks?"

"No. They've had enough until tonight." Dani smiled. "See you soon."

"See you soon."

"Do you think she'll be okay?" Jake asked as they walked to the truck.

"I think so. And she needs somebody to trust in her abilities. By the way, it's great that someone noticed the pinstriping on your truck."

"Actually, I took a few people over to see it, hoping I'd get a response like that."

She glanced at him. "You did? That's terrific."

"Paula deserves a break."

Dani held his gaze for a moment. *So do I*, she thought, looking away.

The ride to Evelyn's shop, in such close quarters, was short and silent. In an effort to block out Jake's sensual power over her, Dani reviewed her tentative price list. Evelyn might think that because Dani had no outlet, she'd be desperate to sell cheap. She wasn't that desperate.

They found the address with a temporary sign propped in the window identifying it as The Silver Coyote. Dani let out a little sigh of relief. "At least she didn't make everything up."

"You thought she might have?"

She turned to him. "I guess you think I'm suspicious of everyone, but coming from the L.A. area, you should understand. Growing up there, I learned that people aren't always what they seem."

"I think you're right to be careful. Keep up the vigilance."

Even where you're concerned, she thought. "You can just drop me off."

He pulled on the emergency brake and opened his door. "No, I can't. My mother didn't raise me that way." Before she could protest further, he'd opened her door and taken the cases and sketchbook she held in her lap. Then he offered his hand to help her down. "Watch the running board. Don't want dirt marks on those slacks."

"My goodness, what a gentleman you are." She had to joke with him to mute the effect of his hand gripping hers. She let go as soon as her feet touched the dirt road. Yet, she appreciated having him there with her. This meeting could mean a great deal to her, and she was a little nervous. Jake's presence took her mind off the importance of striking a deal with Evelyn.

A bell tinkled when Dani opened the shop door and Evelyn turned from her supervision of a painter, who was coating the walls of the shop in deep turquoise. "Don't you love this color?" she asked, in lieu of a greeting. "The shelves and counters will be white, and the interior of the display cases will be covered in black velvet, of course, to set off the jewelry. Your jewelry."

"It should be stunning," Dani agreed.

"And who do we have here? Is it the bartender?"

Dani turned back to Jake. "This is my friend, Jake Clayborn, and yes, he tends bar at Canada Verde. You might have seen him there."

"Indeed I did." Evelyn smiled archly. "You mix a mean margarita, Jake."

"Thank you."

"Ever had sex on the beach?"

Dani stared at her. Surely Evelyn hadn't really said that!

"Once," Jake replied.

Dani's attention snapped back to Jake. And surely he wasn't answering the question!

He smiled. "I didn't like it." Then he glanced at Dani. "It's a drink. Vodka, Peachtree schnapps, orange juice and cranberry juice."

Dani's cheeks felt warm. "Oh."

"I always like to ask bartenders that," Evelyn said. "Separates the men from the boys."

Jake studied her for a moment. "If you say so."

Evelyn's eyes narrowed. Dani remembered the expression. Evelyn had looked that way when Dani had told her she couldn't make it on Monday morning. Maybe Evelyn's wealth caused her to expect deference from others.

Then the look was gone and Evelyn smiled. "Are you planning to stay for Dani's presentation? I only have two chairs in the back room, but we can—"

"No, actually I just came in to bring her jewelry cases. If you'll show me where to put them, I'll be on my way. Dani's car is being pinstriped today, so she needed a ride."

"Pinstriping? How fascinating." Evelyn led the way past the painter on his aluminum ladder. She didn't bother to introduce him. "You can put the cases on this desk," she said, moving a couple of file folders to make room. "I can hardly wait to see what Dani's brought me."

At Jake's mention of pinstriping, Dani had a brainstorm. Evelyn had said the showcases and shelves would be white. What a perfect backdrop for some of Paula's work! Dani envisioned thin swirls of turquoise and black, or even better, geometric patterns echoing Indian border designs. Paula would love doing it.

Dani could hardly wait to find an opening to suggest the idea to Evelyn. Evelyn certainly had the money to pay Paula, and Dani would arrange to be around while she worked, so the job might not be as intimidating as working on strangers' cars.

Jake set the cases on the desk. "What time should I pick you up?"

Dani thought they'd be able to cover everything in a half hour, but she glanced at Evelyn for direction.

"Ten-thirty," Evelyn said. Then she smiled. "So we can get to know each other."

"Of course."

"Ten-thirty it is," Jake said. "See you then."

As he walked out of the shop, Dani realized that she didn't want him to go. But that was silly. She didn't need Jake to conduct this business. In fact, he might get in the way. Taking a steadying breath, she reached for the first jewelry case.

JAKE STARTED the truck and pointed it out of town toward the country club. This was turning into one hell of a morning. First Evelyn and now Perrine.

Jake had met women like Evelyn before. She had the mistaken impression that she had charisma, when all she had was a large bank account. Of course, she hadn't really been out to charm him. Maybe she could do a whole lot better when she wasn't feeling antagonistic. He wasn't sure why she didn't like him, but she obviously didn't.

Not that it mattered. She seemed to have the resources to get Dani's reputation established in Tubac, and that was what Dani wanted. For a while he allowed himself to fantasize about what life would be like if he really were only an itinerant bartender who happened to meet Dani because they both worked at the same restaurant.

Dani had found her niche: she'd be happy settling into the life in Tubac and creating her jewelry. But could he be content to spend his working hours as a bartender? He knew the answer. Already the job was starting to get on his nerves. He liked fresh air and movement. Being cooped up behind that bar for hours wasn't his idea of fulfilling employment.

He liked the challenge of being a bodyguard, but he didn't expect to do that all his life, either. And he certainly couldn't work as a bodyguard in the sleepy little town of Tubac. Tucson, maybe, but that was a long commute. He didn't know enough Spanish to work in Mexico.

Eventually, his job guarding Dani would be over, either because the bad guy showed his hand or because Helen finally admitted she'd engineered a hoax. Then, because of his respect for Dani, he'd have to admit he'd been withholding the truth all along. She'd tar him with the same brush as her mother and never want to see him again. He tried to imagine a different scenario, but no other outcome seemed logical.

Jake parked the truck in front of the pro shop and walked in. Perrine was straightening a rack of golf shirts and glanced up when Jake entered. Jake thought of the flowers and wanted to punch him in the mouth. Instead, he decided to finesse this encounter. "How's it going, Larry?" He made himself smile.

"What up, Jake? Gonna play nine holes before work?"

"No, I came to talk to you."

"Oh, yeah?"

"About Dani Goodwin."

Perrine's open expression closed down. "What about her?"

"I understand you're interested."

"What's it to you?" Perrine hunched his shoulders.

Jake wondered if this discussion might turn into something physical, after all. A brawl in the pro shop would start some gossip, and Dani would hear about it, which wouldn't be good. "I've known Dani a long time," he began. "Friends of the family, and all that. Just wanted to warn you, man-to-man."

"About what?"

"Listen, I can't be specific and betray her trust, but she . . . probably shouldn't be dating at this point."

"Why not?"

"I can't tell you, Lar. I really can't. Just take my word for it. Dating her is a bad move—for both of you."

Perrine fiddled with a button on his sport shirt. "This is some scam, right? To keep the field clear for yourself."

"Absolutely not." Jake gave him the same look he once reserved for the toughest batters in the league. "You can choose to disregard what I'm saying, but I wouldn't if I were you."

Perrine swallowed. "I don't get it. What could be the problem?"

"Use your imagination."

Perrine gazed at him and gradually his eyes widened. "Lord."

"I think you're beginning to understand. And I sure hope I didn't judge you wrong, Lar. If she finds out I've talked to you, all hell will break loose, but I felt I had to warn you, especially after the flowers."

"What flowers?"

"The ones you sent on Sunday."

"I didn't send any flowers."

"My mistake. I thought they were from you."

"Better find out who sent them, Jake. Quick. Some other poor sucker may be getting ready to—"

"Yeah. I'll do that, Lar. See you." As Jake got back into the truck, his thoughts whirled as he tried to imagine who else might be trying to woo Dani.

He'd just have to ask her. She wouldn't like it, and she'd probably jump all over him the way she had last time, but he had no choice. He had to keep men away from her. For professional reasons, of course.

CHAPTER TEN

DANI BASKED in Evelyn's praise of her work. When she showed Evelyn the sketchbook, Evelyn went crazy.

"The peacock designs are fabulous!" she cried, holding the book away from her to gain perspective. "I can see all sorts of possibilities—turquoise, of course, but how about abalone shell? If you find some with enough blue in it, and with that iridescent quality—"

"I thought of abalone," Dani interrupted, excited that someone shared her vision. "Or maybe turquoise and abalone together."

"Yes!"

"And a touch of obsidian for the eye."

"Can you do that? The work would be so delicate. But of course you can do that. You're a real artist."

"I think I can."

"Dani, you must get started right away on this. It could be the best thing you've done so far. I've half a mind to rename the shop The Silver Peacock."

"Oh, no." Dani tried to contain her swelling ego. "You already have business cards and everything. The Silver Coyote is more southwestern-sounding, anyway."

"And more ordinary. You have such a creative gift."

"Thank you." Dani had been saying that a lot during the past hour and fifteen minutes. She'd started by thanking Evelyn for the flowers, belatedly, she thought, but Jake's presence and the remark about sex on the beach had distracted her.

Later, Dani had thanked Evelyn for not quibbling over prices, and for agreeing to Dani's suggestion about having Paula pinstripe the display cases and shelves. She could hardly wait to tell Paula. She glanced at her watch, thinking Jake should arrive soon. Her pulse quickened.

"When can I see the rest of your inventory?" Evelyn asked. "How about a late dinner after work tonight?"

"Well, I— Sure, why not. In fact, why don't you come by my house and we'll eat there? Four cases would be difficult to carry around, and you can see the pinstriping on my Mustang."

"Wonderful. Do you have a blender? We could have margaritas."

Dani thought about her mother; she liked margaritas, too. "Sorry, no blender," she said. "Or any of the ingredients, either. I just have the basics in my kitchen."

"Then I'll bring mine and all the fixings. We can have a regular girls' night out."

"Sounds fun." And it did, Dani thought. Evelyn had opened up so many dazzling possibilities to her. Paula was wonderful, but still very young. And Jake— well, Jake was a different kind of problem. Lovely to be with, impossible to hold.

As if in tune with her thoughts, Jake came in the front door of the shop in a flurry of jingling bells.

"I have to go," Dani said, rising from her chair and gathering the jewelry cases and her sketchbook into a pile. "I have to change for work."

"You don't belong in that ridiculous costume," Evelyn said.

Dani had grown secretly fond of the peasant blouse and skirt, because they reminded her of Jake and Paula and all the fun times they'd shared. But she nodded, anyway. "I know, but the management thinks we should look like *señoritas* or something."

"The way I see it, you won't be working at Canada Verde much longer." Evelyn glanced toward Jake as he stepped into the back room. "What do you think, Jake? She's destined for more than waitressing, wouldn't you agree?"

"I'd agree."

Dani hated the emotional distance she heard in his voice, as if he'd already resigned himself to their drifting apart. When she stopped working at the country club, she wouldn't see him as often. He hadn't hit it off with Evelyn, so he probably wouldn't drop by the shop. The prospect of leaving her job became mildly depressing.

She shook off the vague uneasiness and turned to Jake. "Guess what? We're going to ask Paula to pinstripe the display cases and shelves."

He was maddeningly polite. "She should enjoy that."

"I thought it might make a good transition, from this to the cars you were talking about."

"It might. Listen, we'd better go."

"You're right." She picked up the cases, but Jake immediately stepped forward and took them for her.

Dani turned back to Evelyn. "Is nine-thirty too late? I'll need some time to get home and throw a few things together. Maybe a stir-fry."

"Sounds perfect. See you then. Goodbye, Jake."

He gave her a nod. "Goodbye, Evelyn."

With a wave to Evelyn, Dani followed Jake out to the truck. He helped her into the passenger seat and gave her the cases to hold before closing the door. Their hands brushed. She had the ridiculous urge to clutch his hand and...what? Force him to kiss her, make love to her? She sighed and folded her hands around the boxes.

Jake closed the door and came around to his side. He got in and turned the key without a word.

"I guess you two won't be fast friends," Dani said as he backed the truck away from the shop.

"No, but so what?"

"She's being extremely generous to me."

"She should be. You're very talented. You may be doing her a bigger favor than she's doing you."

"I really doubt that, Jake."

"I don't. Consider how hard it must be to start a jewelry shop in an artist-intensive community like Tubac. She needs a fresh new talent if she expects to stand out from the crowd."

"Okay, but she didn't have to pick me." Dani wanted to fight with him, probably because she wasn't able to do what she really wanted.

To calm herself, she rolled down the window and breathed in the spring air. Palo verde trees held a trace of yellow blossoms in their feathered green branches. A few orange poppies mingled with purple mountain lupine in a grassy field on the outskirts of town. Their fragrance was subtle but compelling. Maybe the season of the year had something to do with her longings for Jake. Or maybe she just wanted what she couldn't have.

Jake broke the silence. "What was all that about stir-fry at nine-thirty tonight? Are you two having dinner?"

"At my place," Dani replied. "She wants to see the rest of my inventory and that's the easiest way. Plus, she can look over the job Paula did on my Mustang, so she won't be flying blind in hiring her for the work in the shop."

"Is she going to pay Paula?"

"Of course." Dani's anger resurfaced. "She wouldn't take advantage of someone like Paula. I suggested a flat fee for the whole job."

"How much?"

Dani told him and he nodded. She felt relieved that he thought she'd priced Paula's services fairly. And after all, his questions had all been in Paula's interests. She shouldn't be angry about that. "I hope Paula's been getting along okay without us," she offered as a gesture of peace.

"So do I." He was quiet for a while. "She suggested I get some flowers like yours to brighten up my house. Did you buy that bunch somewhere?"

"No. Evelyn sent them."

"Evelyn?"

"Don't sound so surprised. She sent them as a sort of apology for being abrupt on Sunday night. That's what I mean, Jake, about the kind of person she is. She may rub you the wrong way, but she means well, and sometimes what she says doesn't come out right."

"If you say so."

"I wish you'd try to like her."

"Why?"

Dani glanced at him. Why should she care? Except that she valued Jake's opinion and if he felt good about Evelyn, she'd feel more comfortable. "I just wish you would."

"Okay. I'll try." He pulled into the yard and drove carefully past Dani's Mustang so dust wouldn't settle on the new paint job.

"Wow," Dani said, gazing at the swirls of black, purple and red along her fenders and around her tail-lights. "I think she's created a masterpiece."

"Sure looks like it."

"I wonder where she is?" Dani gazed beyond the car to the porch and noticed Paula's bike still leaning against it. "She must be inside."

Jake turned off the engine and opened his door. "I'll help you carry those."

Once again, he helped her from the truck with an outstretched hand. His touch was warm and reassuring, and gone too quickly. As she mounted the steps, she heard Paula's voice and paused. She'd never known Paula to talk to herself, yet that's what it sounded like.

"She went with Jake," Paula said as Dani opened the door. "They're back."

She walked into the kitchen and discovered the explanation. Paula was on the phone.

"Hee—rre's Dani!" Paula said. Then she held out the receiver. "It's your mother."

Dani stared at the receiver without taking it. Behind her in the living room, Jake called out that he'd put the jewelry cases in the corner. His voice would have carried easily to the phone.

Her mother didn't know about Jake. Or rather, she *hadn't* known about Jake.

Paula pushed the receiver at her again. "It's your mother," she repeated.

"Right. Thanks." Dani took it gingerly and put it to her ear. Then she pumped some frivolity into her voice. "Hi, Mom! What's up?"

"Who's Jake?"

"I hate it when you beat around the bush like that. You really should learn to be more direct." She glanced at Paula and mouthed silently, *"The car looks great."* Paula grinned.

"Sarcasm doesn't become you, dear. Your friend Paula tells me Jake lives there."

Jake came and stood in the kitchen doorway. He lifted an eyebrow and Paula told him who was on the phone. He nodded and walked back into the living room, but Dani was very aware that he was close enough to hear everything she said. Not that she had anything startling to reveal to her mother. Unfortunately.

"Jake lives across the way, Mom. He tends bar at the country club. He gave me a ride to Evelyn's shop—you know, the woman I told you about? She's going to sell my jewelry. She really likes it, and I think—"

"Why did he give you a ride? Is something wrong with your car?"

"Exactly the opposite." Dani looked at Paula and smiled. "Paula pinstriped it this morning. It's gorgeous."

"Pinstriped? What is that? That car's a classic, Dani, and you shouldn't—"

"Trust me, if it was a classic before, it's a collector's item now."

"Do you like this Jake fellow?"

Dani should have known her mother would return to that topic. The car was only a momentary concern. Did she like Jake? *Like* was too generic, too pale a word for how she felt about him. But she didn't want her mother to know that. "He's been a good friend."

"Is he handsome?"

She pictured him as he'd looked sitting at the breakfast table that morning—his grin, the devilment in his brown eyes, the seductive curve of his fingers as he'd picked up another muffin. As an artist, she appreciated how beautifully he was put together; as a woman, she longed to touch that perfection, to claim it somehow. "He's okay."

"Dani, I want you to be careful."

"I know, Mom. You think—" She started to say *someone's out to get me* and then she remembered Paula didn't know anything about the notes. Dani hadn't wanted to scare her. "You think I don't take care of myself," she finished.

"This isn't just about your physical safety. If this Jake person wanted to harm you, he's had enough chances already, so I'm not worried about that. I'm concerned with your emotional safety."

Dani thought this was the pot calling the kettle black, but she held her tongue.

"You're in a strange place, and you might form an attachment too quickly. Don't fall in love just because you're lonely."

"Don't worry." Despite Dani's nonchalance, the word *love* startled her. She couldn't be in love with Jake. It would be too humiliating. But she'd have to be on guard to make sure that didn't happen, because Jake sure as hell wasn't falling in love with her. If anything, he was running in the other direction. "Anything new with you?"

"No more notes, if that's what you mean."

"I'd be delighted if we had something else to talk about."

"Okay. *The Unvanquished* has been optioned by Warner Brothers."

"No kidding! That's great!"

"Remember that an option is a long way from having a movie made."

"I know, but still. Aren't you excited?"

"Movies have been made of my books before."

"Yeah, but for television, not by a major studio. That's terrific, Mom. I'll bet Rudy's bouncing off the walls."

"He is a bit manic, but you know agents. At least my agent."

"Well, I'm happy for you." Dani hesitated. "Any ideas for a new book?"

"I don't know how you can expect me to concentrate on a new book when someone's stalking you and you insist on living five hundred miles away from me, where I can't properly protect you."

"A new book would take your mind off things."

"Dani, you've never had children of your own. When you do, you'll understand why I can't work right now."

"Mom—" Dani realized the futility of the argument. "Okay. I just hope this business ends soon so you can start a new project. Your fans will be very unhappy if another Helen Goodwin book doesn't show up next year."

"I understand that, and I'd work if I could, but I just can't."

Dani decided they'd traded guilt trips long enough. "Well, thanks for calling. I have to get dressed for work now."

"All right, dear. And guard your heart."

It was an old-fashioned expression, but for the first time in a while, Dani agreed with one of her mother's cautionary statements. "I will," she said.

WHEN JAKE HEARD Dani hang up the phone, he grabbed one of her magazines and pretended interest in it as she walked into the room with Paula. With a practiced look of boredom, he glanced up.

"My mother," she said.

"Oh." He returned his attention to the magazine and flipped another page, as if he didn't much care, as if he hadn't been straining to hear every word. *He's been a good friend. He's okay.* Both delivered as if Dani hadn't given him any more thought than... than *Perrine* for crying out loud. Of course he hadn't wanted Helen Goodwin to get the wrong idea about his behavior, but *still.* Dani could have shown a little more enthusiasm when talking about him.

"Come on." Dani walked toward the screen door. "Let's go take a better look at Paula's job."

He followed the two women outside. Then he and Dani heaped congratulations on Paula, whose face became all pink and happy-looking. The job was damn good. He had no reservations about scaring up business for her after seeing this.

Paula left, and within half an hour he was driving Dani to work. Then a thought struck him. "If you're supposed to be here for Evelyn at nine-thirty, and I won't get off until about eleven, how will you get home?"

She glanced at him. "Damn. You're right. In all the confusion, I forgot the logistics of this."

"I thought so." He spent too much time gazing into her gray eyes and ran the truck through a pothole, jouncing them both quite a bit. "Sorry."

"That's okay. The roads aren't great. Anyway, let me ask around. I'll bet there's someone else who can give me a ride. Maybe even Jean, or that busboy who lives out this way, I think."

Jake didn't like the last idea. The busboy she'd mentioned was no boy. He was thirty if he was a day, and a real Latin-lover type. For some reason, he hadn't made it to the picnic, or Jake would have had to watch out for him, too. "I can probably get off early. The part-time bartender, Jeff, has been asking for more work. I could get him to come in for a couple of hours tonight."

"Jake, that's silly. I'll find another ride."

"It's not silly. I wouldn't mind knocking off early."

She gazed at him.

"Seriously."

She shrugged. "Okay, if you say so. Makes my life a lot easier."

He nodded. "Good."

"I'd...I'd invite you to join us, but this is supposed to be a business discussion, and—"

"No problem. While I was out this morning, I picked up some more groceries. I'll just make myself some beans and wienies and kick back with a book." He didn't tell her it would be *The Unvanquished,* which he'd found in paperback. He hoped that reading the book might give him some insight into the mind of the note writer. He still didn't know if there was some sicko after Dani, or whether it was indeed Helen Goodwin herself.

PAULA RODE HOME feeling both happy and sad. Happy because she'd done a good job pinstriping. And also because Dani had said her new friend Evelyn wanted Paula to pinstripe something in a store. Indian designs. Something new to try. Dani would be there, so it wouldn't be too scary. Fun, maybe.

But Paula was sad because Dani and Jake weren't cozy together as she wanted. She could tell they liked each other. A lot. Jake looked at Dani as if she were the last M & M in the bag, and somebody else got her. Dani looked at Jake as if he were Kevin Costner and Mel Gibson rolled into one. Paula thought Jake was cuter than both of them.

The pinstriping had made them have to ride together a lot. That was good. But the pinstriping was over, and they still weren't holding hands and stuff. Paula knew they had to at least hold hands first. Then kiss. Then that other junk she'd read about in her mother's books, the ones with people kissing on the cover. She didn't understand all of it. The words were hard. But she got the idea. Dani and Jake weren't even close to doing that.

She'd have to think of something else. She'd watch and wait for the right time, and do something so they had to be together. Maybe when that cactus thing was going to bloom. The books talked about flowers and sweethearts.

She'd tried to make Jake get some flowers. But he wouldn't. She'd get some and say they were from Jake, but that wouldn't be any good. They had to be really from Jake. Anybody knew that.

Jake and Dani were perfect together. They just didn't know it. But she'd fix things so they'd know.

CHAPTER ELEVEN

THAT NIGHT, after Jake took her home, Dani changed into jeans and a knit top, not wanting to meet Evelyn at the door in what Evelyn called a "ridiculous costume." Then she hurried around her small kitchen, setting the table and stirring the vegetables in the skillet. Evelyn's flowers were too big for a centerpiece, but Dani teased a few out of the arrangement to put in a bud vase she found in a high cupboard.

As she worked, she kept glancing through the window at the little white house across the clearing. A faint light glowed, probably coming from the kitchen. She pictured Jake eating a lonely dinner and sitting down with a book. If he and Evelyn got along better, she might have invited him, at least for dinner. But his presence would have cast a pall over the evening. Dani suspected Evelyn didn't like Jake any more than he liked her.

Dani turned away from the window and decided not to think about Jake anymore tonight. She'd found out a long time ago that just because she liked someone didn't mean everyone she knew would like them, too. She hoped Paula would get along with Evelyn, though. When Dani had described the inside of Evelyn's shop, and the possibilities for pinstriping there, Paula's eyes had sparkled. As long as Evelyn agreed, Dani planned to take Paula over to The Silver Coyote the next morning.

Evelyn arrived twenty minutes late. Her denim skirt, silk blouse and denim vest looked casual, but Dani knew expensive boutique clothes when she saw them. Evelyn didn't apologize for being late.

"You look wonderful, Evelyn," Dani said as she took the canvas sack containing Evelyn's blender and the margarita ingredients.

"Wonderful." Evelyn paused. "That's the word people use for 'women of a certain age,' isn't it? Just the other day I heard someone say that George Burns looks 'wonderful.'"

Dani flushed. She always seemed a little off balance with this woman. "I meant you look terrific, and a heck of a lot better than George Burns."

"I should hope so." Evelyn glanced around her. "What a charming little place. I passed the peacocks on my way in. They didn't look very regal squatting on your porch railing."

"You don't get the full effect unless the male spreads his tail in the sunlight. Then he's breathtaking." Dani tipped her head toward the kitchen. "Let's mix up the margaritas. If it's not too cool for you, we can sit on the porch and listen to the river."

"Perfect. If you'll direct me toward a plug, I'll do the mixing. Creating margaritas is not a job for amateurs."

Dani did as she was told, all the while fighting the feeling that she was being treated like a child. Apparently, that was Evelyn's manner, probably because she'd had money for a long time and was used to being in charge. While Evelyn mixed the drinks, Dani turned down the heat under the skillet. She shouldn't have started dinner so soon; the vegetables would be limp by the time they ate. Maybe after a couple of margaritas Evelyn wouldn't notice.

In a few minutes, they were settled in wooden lawn chairs on Dani's porch, a pitcher of margaritas on a small table between them. The only sounds in the night were the crickets chirping in the nearby mesquite tree and the ripple of the river sliding through its banks.

Evelyn raised her glass. "Here's to successful endeavors."

"To successful endeavors and The Silver Coyote." Dani sipped from her salt-rimmed glass. The margarita was strong. She'd have to limit herself to one if she expected to serve dinner and show Evelyn the rest of her inventory.

"Who lives in that little house across the way?"

"Jake Clayborn, the man you met today."

"Oh, really? I had no idea he was your neighbor, too. He's a trifle possessive, don't you think?"

"I'm not sure what you mean."

"It's just an impression I have, as if he's keeping track of you, somehow. I'm assuming that he has the hots for you."

Dani grimaced. "I hardly think so." Yet she had thought so, at one time. And Evelyn was right—Jake did seem to be keeping track of her. If their relationship had progressed as she'd hoped it would, his behavior would make more sense. As it was, he acted like a dog in the manger, not wanting her, but not wanting anyone else to have her, either. "Jake's an unusual man," she said.

"If he's not giving you the rush, I'd say he's more than unusual. I'd say he's strange."

Dani felt the need to change the topic before the tequila prompted her to say more than she wanted to about Jake. "Did you happen to notice the pinstriping on my car as you came in?"

"Not really."

"We should go look at it." She stood. "I'll get a flashlight and—"

Evelyn waved her back down. "Sit, sit. I believe you when you say that this Paula person is talented. I don't need to see the evidence. Besides, I'm happy to give a budding young artist a boost. If I don't like what she does, I can always have someone paint over it."

Dani winced at the thought. "I don't think that will be necessary. The work she did on my car is beautiful. I'm almost afraid to drive it, for fear something will happen to the paint job."

"That's the trouble with all original artwork. It can be easily destroyed. The only way to gain immortality is to write something and get it published, with thousands of copies in circulation. Then your name will live on."

"I suppose." Dani thought of her mother. She'd never imagined her mother's work as making her immortal, but perhaps it did, for a few years, anyway. She thought of telling Evelyn she was Helen Goodwin's daughter. Evelyn would be impressed. Dani rejected the impulse as unworthy. She'd earn Evelyn's respect on her own terms.

"I'm writing a detective story," Evelyn said. "Did I tell you that?"

"No, you didn't. How interesting." Dani was glad she hadn't mentioned her mother. Next thing, Evelyn would ask if Dani would send the manuscript to her mother for a critique. Dani didn't want to put her mother in that position. With Evelyn's offer to market Dani's jewelry, too much was at stake.

Evelyn poured herself another margarita. "It's a murder mystery. I've been writing for years, but this time I think I'm on to something that will sell."

"Mysteries are big these days." Dani felt more and more uncomfortable. If she had a long association with Evelyn, Evelyn would inevitably find out about Helen. Better to face the problem now and deal with it. "My mother's a writer," she said at last.

"Really? What does she write?"

"Mainstream fiction. You may have heard of her. Helen—"

"Not Helen Goodwin? I've read all her books! *The Unvanquished* is the main reason I came down here. After reading about Tubac, I had to see the place."

"I came here because of that book, too, in a way."

Evelyn settled back in her chair and stared at Dani. "So you're Helen Goodwin's daughter. How absolutely amazing. What a small world."

"I normally don't mention my mother to people, but if we're going to be working together, you'll find out sooner or later. And the thing is, my mom doesn't like to critique other people's work, so—"

"Goodness, you think I'd presume like that on someone I don't know? I wouldn't dream of it." Evelyn leaned forward and patted Dani's knee. "Put your mind at rest. Besides, I already have a dear friend who is enormously helpful."

"That's good." Greatly relieved, Dani took a long swallow of her margarita. At least that hurdle was crossed. She hoped there wouldn't be too many more standing in the way of a successful business relationship with Evelyn.

"Your father died not too long ago, didn't he?"

"Yes."

"I was so sorry to hear that. I read in an interview once that your mother was devoted to him, and he to her."

"That's right." Dani drained her glass and decided on just a half a glass more. This conversation seemed to require it.

"It must have been hard on you, too. He wasn't that old."

"Not really. Although he was fifteen years older than Mom, but I never thought about that, never realized he was getting to an age when he might die." Dani felt the old lump in her throat, but the pain was more bearable now than it had been six months earlier. She was healing from the loss.

"What a shame that he's gone. But what surprises me is that you're down here and your mom is up there. I would have thought you might cling together a little more."

Dani took another swallow of her margarita to silence the voice of guilt Evelyn had awakened. She'd wanted to be a comfort to her mother. But her mother had seemed to suck her dry.

"You're getting mighty quiet over there," Evelyn chided. "Did I hit a nerve?"

"I think you hit an artery."

"Troubles between you and the bestselling author, perhaps?"

Dani grimaced. "I had to get away from Mom for a while. We had some . . . problems."

"Sounds like an understatement to me."

"Yeah." Dani sighed. Why not explain? If she and Evelyn were to be partners, Evelyn probably deserved to know exactly why Dani had escaped to Tubac. Condensing the details, she told Evelyn about the notes and her belief they were a product of her mother's imagination.

"I've never heard anything so amazing," Evelyn said when Dani had finished. "It does sound like something out of a book, doesn't it?"

"You can see why I think she made it up."

"Well, yes, but what if she didn't? To think of some crazed person following you here to Tubac is—" Evelyn shuddered. "It's bizarre. I'd be pretty nervous if I were you."

"I vacillate. Sometimes I tell myself to forget it, that Mom's pulling some stunt, and other times I get a little scared. But I'm hardly ever alone. Jake's right across the way if I get into trouble."

"How convenient."

Dani chuckled. "He's less trouble than a guard dog."

"I wonder."

Dani glanced across at the other house. The light was out, so Jake was probably in bed. She thought of him stretched out beneath the sheets. He wasn't the sort of man who wore pajamas to bed. She took another sip of her margarita. "Sometimes I wonder, too. Listen,

Evelyn, if we don't eat that stir-fry pretty soon, it'll be mush."

"Fine with me. The margaritas are all gone, anyway."

Dani glanced at the pitcher and discovered Evelyn was right. While Dani had been talking, Evelyn had finished off the rest of the mix. Yet she stood from the chair and walked into the house with nary a wobble, while Dani felt very unsteady. Evelyn was used to drinking these, Dani decided, and she wasn't. With luck, she wouldn't drop a plate of food in Evelyn's lap.

Dani managed to serve the dinner without mishap, and it tasted better than she would have expected. She was pouring coffee for Evelyn when the peacock screamed.

"My God!" Evelyn leaped from her chair and jostled Dani, who poured the coffee on Evelyn's denim skirt.

"Oh! I'm so sorry! It's the peacock." Dani set the carafe back on the burner and tore paper towels from the holder. "Here, your skirt—"

"There it is again! That's a horrible sound. Are you sure it's not someone out there screaming for help?"

"No, it's the peacock. Look out the window and you'll probably see him in the yard, strutting around. Something startled him. Something—" Dani glanced outside and froze. Someone *was* in the yard. Someone was walking toward her porch.

She peered at the figure, her heart pounding. Then she let out a sigh. It was Jake. She hurried to the door and opened it. "You scared me half to death, Jake Clayborn."

"That peacock scared *me* half to death. I had to come out and see what was going on, make sure you were okay."

Dani stood in the doorway debating whether to invite him in. After all, he had charged out into the night, thinking she might be in danger.

He sniffed. "Do I smell coffee?"

She made her decision. "Probably the half a pot I spilled all over Evelyn." Dani glanced into the kitchen and saw Evelyn sponging at her skirt. "But come on in. I have cookies, too."

"I'm game. I skipped dessert." He mounted the steps and walked toward her.

"How's your book?"

"Pretty engrossing."

She stepped back and let him come in. "What is it?"

"Just some paperback I picked up in town." He walked into the kitchen ahead of Dani. "Looks like the peacock got us both upset, Evelyn."

Evelyn dropped the sponge into the sink. "Fortunately, I've found a good dry cleaner in Tucson. So... you bolted out to make sure Dani wasn't being murdered?"

Jake walked over to a cupboard and took out a mug as if he'd done it dozens of times before. "Something like that."

Dani watched him carefully as he poured himself a cup of coffee and settled into the chair she'd been using. He moved with studied nonchalance as he established that this kitchen was familiar territory for him. He was acting, as Evelyn had put it, "a trifle possessive." Maybe more than a trifle.

"I warned you about that peacock, Jake," she said.

"I know. But this time it sounded different. So I thought I'd make sure everything was okay."

"Thanks, everything's fine."

Evelyn reclaimed her chair opposite Jake. "I never realized peacocks had this other side to them. How can such a frightening sound come from such a magnificent bird?"

"One of nature's little jokes, I guess," Jake said.

Dani reached for the coffee carafe. "Can I pour you some more, Evelyn?"

She held out her cup. "Please."

Dani came over with the coffee, poured some for Evelyn, and moved her own cup from in front of Jake. "Guess I'll have some, too." After returning the carafe to the burner, she sat in the chair facing the window, between Jake and Evelyn.

Jake glanced at her. "Did I take your seat? I'm sorry."

No, you're not, she thought. For some reason, he'd wanted to be right across from Evelyn so he could look her straight in the eye. "It doesn't matter," she said.

"Did you two have a nice dinner?"

"Delicious," Evelyn said. "Dani is a marvelous cook."

"I know. You should taste her bacon and eggs."

Dani felt like kicking him for implying that he'd spent the night with her. And after he'd gallantly defended her honor in front of Ed Jordan, too. "Paula came over early this morning to work on the car, and we all had breakfast together before she started," Dani explained.

"How neighborly."

Jake nodded as if he hadn't noticed the sarcasm in Evelyn's voice. "We all get along pretty well. Tell me,

Evelyn, what made you decide to open a shop in Tubac?"

"I was just telling Dani that her mother's book inspired me to come down here. Do you know who Dani's mother is?"

"Dani's told me all about her."

"Not *all* about her," Dani cut in.

"Dani needed someone to talk to," Jake said. "You know how that is, Evelyn."

"And she found you. How sweet."

Dani slammed her cup down. "Will you two cut it out?"

Like feuding children, Jake and Evelyn eyed each other across the table.

Then, Jake lazily stretched before pushing back his chair and getting up. "Okay, Evelyn. You don't like me and I don't like you. But we both think a lot of Dani. As long as you give her a fair shake, I won't bother you. But if something goes wrong, I'll be knocking on your door."

Evelyn glared at him.

Dani stood, shaking with anger. "Jake, that was the most arrogant, rude—"

"Maybe, but it was the truth. See you later."

As the door closed after him, Dani sank back to her seat. "Evelyn, I apologize for—"

"No need. But I warn you, that man is trying to build a fence around you."

"That's what he thinks."

Evelyn smiled. "I'm glad to hear you talk like that. I'd hate to think you could be manipulated by a possessive man."

"Not in a month of Sundays."

JAKE THREW HIMSELF on the bed fully dressed. Damn, but this wasn't going well. He'd tried to spy on Dani and Evelyn's dinner, just to get a better angle on what Evelyn was up to. The flowers bit had thrown him for a loop. Dani hadn't acted as if Evelyn had insulted her or been particularly rude, and yet here came an armful of orchids.

Then, as he'd been eavesdropping at the window, the stupid peacock had started crowing his head off. Jake had been forced to maneuver himself across the yard so he could walk back toward Dani's house as if he'd just been rousted out of bed.

Then he'd decided to wangle an invitation to coffee, for some reason he couldn't think of now. Probably it was his growing urge to be near Dani at all costs. He'd pretended to himself he was only doing his job, but it was more than that. And it was affecting his judgment.

He wanted her. Lord, how he wanted her. Under other circumstances they'd be lovers by now. He wondered if that was part of this obsession he had—that she was off-limits to him. He hadn't often been thwarted when it came to women. Maybe, as the old saying went, forbidden fruit seemed sweeter.

Jake groaned and rolled over. Right now, Dani seemed like the sweetest thing in the world to him. And the most remote.

CHAPTER TWELVE

DANI PULLED UP in front of Paula's house at eight-thirty the next morning. She hadn't seen Paula's parents since the morning Paula had defiantly snuck over to Dani's house, and she didn't relish seeing them now.

Nevertheless, she'd wanted to drive Paula to The Silver Coyote rather than have her arrive hot and dusty after a bike ride. She wanted Paula to create a good impression and get off on the right foot with Evelyn, especially after Jake's animosity toward the woman last night.

The incident between Evelyn and Jake had apparently distracted Evelyn from her purpose in coming to Dani's house; she'd left without seeing the rest of the jewelry. Dani had the other four cases in the back seat with her now, to show Evelyn this morning.

Dani still couldn't believe Jake had practically threatened Evelyn to do right by her. His behavior could only hurt her chances with Evelyn, not help them.

This morning, Dani had considered marching over there to tell him off, but had finally decided the best response was no response. She'd ignore him. When he'd called out a greeting as she'd gotten into the car, she'd gunned the engine and driven off without a word.

Now, perversely, she wished he could be here to help her face the Jordans. She turned off the engine and stepped out of the Mustang. The spring sky held the depth of polished azurite, and in the Jordans' flower beds, topaz-colored African daisies opened their petals to the sun. Dani had once heard that gazing at the color yellow fed creativity. She hoped Paula would come out and stare at these flowers every day this spring to counteract the negative vibrations from her parents.

Dani's heels echoed on the tile steps, and the doorbell sounded like a gong in some forbidden temple. Strange how she'd once admired this house. Now, knowing it lacked loving spirits within, the house seemed a hollow shell of ostentation to her.

Madge came to the door dressed in a lime-green jogging suit. "Paula's not feeling well."

Dani's hopes sank. "May I see her?"

"I don't know if she has something contagious."

"I'll take my chances."

"As you wish." Madge stepped aside. No smiles this time. No offers of coffee.

Dani made her way down the hall toward Paula's room. The house could have been a model home, except there was no piped-in music. Instead, the quiet seemed to smother any instinct toward joy. No sign of Ed Jordan. Dani figured he was probably out on the golf course. No wonder Paula loved working at the restaurant. At least there she found noise and laughter, *life*.

She rapped on Paula's door and heard a faint call to come in. The miniblinds, which Paula had also pinstriped, were closed, casting the room into twilight.

Dani could barely make out the vibrant colors on the wall. She approached the huddled form under the bedspread. "Paula?"

"My tummy feels bad."

"Gee, I'm sorry. Do you think it's stomach flu?"

"Don't know."

Dani eased carefully down and sat on the edge of the bed. "Well, don't worry about the appointment with Evelyn. I'm sure she can wait another day. I don't think she's ready for you yet, anyway. And I'm sure you've got the job."

"Maybe I shouldn't."

"What?"

"Pinstripe Evelyn's."

Dani had a growing suspicion this tummy ache had something to do with Madge and Ed Jordan. "Why not?"

"I might mess up."

In the dim light, Dani could see that Paula was turned toward the wall. Dani reached out and rubbed her shoulder. "You won't mess up. You'll do a wonderful job. I know you've never met Evelyn, but I'll be there while you work, so you won't be alone with her."

Paula didn't answer.

"Remember what I told you about the inside of her shop? It's deep turquoise, like being under the sea, almost, and the shelves are white as...as Jake's teeth when he smiles."

Paula gave a little snort of amusement.

Encouraged, Dani kept going. "The white against the turquoise is a nice contrast, but the whole effect is basically...plain." She continued to rub Paula's shoulder. "If you added some black and turquoise on the white shelves and cases, the place would be dynamite. And that's what we want, so people will come in and buy my jewelry."

"I want to, Dani, but..."

"What is it?"

"My tummy hurts."

Maybe she really was sick, Dani thought. "That's okay. We can go another time. I guess you won't be at work today, either."

"Guess not."

"Anything I can do for you?"

Paula rolled over and gazed at Dani. "Come and see me tonight? After work?"

"Sure thing." Dani squeezed her shoulder. "Get better soon. I'll miss you."

"Okay."

Dani rose from the bed and started toward the door.

"Dani?"

She turned and glanced back at Paula.

"Pinstriping would help you?"

"Absolutely. It would add some real class to the cases. People would be drawn to them, and then, when they see my jewelry inside—*Bam!*—we've got them."

There was a pause. "Tomorrow," Paula said.

Dani acknowledged the resolution in her voice. "Tomorrow for sure. I'll be back to check on you tonight, though."

"Bring Jake."

Dani thought fast. "Jake doesn't get off until later. I don't think your parents would want us here then."

Paula sighed. "Okay. Just you."

"See you then." Dani left the room feeling as if she'd dodged another bullet. Maybe after Paula had recovered, and after she'd begun her job with Evelyn, Dani would have a heart-to-heart talk with Paula about Jake. Surely Paula would be able to understand why Dani needed to stay away from him for her own peace of mind.

The living room and entry hall were empty, and she was about to let herself out the front door when Madge appeared from the vicinity of the kitchen.

"Your friend called here," she said.

"My friend?" Dani wondered if she could mean Jake.

"Evelyn something. She called last night and wanted to talk to us about Paula's work."

"She did?" Dani hadn't expected that. Of course, she'd given Evelyn Paula's name, and Evelyn wouldn't have had much trouble finding the Jordans in the phone book, but why would she call after professing such confidence in Dani's opinion?

"She just said she was thinking of hiring Paula for some work around her shop, and she wondered how much experience Paula had in that sort of thing. Of course, I didn't know anything about the job. Paula had failed to mention it."

"Well, it just came up yesterday, so I can understand if it slipped her mind."

Madge smiled sadly. "Oh, it didn't slip her mind. Paula has become very secretive lately." The implication was clear that Dani had made her that way.

"I see. So what did you tell Evelyn?"

"The truth. That Paula has pinstriped the walls in her bedroom, an old dilapidated truck and your Mustang, none of it for pay. That Paula can be emotionally unstable and I couldn't in all good conscience recommend her to someone for an important job like painting the inside of a business establishment."

Dani stifled a groan.

"Then I told Paula the same thing."

"And now she has a stomachache." Dani wanted to slap Madge. "How could you ruin her chances like that?"

"How can you take such chances with her?" Madge's eyes were bright, as if with unshed tears. "You haven't lived with her for twenty-two years. You haven't seen her try and fail at everything. You haven't been humiliated because the rest of the family have smart, talented children and you have a...a..."

"Dummy?" said Paula. She stood in the hall dressed in Batman pajamas.

"No!" Dani ran to her without thinking and grabbed her in a fierce hug. "Don't ever say that again!"

"It's true," Paula said, her words muffled against Dani's shoulder.

"It's *not* true. You can fill the world with beauty. All you need is the chance."

Madge finally found her voice. "Paula, sweetie, you're ill. Go on back to bed."

Dani tightened her grip. "If you want to come with me, I'll wait."

"My...tummy still hurts." She squirmed a little, and Dani released her.

"Why did you come out here, then?"

"Heard you talking. And I wanted to tell Jake..." She chewed on her fingernail and glanced at her mother. Madge looked away.

"You wanted to tell Jake something?" Dani prompted.

"I think . . . his truck needs one more stripe."

"I'll tell him," Dani said, and then realized she hadn't meant to talk to him. Oh, well. "But we'll still go to Evelyn's tomorrow, right?"

Paula glanced at her mother again. "It helps Dani."

Madge sighed. "I think it's too much for you. I worry so that you'll have a hard time. So does your father."

Paula looked back at Dani. Her gaze was troubled. "Are you sure I'll help you?"

"Very sure. And I'm not the least worried about the job you'll do."

"Okay." Paula started back down the hall. Halfway to her room she stopped and turned around. "Don't forget to tell Jake. About the stripe. Gold."

"I won't." Dani sent her a smile of encouragement. As she watched Paula walk down the hall, she wondered if her interference was a mistake. After all, Paula's parents had known her for twenty-two years, and Dani had only been around a short while. But sometimes it took an outsider to see what needed to be done. And what Dani saw was that Paula needed an ally.

Straightening her shoulders, Dani vowed to be that ally. When Paula was back in her room, Dani nodded to Madge and left the house. She was afraid of what she might say to Paula's mother if she stayed a minute longer.

WHEN SHE HEARD Dani leave, Paula snugg. down into her covers. Her tummy still hurt, but not so bad.

Dani needed her to pinstripe so her jewelry would sell better. Tomorrow she'd go and help Dani.

She was helping Dani in another way, too, but Dani didn't know it. The idea about Jake coming with her tonight hadn't worked. So Paula had thought of the stripe. She had to keep thinking of ways for Dani and Jake to be together. Now Dani had to talk to Jake about the stripe. And when the painting started, Dani had to give Jake a ride to work.

Paula closed her eyes and sighed. She had a dream that nobody knew. A dream that Dani and Jake got married. Then they'd build a house. Then they'd build another house. A little house near the big one. Paula would live there. Paula thought about the little house, filled with pinstriping, and her tummy ache almost went away.

DANI TOOK the rest of her jewelry to Evelyn's shop and explained that Paula didn't feel well, but that she'd be there the next morning. She insisted Evelyn come outside to see the pinstriping on her Mustang.

"Did she use a stencil?" Evelyn asked.

"No."

"My, she has a flair."

"She needs nurturing," Dani said. "She's easily crushed at this stage, and her parents do nothing to build up her confidence."

"Her mother didn't sound the least encouraging on the phone. I'll say that."

"It's...unfortunate you called them. After your call, Madge convinced Paula she couldn't do the job. Which is ridiculous. You can see from this work she'd be wonderful. But this morning Paula had a stomach-ache. I think it's just nerves.''

"Heavens, I wish you'd have said something! It's just standard business procedure to check references, but if I'd known . . .''

"I think everything will be fine by tomorrow." Dani hoped so.

"Good, because I'd like to open the shop sometime next week.''

Dani glanced at the storefront and imagined customers coming through the door, admiring her jewelry, buying pieces they loved. She missed that more than she'd realized. "We'll be ready by next week," she said.

Dani stayed at the shop far later than she'd planned, and she was running behind when she returned home to get ready for work. She passed Jake on the road. He tooted his horn and waved and she lifted her hand in a lukewarm response. No point in completely snubbing him now when she'd have to talk with him at the restaurant, anyway. Her idea of ignoring him was already going astray, thanks to Paula.

Soon after she arrived for work, she found a spare moment and decided to get the conversation over with. She walked quickly into the bar, as if she didn't have a second to waste. Jake glanced up from rearranging bottles and smiled. As always, when he smiled at her like that, her heart hammered in her chest. It would probably be a great relief when she didn't have to work here anymore and see him all the time.

"I have a message from Paula," she said, keeping a couple of feet away from the bar.

"I noticed she didn't come in today. Is she okay?''

"A stomachache."

"The flu?"

"No. Her parents again." She hadn't meant to go into it, but Madge's treachery was eating at her. "Evelyn called the house to ask Madge about Paula's pinstriping experience, and Madge basically told her not to hire Paula. Then she told Paula she shouldn't accept the job."

"Damn."

"But I think Paula's going to do it. I convinced her I needed the pinstriping to help show off my jewelry so it would sell better."

"Good thinking. But why did Evelyn call in the first place?"

Dani shrugged. "She's used to doing things in a big-city way, I guess. She wanted some sort of reference for Paula's work, beyond what I told her."

"She didn't ask for any references from you."

Dani thought about that. "Maybe because I had all this stuff I'd made."

"You could have lied, said the jewelry was yours when it wasn't. You could be a total fraud. She doesn't know."

"Yes, well . . . for some reason, she believes me. Anyway, she was really sorry she screwed things up."

"Does that mean you'll get another nifty bouquet of flowers?"

Dani glared at him. "I don't even know why I talk to you."

"Because you're crazy about me."

The accuracy of his statement paralyzed her for a second, but she recovered quickly. "Right. I adore having people around who come into my house and insult my guests. Especially when that guest is trying to further my career. You're a prince, Jake."

His brown eyes grew darker. "Last night I wasn't very nice and I apologize. I know you need to market your work. But I wish you'd found someone besides Evelyn to help you. Have you asked around the other shops again? Maybe enough time has gone by and they—"

"No, enough time hasn't gone by. And Evelyn's like some gift from the gods. She may not have the most diplomatic manner in the world, but she loves what I do, and that counts for a lot."

"You're right. Now, what was it Paula wanted to tell me?"

Dani was startled to discover her hands resting on the edge of the bar. As she and Jake had been talking, she'd drifted forward until now, with Jake leaning on his side, their faces were only inches apart. As she gazed into his eyes, she tried to remember what had brought her into the bar in the first place.

"A message?" Jake asked softly.

"Why haven't you ever kissed me again?" she murmured.

"Too many reasons. None of them seem worth a damn at this very moment."

"Oh, Jake. You confuse the heck out of me."

"I know. I'm sorry." His hand slid slowly across the bar and their fingertips touched. "I wish we were in a different time, a different place."

"Dani!" Jean called from the kitchen. "I need you in here."

Dani snapped out of her daze. "But we're not," Dani said, and pushed away from the bar. "The message is, Paula wants to paint another stripe on your truck. Gold this time.''

"She can paint a rainbow on it for all I care.''

Dani backed toward the kitchen, unwilling to let her gaze leave his face. "If you tell her that, she will. She'd do anything to please you.''

"I'd do anything to please her.''

Dani didn't think they were talking about Paula any longer. Jake cared for her. She knew it. Yet something stood between them, something mysterious. If only she could discover what it was. Jean called her again, and with a last glance at Jake, she went into the kitchen.

AFTER THE WAY Jake had looked at her in the bar, Dani half expected him to knock on her door that night after he came home from work. She visited Paula and convinced herself Paula would be ready to go to Evelyn's the next morning. Then she hurried home and changed into a soft lounging outfit, just in case. Then she found a book and prepared to read until he arrived. The words kept jumping around on the page, but she managed to drag herself through a couple of chapters.

When she heard his truck in the driveway, she put down her book and listened. The truck moved past her house and over to his. Then the engine stopped. She heard the door of his house bang shut. Maybe he'd decided to change, too. Maybe he was picking up a bottle of wine. Or maybe . . . as the silence lengthened she entertained another possibility . . . he wasn't coming.

Dammit, what was wrong with that man? He practically drooled over her one minute, then scampered away the next. He was crazy, and quickly making her that way, too. She was furious with herself, and even more furious with him. She'd had enough. She wasn't pining after him another second. Whatever game he was playing, she was cashing in her chips. Snapping the switch on the lamp so vigorously she almost knocked it from the table, she stomped off to bed.

JAKE STOOD at his window and watched her lights wink out. He'd let his guard down again today. He didn't know how much longer he could keep this charade going. If someone was after Dani, that person wasn't anxious to show his hand. As much as he didn't want Dani in any danger, he almost wished the note writer would show himself. Then everything would be resolved.

Of course, if there was no real threat and the note writer was Helen, then this situation could continue indefinitely. Except he knew that wasn't possible. His need grew stronger and Helen Goodwin's restrictions seemed less important with each passing day. He'd have to tell Dani how he felt about her very soon. He had to show her. Lord, how he wanted to show her. But not tonight. For one more night he'd be strong.

CHAPTER THIRTEEN

DANI WAS TOUCHED by how carefully Paula had dressed for her meeting with Evelyn. Dani knew the arrow-straight part in Paula's hair and the polished white shoes had to be the young woman's doing. She would have choked before asking either of her parents to help her get ready. She wore white slacks and a pullover knit top covered with multicolored swirls.

"You look wonderful," Dani said when Paula answered the door.

Paula pointed to her top. "I picked this."

"I can tell. It looks almost like pinstriping."

Paula nodded enthusiastically.

"Are you ready, then?"

"Do I need paints?"

"Not this time. This is just to scope out the job."

"Then let's go."

Dani hesitated. "Shouldn't you tell your mother you're leaving?"

"I guess." Paula turned her head and yelled out "Leaving!" Then she stepped outside, looked around and sighed. "Leaving," she repeated.

Dani wished she could tell Paula to pack a bag, that she was coming home with her after work that day. But Dani could barely support herself, and her future wasn't stable enough to take on responsibility for someone like Paula, even if her parents would agree, which they probably wouldn't. Dani acknowledged that in their own way Madge and Ed loved Paula, even though they were stifling her. Much, Dani reflected, as her mother had tried to stifle her.

"Did you tell Jake about the stripe?" Paula asked as they drove toward town.

"Yes." Thinking about Jake gave *her* a stomach-ache.

"Did he say okay?"

"Yes."

"Dani! You're mad at him."

"Yes."

"Why?"

Dani gripped the wheel. Now was as good a time as any. "Because he acts as if he likes me, and then poof, that's the end of that. He comes forward and backs off. I don't know what his problem is, but I'm sick of never knowing how he feels about me. I'd rather have nothing to do with him than be on this seesaw."

"Seesaw." Paula stared out through the windshield and chewed on her fingernail. "He has a secret."

Dani's pulse quickened. "He told you that?"

"Sort of. Not really."

"Oh." Dani's shoulders slumped with disappointment. "Then you're as much in the dark as I am."

"He likes you."

"Well, he has a funny way of showing it. Or *not* showing it, to be more exact. And you may be right about the secret. But if he has something to hide, I don't want anything to do with him, anyway."

Paula chewed on her fingernail some more. "Maybe he can't decide something."

"Oh, great! Just what I need, an indecisive man. Paula, I understand what you like about him. He has some wonderful qualities, but he's not the one for me. So the upshot is, I'm not eating lunch with him today."

"What?" Paula turned toward Dani as far as her seat belt would allow. "Not eating lunch? But... the Three Musketeers!"

"I'm sorry, but it's too hard on me. I... well, I do kind of like Jake. If I let myself, I could like him a lot. But the way he's acting, being around him is just...my ego can't take the beating."

"He makes you feel bad?"

"Sometimes. Not all the time, but when he stays away from me, and I don't understand why, then it hurts."

Paula nodded. "Okay."

"I'm eating lunch with Jean today."

"Okay."

Dani swung the car into the parking space in front of The Silver Coyote. Evelyn had recently traded in her rental car and bought a Jeep CJ-7, and it was parked there, too. "I'm really sorry it didn't work out for Jake and me," Dani said, putting a hand on Paula's arm. "I know you tried to be a matchmaker, but sometimes people just don't click."

Paula glance was unsmiling. "It's okay."

Dani squeezed her friend's arm and opened the car door. "Come on. I want you to meet Evelyn."

The inside of the shop smelled of fresh paint. Dani paused before taking Paula back to the office. "Isn't it a beautiful color?"

Paula glanced around, and when she looked at Dani, her eyes were shining. "Pinstriping would work perfect."

"I knew you'd think so."

"Do I hear voices out there?" Evelyn walked through the office door and came over to hug Dani. "Here you are. I've been counting the minutes."

Dani tried not to choke on Evelyn's heavy perfume. "This is Paula," she said when Evelyn released her. "Paula Jordan. Paula, I'd like you to meet Evelyn Ross."

"What a funny little top you have on," Evelyn said.

Paula blushed bright pink.

Dani rushed to the rescue. "It's her way of suggesting what she does. The top almost looks pinstriped, don't you think?" She wished Evelyn wouldn't say the first thing that popped into her mind. Dammit, she'd embarrassed Paula already.

"I suppose you could view it that way," Evelyn said. "Well, Paula, do you think you're up to this job?"

Paula glanced at Dani, who gave her a thumbs-up sign. "Yes," Paula said, with only a trace of a quiver in her voice.

"She can work early mornings for about two hours, I'd say, before we go to Canada Verde." Dani put her arm around Paula's shoulders. "Does that sound okay?"

"Fine. You'll be bringing her, Dani?"

"That's the easiest."

"Great. I have a terrific idea. Why don't you transfer your equipment to the shop? You can work on those peacock earrings we talked about while Paula's painting the shelves and cabinets."

Dani couldn't think of a good argument against the idea, although housing her precious equipment in someone else's shop didn't feel quite right. But the plan made sense. She needed time for the peacock jewelry, and working during the early-morning hours here with Evelyn and Paula was a logical solution. "Sure, I'll do that," she said.

"Then I'll see you both bright and early tomorrow morning."

"Sounds good to me." Dani glanced down at Paula. "Does it sound good to you?"

Paula nodded. She looked scared but determined.

Dani said goodbye to Evelyn and Paula managed a little wave. When they were outside again, Paula slumped with relief.

"You did it!" Dani said. "You went in there and clinched the deal. Let's have some hot chocolate and celebrate."

"Okay!" Paula grinned and hopped into the Mustang.

They drove a short way down the street to an aromatic little coffee shop with rust-colored dried chili peppers hanging from the eaves. Only a couple of other customers were in the shop drinking mugs of coffee. Dani chose a table for two by the window and ordered two hot chocolates with marshmallows on top. Paula ended up with a frothy mustache after the first drink, and they both laughed as she wiped it off.

"Pretty nice to be served for a change, huh?" Dani said.

"Pretty nice."

"You'll do a great job on the pinstriping."

Paula's smile faded. "I guess."

"Look, something you'll have to realize about Evelyn is she speaks without thinking. She has a good heart, but she doesn't always say the right things."

Paula gazed at Dani for a long moment. "Okay."

"Tomorrow will be fun. You'll be working on your stuff, and I'll be working on mine."

"What about Evelyn?"

"Evelyn will—I don't know—maybe catalog inventory. She has some gift items she plans to sell along with my jewelry."

"She'll watch me?"

Dani knew Paula would have to get used to scrutiny sometime, but maybe Evelyn wasn't a good place to start. "I'll ask her not to."

Paula relaxed. "Good." Then she finished off her hot chocolate in one big gulp and stood. "I need to go home. I need practice."

"Paula, you're already great."

"I can be super-great."

"If you say so." Dani paid the bill and followed Paula out into the sunshine.

THAT AFTERNOON, Paula ate alone with Jake. She missed Dani. She knew Jake did, too. Painting the gold stripe wouldn't work. She had to paint shelves instead. For Evelyn. Dani said Evelyn wouldn't watch. And Dani would be there the whole time. That was a good thing.

But Dani and Jake, that was a bad thing. After the lunch with no Dani, Paula looked at the calendar hanging in the restaurant kitchen. It had names written on the squares, telling who worked what days.

Paula wanted to write "No Three Musketeers" on today's square. But she didn't.

Today was Thursday. There was a round circle beside the number. Paula remembered that meant a full moon tonight. Full-moon nights were good for kissing. The books said so. Paula sighed. This was getting harder and harder to figure out.

THURSDAY NIGHT was slow behind the bar, and Jake was restless from the inactivity, or at least, he told himself boredom was his problem. He didn't want to think about the other possible reason. Dani had decided to shut him out. That was just as well. He could do his job without talking to her every day; living near her and working where she worked kept him aware of her activities.

Paula had quizzed him unmercifully and he'd finally had to tell her gently to lay off. The hurt look on Paula's face had just about killed him, but what was he going to do, tell Paula everything? Someone like Paula, who was just testing her wings in this world, didn't need to hear that some crazed person might be after Dani.

Dani. She moved through her routine at the restaurant with the grace of an angel. When she came into the bar to fill a drink order, he treasured every moment she stood there, even though she avoided his gaze and stood away from the bar, away from any contact with him. Covertly, he'd study the tilt of her head, the fullness of her lower lip, the curve of her breasts beneath the peasant blouse.

Then he'd open his mouth to say something, anything to break the ice, but before the words were spoken, he'd call them back. They were both better off this way. Yet the ache inside him grew, and he daydreamed of her kiss, her touch, and the quenching love he knew she could give his thirsty body and soul.

He would abandon the assignment and end this torture, except that he no longer trusted her safety to someone else. He'd finished her mother's book and had formed some ideas about how the note writer might think. He even had some ideas of where they might strike, if the threat was real. If it wasn't, he was in for interminable torture as he waited for Helen Goodwin to play out whatever crazy game she'd begun.

Jake glanced at the Budweiser clock behind the bar. Dani would be going home soon and he still had another hour or so to work. He'd never liked the gap in his surveillance, and he'd talked management into letting Jeff, the part-time bartender, cover the last couple of hours, starting tomorrow night. Then Jake would be able to cover Dani's activities pretty much around the clock. Fortunately, she hadn't noticed him following her to Paula's and then to Evelyn's, but then she wasn't used to being tailed.

He'd had to piece his program together, and he'd done the best he could without blowing his cover. Helen seemed to think he was doing a good job, and she counted Evelyn as extra protection. Jake didn't. He wanted to be on the scene all the time, Evelyn or no Evelyn. He might not be able to hold Dani, or tell her how much he cared about her, but he damn sure wasn't going to let anything happen to her.

He realized he'd been polishing the same glass for at least five minutes, and he replaced it on the shelf behind the bar. He'd picked up another one when Paula raced in, her nylon jacket flying out behind her.

"Come see Dani's car! Come see Dani's car!" she cried.

He dumped the glass and towel on the bar and vaulted it. He was vaguely aware of a buzz of excitement from the customers as he tore back through the kitchen and banged out the door.

Dani was standing in the employees' parking lot staring at her Mustang. The light from the full moon gave him a clear view of two flat tires. The car wasn't tilting to that side, so he assumed they were all flat. His stomach clenched. Was this how it would start?

He caught her arm and spun her around. "What in hell are you doing out here alone?"

Her jaw jutted forward as she wrenched her arm free. "Trying to drive home! But I'm finding it a little difficult!"

"Poked," Paula said, almost jumping up and down in her agitation. "Tires poked."

Jake glanced around the parking lot. If someone planned to waylay Dani, this wasn't a very good night to do it. The moon lit up the place like day. He crouched next to one of the tires and found the spot where someone had stuck a knife through it. He controlled a shudder of fear. A knife had been the weapon used in an attempted murder in *The Unvanquished*. The thought of someone coming at Dani with a knife made his stomach roil.

He stood and looked at her. "We're calling the police."

"No!"

"I know it's a longshot but maybe they can—"

"I don't want them asking a lot of questions," she said in a low tone.

He hesitated. If she didn't want to tell the police about the notes, he couldn't force her to, and without that information, they wouldn't be able to do much.

"All right," he agreed reluctantly. "I'm taking you home."

"That's okay. I'll ask Enrique to take me."

"No." The Latin lover was definitely not taking her home tonight.

She glanced over her shoulder. "You have nothing to say about it."

He cursed under his breath and ran after her. Paula followed behind, puffing from the effort.

He caught Dani by the door and grabbed her arm. When she turned, her hazel eyes reminded him of a frozen lake he used to skate on as a kid. "Dani—"

"Let go of me, Jake."

He didn't. "Listen." He kept his voice low. "You may have a problem here. Enrique is not the guy to handle it."

"And you are?"

"At least I have some idea what you're up against. Unless you're planning to tell Enrique all about it?"

Beneath the ice of her stare he saw fear lurking. The tire incident had shaken her, but she didn't want to come to him for help. Too bad. She was getting it, anyway.

"You aren't off for another two hours," she said, "and I'm not waiting around." She sounded tough, but he could tell her resistance was ebbing. "I need my rest," she added. "Paula and I have a lot of work to do tomorrow morning."

"I'll call Jeff. He should be able to cover for me."

"That's silly. Enrique can—"

"Dani, suppose he takes you home? I won't be there for a while yet. It's possible...certain people know that and are using that information to get you alone."

Paula inserted herself between them. "What people?"

Jake glanced at her and wished, just this once, that Paula would go away. He wanted to convince Dani she was in danger, but he couldn't do that if he had to worry about scaring Paula.

Dani shrugged. "You know men, Paula. They're paranoid. They imagine bad people are hiding everywhere, ready to jump on women."

Paula's glance swerved from Dani to Jake and back again. "I think you should go with Jake."

"She *is* going with me. I just need a minute to arrange for my backup."

"Oh, all right," Dani grumbled. "You can unhand me now. I'll go peacefully."

He released her with regret. The firm flesh of her arm, covered only by the cotton of a light sweater, had felt wonderful under his fingers.

The three of them went back into the kitchen while Jake made his call. Then they waited in the bar for Jeff to show up. Somewhere along the way, Jake had decided to run Paula home, too. If bad spirits were out and about, he didn't want Paula blundering into something dangerous, either.

After Jeff arrived, Jake ushered Dani and Paula out to his truck. He loaded Paula's bike into the back then opened the passenger door and smiled to himself as Paula and Dani argued over who would get in first.

Each of them had an agenda and both were stubborn. He got in the truck and started the engine. Neither of them were in the truck yet.

Finally, he leaned over the seat toward them. "Ladies? Could we get on with this?"

"I get out first," Paula said. "I should go in last."

Dani glanced up at Jake in mute appeal.

He didn't feel particularly charitable. "She's right."

Without another word, Dani climbed into the truck. She tried to keep her distance from him, but once Paula got in and slammed the door, she was wedged tight against his arm and thigh. "Did you plan this?" she asked in an undertone.

"No." He would never have planned this. No man should have to endure such tantalizing pressure from a woman he wasn't supposed to touch. Her skirt and petticoats billowed around the gearshift and he had to search through them to find the damn thing. Sometime during the search, he encountered her bare knee and heard her quick intake of breath. He swore he could also hear her heart pounding, but it was probably just his own thundering along like a freight train.

"Cozy," Paula said from the other side of the cab.

Impossible, Jake thought. Dani shifted her weight on the seat and suddenly the softness of one breast met the tense muscles of his arm. He almost groaned aloud, and Dani quickly shifted back. Jake gave thanks that Paula lived close to the country club. Sweat dampened his armpits and the zipper on his jeans was beginning to pinch as he reacted to the heady scent of Dani's perfume and the uneven tempo of her breathing.

"The Three Musketeers ride again," Paula said into the charged silence.

Jake didn't trust himself to make small talk, so he remained silent. He figured Dani was in the same boat.

"Full moon tonight," Paula said. She sounded like a kid on a trip to Disneyland.

"Mm." Jake stepped on the gas and exceeded the speed limit down the narrow road to Paula's house. He pulled in with a squeak of brakes and was out the door to unload her bike before the sound of the engine died. The cool air helped, but another ride with Dani awaited him. He prayed for willpower.

He lifted the bike over the tailgate and set it on the circular driveway in front of Paula's house. Her parents must have heard them drive up, because the garage door slowly opened and a light snapped on inside. Paula came around the truck and took hold of the bike's handlebars.

"There you go," he said. "I'll stay here until you get the bike put away."

She glanced up at him and spoke in a stage whisper. "Full moon tonight!"

"I noticed, Paula."

"Don't blow it!"

"Paula…" He couldn't think of anything to say that would dissuade her. And if he didn't agree with her, she might never go inside. "Okay, I'll try not to blow it."

Her smile was brighter than the moonlight flooding the driveway. "All right!"

"Now get inside."

Paula winked at him. She had to almost close both eyes to do it, but he recognized it as a wink. Then she wheeled her bike toward the garage. He waited until she was inside and the door closed again. Then he took the long walk back to the truck cab.

Dani was hugging the far door, as he'd expected she would be. He got in without a word and started the engine.

"I guess I should be thanking you, or something. For coming to my rescue."

He winced. Of course, she didn't know he was being paid to come to her rescue. Even though the money meant nothing to him now, but when she found out... "You don't have to thank me," he said.

"What I really don't understand is why you're always so concerned about my welfare."

She was belligerent with good reason, he supposed. "I'm just that kind of guy."

"Oh, really? And what kind of guy is that? The kind who leads women on and then turns away?"

He clenched his jaw. "I didn't lead— Okay, I didn't *mean* to lead you on."

"Then what *did* you mean? Two nights in a row, you gave me a very soulful kiss. Usually that's the start of something, not the end. Or maybe you don't like the way I kiss. Is that it?"

Dani, don't do this.

"Maybe you're used to women with a more practiced technique. I guess baseball has groupies like every other sport. Maybe the women you're used to have a more sophisticated way of—"

"That's enough!" He drove the streets of Tubac as fast as he dared. He had to get her home and behind her own locked door. And fast.

"Oh, is the big bad man all upset? Well, good! At least I've aroused some emotion in you. The way you've been acting, I was beginning to think you were made of stainless steel. Or tin. I don't know, Jake, what are you made of?''

He wheeled the truck down the driveway and braked to a stop in a cloud of dust that glittered in the moonlight. With an angry twist he shut off the engine and punched the knob to turn off the lights. Then he gripped the wheel to keep from grabbing her and doing all the things he'd been dreaming about for endless nights in a lonely bed. He lowered his head to avoid looking at how the moonlight silvered her soft skin. "Get inside," he muttered.

"Don't worry." She threw open her door and started out. "I wouldn't want to inflict my presence on you any more than absolutely— *Oh!*"

Her soft cry of wonder brought his head up.

"Jake, look! Have you ever seen anything so beautiful in all your life?"

CHAPTER FOURTEEN

AT FIRST he thought kids had draped her mesquite tree with a roll of white toilet paper. Except the white was in splashes the size of softballs, not strung the way toilet paper would be. Then he remembered the night-blooming cereus.

Dani walked beneath the tree and lifted her face to the blossoms. Hundreds of them glimmered in the moonlight. From a branch of the tree, a shadow fluttered to the ground, and then the peacock turned...and spread his tail. The cock's blue-and-gold feathers glowed with the phosphorescence of some deep-water creature as he moved gracefully toward Dani.

Jake sat bewitched by a scene that seemed ripped from some other-world fantasy. All that was missing was the man to free the maiden's hair from its confining net, and kiss her soft lips, and hold her warm, yielding body, and never let go...never...

He wasn't conscious of leaving the truck, of crossing the distance between them. The flowers had no scent, he thought dazedly. Yet they were compelling, sensuous, spreading their delicate petals for the moon, not the sun. For a moment, he believed he was dreaming. When he reached for the net that bound Dani's hair, he was almost surprised his hand didn't go through thin air, so ethereal she seemed standing there, watching him with luminescent eyes.

He pulled the net away and her hair tumbled down her back. The net fluttered to the ground and he slid both hands beneath the weight of her hair and combed out the silken strands. This was no dream. As if to convince himself, he lifted a handful of those glorious tresses and brought them forward over her shoulder. Then he let his touch drift gently down over her breast. No dream. She was warm, quivering. Real.

Her breath caught, then came faster. "What do you want from me?"

"Everything."

"I don't understand you."

He moved closer, cupped her face in his hands. "You'll understand this." As his lips touched hers, his eyes closed in ecstasy. She was everything he remembered, and more. He dipped his tongue inside the sweetness of her mouth and moaned at the delicate way she met his advance, at the subtle parting of her lips, the seductive motion of her tongue against his.

He caressed the line of her jaw, the curve of her throat. When his grip closed over her shoulders, he steadied himself to keep from crushing her to him. All the hours of wanting and not having hammered at him, demanding that he take her now, here under the tree, with no softness, no tenderness, just grinding, driving need. He pushed the red mist of lust away and released her.

Then he stepped away, to give her time, to let her choose. She stood watching him, her breath coming in little gasps, her eyes wide and deep. He gazed into them and found what he wanted there. Slowly, he held out his hand.

Just as slowly, she placed hers within it. They walked to his door without speaking, accompanied by the sound of the river and the steady chirp of crickets. His key slid into the lock and he glanced at her. Once inside, there would be no turning back. She had to know that, but he'd give her one more chance to run away.

She met his gaze without flinching. He'd hoped communication could be like this between them and he wanted to shout in triumph. Tomorrow he might regret what was happening now. Tomorrow was soon enough. Tonight he would love this woman.

Moonlight flowed in through all the windows in the house. In his bedroom, a silver square of light rested on his bed, as if guiding them.

He turned to her and caught her other hand. "Paula told me to bring you flowers. I have no flowers."

She tilted her face upward. Her eyes were in shadow, but he could see her faint smile. "No, but *we* have them. Dozens of them."

"Tomorrow they'll be gone."

"Yes. It doesn't matter. We saw them tonight."

He listened in wonder to the meaning beneath her words, that she would take tonight with no guarantees. He was awed by her bravery. All his life he'd dreamed of a woman with the strength to live life as it came. He'd thought she'd need explanations before he made love to her. He'd held back because he knew he couldn't give any. But he'd been wrong. She needed none.

Slowly, he undressed her until she stood before him, her pale skin seeming to glow with a light of its own.

She was exquisite. He searched for the words to tell her, but words seemed such lifeless things to use. She threw back her hair and challenged him with her gaze. Without a word, he removed his own clothes.

After he'd tossed them aside, she began to touch him, her fingertips brushing seductively over his skin as she explored his quivering body. When he was afraid his legs would no longer support him, he caught both her hands and pulled her down to the bed.

They lay facing each other, both of them breathing hard. He splayed his hand across the small of her back and drew her gradually closer, until their bodies just barely met—her nipples touching his chest, the swell of his desire nudging her thigh. As she breathed, her nipples rubbed back and forth, back and forth, tantalizing him almost beyond endurance.

He concentrated on her eyes. He wanted her to understand the reverence he felt as he caressed her. In the moonlight her skin looked cool, but under his hand it was warm and damp. Now was his time to explore, and he celebrated the wonder of teasing her nipple to erection as he cradled the weight of her breast in his palm. As his touch moved lower, her eyes darkened and her nostrils flared.

He sought her heat and she whimpered when he found it. He pressed inward, following the invitation in her eyes. If he could have no more than this, he would die a happy man. But he could have more. She moved beneath his caress, telling him without words that she wanted more.

He withdrew his hand and rolled to his back, pulling her with him. Her hair fell around his face and neck and he breathed in the fragrance of it before she tossed it back over her shoulder. He gazed up at her. Would she follow his lead?

He needn't have wondered. She was his match. He'd sensed it all along. Shifting her weight away from him, she slid her hand down his belly. She teased, stroked and cradled him until his control threatened to disappear. All the while she gazed into his eyes and he held her gaze as the intensity built.

He grew wild with wanting her. At last, gasping from the strain, he grabbed her hand. Now. He had to be inside her now. He leaned over and wrenched open the bedside table drawer. She watched the entire process as he sheathed himself with shaking hands. No false modesty for this woman. When he was finished, he reached for her. The brief moment of not touching her had been enough for him to remember how fragile and uncertain their union was. He might never have another night with her. As he eased her to her back, he could read in her eyes what she wanted, expected, what he'd wanted a moment ago. Now he wanted more. He decided to take the full measure of Dani Goodwin.

He brushed a strand of hair from her cheek. Then he leaned down to kiss her there. He kissed her nose, her chin, her throat.

Kneeling between her thighs, he ran his tongue down the valley between her breasts. He sucked on each nipple until she writhed beneath him. Then he slid down and claimed the most intimate caress of all. She cried out in surrender. He brought her close, very close.

Before she came flying apart beneath him, he kissed his way back up her passion-slicked body and buried his throbbing member deep within her. She quivered, and he gazed into her eyes.

"You won't forget me," he whispered, and drove home again as she shuddered. Once more and she was gone, clutching his shoulders and moaning his name. He drank in the sound as he careened over the edge, his control finally shattering like fine crystal against a marble floor. Faintly, through the rushing in his ears, he heard the peacock cry.

A RINGING TELEPHONE woke Dani and she tried to move out of bed. Something was holding her down. She struggled against the weight before she realized it was Jake's arm and one thigh imprisoning her.

She jostled him. "Jake, your phone's ringing."

He snapped awake with a quickness that surprised her. "Thanks." He jumped from the bed and padded into the kitchen.

Dani sat up and stared around at the mayhem of tossed clothes and scrambled bedcovers. So the inevitable had finally happened between them. A slow smile spread across her face as she remembered how completely Jake had loved her once he'd gotten around to it.

She glanced at the lighted digital clock on the bedside table. Eleven-thirty. Who would be calling Jake at this hour? Late-night phone calls always meant trouble. She hoped it wasn't bad news about a member of his family.

She heard his voice in the kitchen, but she couldn't make out much except when he said "I can't talk now." Shortly afterward he hung up the phone.

He walked back into the bedroom and stood looking at her while he ran his fingers distractedly through his hair.

"Is anything wrong?"

He seemed to snap out of his daze and walked over to the bed. "No, nothing's wrong."

Emboldened by what had just passed between them, she chanced another question. "Who called?"

He climbed into bed and pulled her close. "A person I know in L.A."

"At eleven-thirty?"

"Yeah, well, she knows I usually get off later and she thought I'd still be up."

Dani grew very still as a sick feeling crept over her. "Is she a girlfriend or something? Is that why you've been keeping away from me?"

"No, she's not a girlfriend. She's almost twice as old as I am, for heaven's sake."

Dani didn't understand. Why would a woman that age be calling Jake so late at night? Women did that when they had some sort of intimate relationship with a man. Either they were related, or... "Jake, I know you've been low on money, and there are a lot of older women with money in L.A., who would pay you to—"

"Dammit, I'm not a gigolo!" He flopped onto his back.

"Then why all the mystery about who that was?"

He sighed. "I thought we might be able to enjoy what we have together without a lot of explanations. I can see that's not possible."

"I thought maybe we could, too! I wasn't planning to ask you about your secrets, but when some woman calls you at eleven-thirty at night, and we've just made love, it's hard not to ask about that! Especially when you gave me the impression that making love was special, and not just two bodies coming together in the night.''

''It was special.''

''But not special enough to trust me with the details of your life, obviously.''

''Dani, there are things— Oh, hell.'' He turned back and took her by the shoulders. ''I am not involved with another woman. Not a young woman or an older woman. Can you just leave it at that?''

She fought back tears. ''I want to, because tonight was the best ... the best ...'' She sobbed and couldn't go on.

''Oh, Dani.'' He tried to gather her close but she pushed him away. ''It was the best for me, too, Dani. Whatever happens, I want you to know that.''

She spoke through her tears. ''Whatever happens? What *is* going to happen? Why can't you trust me enough to tell me?''

''I'd trust you with my life, but I can't tell you.''

She got out of bed and fumbled with her clothes. ''I think I'd better go home.''

''Dani ...''

''Hey, it was lots of fun, but how does the song go? 'It was just one of those things,' right?'' She sniffed and pulled her blouse over her head.

''Wrong.'' He swung his legs to the floor and reached for his jeans. ''But I can't make you believe that, and I can't force you to stay with me.''

''That's for sure. I'm my own woman.''

He glanced up. ''That's what I love about you.''

She froze. Then she shook her head violently, as if to toss the words right out of her ears. ''Don't say things like that! Things you don't mean.''

"But I do mean them."

"I don't believe you, Jake." She sniffed again and wiped her eyes. "I believe you wanted sex tonight. I can even believe it was the best sex you ever had. But don't go bringing other things into it. Things you can't back up with your behavior." She shoved on her shoes and started for the bedroom door.

"Wait. I'm walking you across the clearing."

"Never mind." She hurried across the living room and flipped the lock open on the front door.

"Dani!"

"I can take care of myself!" She slammed the door behind her and ran across the moonlit yard. Then she remembered her purse was still in his truck. Both doors to the truck were still standing open as they'd left them when they'd walked into his house hand in hand. She sobbed as she dashed around to the passenger door and fumbled on the floor of the cab for her purse. Damn him. Damn him for making love to her like that.

She couldn't find the purse. She groped beneath the seat and still couldn't find it. Then she touched something hard, something that felt like a...a gun. She jerked her hand back as she realized it was exactly that.

"Dani."

She shrieked and scrambled out of the truck. He was standing there in his jeans and shoes, no shirt, and he looked decidedly menacing. "Stay away from me," she managed to say, although her teeth were chattering.

"Look, I don't care what you think of me. Okay, I do care, but something else is more important. Someone may be trying to harm you. Your tires were slashed tonight, which means they may be getting close. Please don't let your anger at me cause you to do something foolish."

Her mind whirled. Who was this man? Not long ago he'd been the person who had taken her to a land of unlimited pleasure. She'd felt closer to him than to any other human being in her life. Now she scarcely knew him.

"I ... need my purse."

He stepped toward the cab. "I'll get it for you."

In a moment, he had it in his hand. He stepped toward her and she involuntarily stepped back. He frowned. "I understand that you're angry, but you don't have to be afraid of me, Dani."

She swallowed. "Maybe I do. Why do you have a gun under the seat?"

His gaze sharpened and he glanced back at the truck.

"It's still there," she said. "I didn't take your precious gun. I hate guns."

"I'm not nuts about them myself."

"Then why do you have one?"

He regarded her steadily without speaking.

"You're not answering that question, either, are you?"

"No."

She stepped forward and snatched the purse from him. "Good night, Jake."

"What do you plan to do about your four flat tires?"

"I'll call a garage in the morning."

"They might not be able to have everything fixed by the time you need to pick up Paula."

"Then Paula will ride her bike, and I will walk." She spun around and walked past the tree full of white blossoms to her front porch. White flowers in the moonlight. She glanced at them again. The magic was gone, and now they seemed cold, lifeless, already wilting as the moon sank lower in the sky.

JAKE PROWLED the inside of his house like a caged animal. With every pass by his living-room window, he looked across the clearing to see if her light was still on. Finally, it went out. She'd gone to bed...her own bed.

Dammit! He smashed his fist against the kitchen cabinet. It might have worked. It really might have worked if Helen hadn't called. But she'd had good reason to call. Another note had arrived, with a difference—it was postmarked Tubac.

At least Helen said it was, and from the panic in her voice he was inclined to believe her. And if he believed her, he had to believe some slimeball was here, maybe somewhere very close, lying in wait for Dani. The tire-slashing was probably the first in a series of terrorizing moves.

Helen had asked where Dani was. She'd tried to call and alert Dani but had reached her answering machine. Jake had mentioned a flat tire on the Mustang and that he'd given her a ride home. He counted on Dani giving roughly the same story to her mother when she returned the call. Dani wouldn't be any more anxious to reveal what had happened tonight than he was. She'd probably called her mother by now, and knew about the Tubac postmark. He wondered if she was scared.

He longed to wrap his arms tightly around her, keep her safe. The scent of her still clung to his skin. If he slept at all tonight, it wouldn't be in that bed. On the living-room couch, more likely, with his window open a crack so he could hear anything happening in the other house. Once he'd thought living as a neighbor was close enough. Now the distance across the clearing seemed like the Grand Canyon. He wanted to be able to see her, touch her, know she was okay. And that privilege had slipped through his fingers in a matter of minutes.

He should go over there and make up some story to satisfy her. If he slept in her bed, or she in his, he would be right there, ready for the next move. But he wasn't good with lies, never had been. He'd been feeding her half-truths instead, and when she'd come out with the important questions he hadn't had any answers.

He was sickened by the image she obviously had of him, that he was some gun-toting gigolo with a shady past. Tonight could have been so beautiful without that call. She was ready to ignore his secretive behavior until she'd had it pushed in her face.

And then she'd had to find the gun. He'd started carrying it under the seat during the day and transferring it to the house when he came home. Except for tonight, when he'd been caught in a spell woven of moonlight and flowers. Now the gun rested on a lamp table next to the door, because he feared he would need it before this was over. All along he'd prayed the whole scheme was a hoax, but it didn't look as if it was.

CHAPTER FIFTEEN

DANI COULDN'T GET her tires fixed because they'd been punctured in the sidewall, not the tread. Putting on new tires and doing an alignment couldn't be accomplished before noon, the garage owner said, so Dani had to call Paula.

"I guess you'd better ride your bike to Evelyn's this morning. If you leave now, you should be there by nine."

"What about you?" Paula sounded dubious.

"I'll walk. I may get there a few mintes after you, but you'll be fine."

"I guess. Can't Jake bring you?"

"No."

"But—"

"It's over between Jake and me, Paula. Really over."

There was a long silence. Then Paula sighed. "Okay."

Dani realized the news disappointed Paula. *Try being in my shoes,* she thought. Still, she wanted to inject some cheer into her voice for Paula's sake. "Don't worry about it. Life goes on. And we have a morning of work ahead, so I'll see you in a little bit, okay?"

"Okay." Paula sounded more discouraged than Dani had ever heard her. Great. Now another person was miserable. All because Jake was acting like such a jerk. Dani wanted to strangle him.

Her feet seemed to weigh more than usual as she started the walk into town. The March sky was strafed with thin white clouds, and a warm breeze brought the scent of new growth that smelled so sweet it nearly made her cry. Although she tried to repress her memories of the night before, they played like a bad movie over and over in her head. She couldn't remember a more emotionally draining night in her life. She'd plummeted from ecstasy to agony in mere minutes.

To top off the horrible ending to her evening with Jake, she'd found a frantic message from her mother on the answering machine. The message demanded Dani call her no matter what time she got in. Dani had called and discovered that a note had been mailed from Tubac.

Would her mother go this far to scare her home? And there was the business about the tires. That hadn't been an accident. The guy at the garage thought maybe something with serrated edges, like a steak knife, had been used. He figured the culprits were vandals who were jealous of her nice car. Dani hoped he was right, but it seemed that vandals would have defaced her paint job and ripped her convertible top. Nothing had been touched except the tires.

She'd walked as far as the bridge over the river when she heard the sound of Jake's truck coming up behind her. Nights of listening for him to come home had made her attuned to the growl of the truck's engine. She took a deep breath and hoped he'd drive right on by.

He didn't. "I guess they couldn't get you new wheels this fast," he called from the window as he cruised beside her.

"No." She kept walking and focused straight ahead. *Go away.*

"What do they think caused the flats?"

"Kids."

"Mm. Well, hop in. I'll give you a ride into town."

"No, thanks."

"Look, walking down a country road alone, even in daylight, isn't a great idea if someone's out to get you."

She fought back the urge to scream at him. "I'll be fine."

"Come on, Dani. Don't be stubborn."

Her control snapped and she whirled to face him. "Stubborn? You're calling *me* stubborn? The man who refuses to answer simple questions?"

He stopped the truck and started to get out. "Bad choice of words. I—"

She held up a hand to ward him off. "Stay in there."

"Can't." He hopped down and came toward her. "Don't be foolish, Dani. Get in the truck."

Dammit, she still wanted him. Looking up into his eyes sent her stomach churning and made her knees weak. Now that she knew what his naked body felt like moving against hers . . . She clenched her hands at her sides. "I was foolish last night. I don't intend to compound that foolishness by having anything more to do with you."

"You need to be with someone, and I'm here."

"Just my luck."

"Be logical. Alone you're more of a target. Let me chauffeur you until you get your car back."

"Leave me alone, Jake." She tried to keep her voice steady. "I'm already running late, and you're making things worse." *Much worse.* She started down the road.

"Dani, wait." He came after her and grabbed her arm.

His touch electrified her and she shook him free in a frantic gesture to rid herself of temptation. How could she want someone who couldn't be honest with her? "Don't touch me."

"Dammit, you could get yourself into big trouble!"

"I'm already in big trouble, and you helped put me there. Now go away!" She turned and walked rapidly over the bridge. Soon the truck's engine started again. He was following her.

After a couple of minutes, she realized he planned to drive behind her all the way to Evelyn's shop. The back of her neck prickled with awareness of his gaze and she increased her stride. The truck hung right behind her, going exactly her speed.

Damn him! Dani held up a fist in a gesture of defiance. He tooted his horn in acknowledgment, but he kept following her. A car passed going in the opposite direction and the occupants stared at Dani marching along with a truck rolling behind her. What was he trying to prove, that he was Sir Galahad? Well, his armor was a little tarnished as far as she was concerned. If he thought she'd be the least bit grateful for this dumb stunt, he was mistaken.

Finally, they reached Tubac Road, and Evelyn's shop was in sight. Jake increased his speed and pulled alongside her. "I'm going down to the coffee shop to get a bite and read the paper. I'll be there until you're ready to go home. The offer of a ride still stands."

"Don't bother."

He grinned. "You have a nice day, too." Then he drove away slowly, as any gentleman would who didn't want to leave a lady standing in a cloud of dust.

But Jake was no gentleman. From the evidence, he was probably a rascal. Dani stared after him and tried to calm her galloping pulse. He parked the truck in front of the coffee shop and walked in whistling, as if he didn't have a care in the world.

It wasn't fair. Jake was the first man who really turned her inside out, but he was missing a very important trait. He refused to be honest with her. And that ruined all the rest of what he was, which was pretty powerful stuff. It just wasn't fair.

Blinking back tears, she started toward The Silver Coyote. Evelyn's CJ-7 was parked outside, but Paula's bike wasn't. Dani hoped Paula hadn't chickened out just because Dani was going to be late. Paula had to outgrow her dependence on Dani and Jake, or she'd never make it on her own with a pinstriping business.

Maybe Paula's mother brought her by, Dani thought as she pushed open the door and the bell jingled. But Paula wasn't inside painting.

Evelyn came from the back room carrying a disposable cup full of coffee. "There you are. Paula said something about car trouble."

"Where is she?"

"Paula?" Evelyn gave Dani a sad smile. "I'm afraid your little Paula has quit."

"Quit?" Dani felt slightly sick to her stomach. "What do you mean?"

"I mean she packed up her paints and rode her bike back home. I got the impression she wasn't coming back."

Dani laughed with relief. "Oh, I'll bet she'll be back tomorrow. She probably got worried about me, or something. She gets ideas in her head, and she's a stubborn little cuss. Maybe she even rode over to my house to find out where I was." Except Dani knew that hadn't happened. She would have met Paula on the road.

"I don't think she'll be back tomorrow. I think she's gone for good."

Dani's relief gave way to growing panic. "I don't understand. Did something happen?"

"I can't imagine what. She came and started working. I went over to the coffee shop to get a cup of coffee to go, like I usually do, and when I came back, she was all in a dither. She said she was 'all done' and then she left." Evelyn gestured toward a display case that was pinstriped halfway around the glass. "As you can see, she's not 'all done.'"

Dani stared at the unfinished lines of black and turquoise. She couldn't believe Paula would quit in the middle of a job. A little voice in the back of her mind whispered that Paula's parents had warned of this, but Dani hushed the incriminating voice. Something was wrong, or Paula wouldn't have left in such an abrupt way. Dani glanced at Evelyn. "You and she didn't have any...words?"

"You mean a fight?" Evelyn laughed. "Goodness, I wouldn't pick a fight with a retarded girl. If I'm going to fight, I'll pick on somebody who's a challenge, like your fellow Jake."

"He's not mine," Dani said with feeling.

"Really?" Evelyn's eyebrows arched. "Well, that's good news. I've been puzzling over Jake a lot, especially after you told me about this thing with notes to your mother."

Dani didn't think she wanted to hear this, but morbid curiosity made her ask anyway. "What's that got to do with Jake?"

"Consider the facts. He's from L.A. and he arrived here soon after you did. He got a job where you work. He moved in next door. Is this all a coincidence?"

A chill went down Dani's spine. All those things had been floating around in her head for days, but she hadn't wanted to put them together. And Evelyn didn't even know about the gun. Dani decided not to tell her, at least not yet. Jake couldn't be the person after her, could he? If he'd wanted to hurt her, or even take her hostage, he'd had dozens of chances already. Last night would have been perfect.

Of course, maybe he'd meant to. Maybe he'd slashed her tires and planned to take her home, seduce her, then carry her off somewhere to... no. It didn't make sense. He would have done that by now if he'd intended to. Their fight wouldn't have stopped him. He could have grabbed her when she was fishing in the truck for her purse. He could have forced her into the truck this morning.

But still, he *was* conveniently around all the time. Now that she considered that, it seemed like more than coincidence, as Evelyn said.

"I can tell you're thinking about the possibility," Evelyn said. "I have no proof, of course. Jake may be perfectly harmless."

No, he's definitely not harmless.

"But I'd be very careful of him if I were you. At least until you know a little more about him."

Dani managed a smile. "Thanks for your concern, Evelyn. And I'm sorry that Paula stopped working today. I'm sure there's some minor misunderstanding. If you're willing to give her another chance, I'll talk with her and see what's going on."

Evelyn shrugged and sipped her coffee. "You can try, but she is a bit unstable. I know you have great hopes for her future, but a reputation for running out on a job won't help her chances any."

"I know that. Let me talk with her. I'll give you a call today and let you know what I worked out." She turned to leave.

"I thought you were planning to finish one of the peacock earrings today?"

Dani paused. "Well, I was, but sorting things out with Paula is important. We need to have that display case finished, too, and—"

"I'll have someone paint over it."

Dani hated to think of Paula's painstaking efforts being covered up with a coat of white paint. "You could, but I'd rather get Paula in here to complete the job. That would be better for us and for her."

"But you'll finish the earrings soon, I hope? I'd like to open the shop."

"I thought you were planning on next week?"

"Except for Paula's work, everything's going faster than I expected. And every day we delay means money going out and none coming in, Dani."

"You're right." Dani's chest grew tight. Paula's behavior was affecting the opening of the shop, and Evelyn was rightfully upset about it. Paula was Dani's responsibility, and she needed to straighten things out and get Paula back on the job. "Look, I'll get right over to Paula's house, and maybe I can have us both back here for an hour or so before we have to leave for the restaurant. How's that?"

"Sounds ambitious. I thought you didn't have a car."

Dani closed her eyes in frustration. No, she didn't have a car, and walking wouldn't cut it in this case.

"I'd loan you the Jeep, but I have several errands to run and I'm late already. I'm afraid your Paula has put us behind the eight ball."

"I'm sorry about that. I'll get her back. Jake can drive me."

"Jake? Is that wise? Maybe I should reschedule—"

"That's not necessary. In spite of all you've pointed out, and I admit it looks suspicious, I don't think Jake's a danger to me." *Just to my heart.*

"I hope you know what you're doing."

Dani gave her a wave as she headed out the door. "I'll be back soon." She closed the door behind her and glanced down the street. Jake's truck was still parked in front of the coffee shop as he'd promised.

She hated doing this. But pride was less important than salvaging Paula's reputation and restoring order to The Silver Coyote. Still, she wished she hadn't been quite so rude to Jake.

If he denied her request, she would have nowhere else to turn. Even if Evelyn's Jeep had been available, Dani wouldn't have wanted to impose on her. And taking Jake to Paula's might help. Paula wasn't likely to refuse Jake if he asked her to honor her commitment.

When Dani walked into the coffee shop, she noticed Jake over by the window at the same table she'd chosen when she and Paula had come in to celebrate the new pinstriping job at The Silver Coyote. So he liked the same table she did. So what? It meant nothing. He was reading a Tucson newspaper and didn't notice her come in.

She walked over to the table, and when she was within about six feet of him, he glanced up. Surprise flickered in his expression.

"Paula's quit her job at The Silver Coyote."

He folded the paper and stood up. "When?"

"Just before I got there. She rode home. I thought we could—"

"Let's go." He tossed a couple of bills on the table along with the folded newspaper. "Do you know what happened?"

"Evelyn said nothing happened." She went out the door he held for her.

"Fat chance of that being true. I'll bet Evelyn said something nasty and hurt Paula's feelings."

"She says she didn't." Dani had privately been afraid of the same thing, but she didn't want to doubt Evelyn's word, either.

"We'll find out from Paula." He opened the truck door for her and she climbed in. He wasted no time getting in himself, and this time he pulled away in a cloud of dust.

"She left a display case half-done, Jake. That doesn't sound like something Paula would do. She's so conscientious."

"She wouldn't do it without good reason, at least. She was proud of that job."

"She should have been. It could have— I mean it *will* lead to more. I'm determined to get her to go back."

Jake glanced at her. "Be careful. If Evelyn said something bad enough to send Paula running home, she's also capable of destroying Paula's confidence in herself."

"We don't know that's what happened."

"Maybe you don't, but I have a pretty good idea. The acid in that woman's tongue would eat the remaining paint off this truck."

"Jake, stop it. You're letting your personality conflict with Evelyn poison your judgment. I was hoping you'd help me convince Paula to finish that job. If you're going to do the opposite, and prejudice her against Evelyn, then . . . then . . ."

He chuckled. "Then what? Want to walk to Paula's and then back into town?"

She clenched her jaw and stared out the window. "I hate it when you have the upper hand like this."

"You didn't hate it last night," he said softly.

She stiffened. "Don't."

"I want you back in my bed, Dani."

"Tough." She clasped her hands together so they wouldn't shake. This is why she couldn't be near him, because she was weak. So weak.

"There will be a time when I can explain everything to you. Can't you trust me until then?"

"Why should I? You don't trust me."

"If it were my decision, I'd give you all the facts in a minute, but it's not. Don't ask me to betray a trust."

She looked over at him. "What are you, some secret agent for the government, or something?"

"No."

"Well, of course if you were, you wouldn't tell me, anyway, so I don't know why I'm wasting my breath asking. But I can't imagine what some government spy is doing in Tubac, unless you're investigating drugs coming over the border, and if you're doing that, I have no idea when you do it."

"There, you see? I have no time to be a government spy. I'm always with you. Trust me, Dani. Please."

"Evelyn thinks it's very strange that you arrived in Tubac from L.A. shortly after I did, and that you found a job where I work, and then moved in next door. What do you say to that?"

"Oh, God."

His heartfelt groan claimed her attention. She watched his jaw tighten as he reacted to the insinuation.

"So she's implying *I'm* writing those notes? What a twisted woman." He pulled into the Jordans' driveway and turned off the engine before he directed his gaze toward her. "And you invited me to move in next door. Let's not forget that."

"I'm not forgetting. It was probably the dumbest move of my life."

"Or the smartest. Dani, we have something precious between us. The rest of the stuff, what you're worried about, isn't important." He glanced away, and when he met her gaze again, his eyes glowed with passion. He spoke in a voice thick with emotion. "Please let me love you."

CHAPTER SIXTEEN

DANI'S HEARTBEAT thundered in her ears. It would be so easy to forget her doubts and surrender to the invitation in those brown eyes. So easy. And so dangerous. She groped for the door handle. Where was it? She had to get out of the truck before she was lost. Finally, her fingers closed around the cold chrome and she opened the door. "We need to get Paula."

His expression closed down. "All right."

They stood together at the massive front door without speaking as the chime echoed through the house.

Madge answered the bell. "I was expecting at least one of you to show up," she said without offering any greeting.

"It's nice to see you again, too, Mrs. Jordan," Jake said.

This was the reason she'd wanted him there, Dani thought. Just for remarks like that, zingers that Jake could deliver so well.

Madge flushed and glanced down the hall. "Paula's in her room. Please don't upset her any more than she already is."

Dani led the way down the hall and tapped on Paula's closed door.

Muffled sobs lessened, then finally stopped. Footsteps shuffled to the door and Paula opened the door a crack. Her eyes were red, her face puffy. Her voice came out in a hoarse croak. "Sorry, Dani."

Dani wanted to cry, too. "Oh, Paula."

"Sorry." The door stayed almost closed.

Dani was suddenly afraid Paula wouldn't let her in. "Jake's here."

The door opened a little wider. "Jake?"

"Hey, Paula," Jake said gently.

Paula's eyes filled with tears. "Hey, Jake."

"Can we come in?"

Paula hesitated, but at last she nodded and opened the door wider. Dani sighed with relief as they stepped inside. Maybe they could smooth this over, after all.

Jake tucked his thumbs through his belt loops and surveyed the room. "Awesome work."

Paula shrugged. "It's okay." She blew her nose and threw the mangled tissue toward an overflowing pin-striped wastebasket. Then she pulled a clean one out of the box on her dresser and blew her nose again.

Dani walked over, put her hands on Paula's shoulders and looked into her friend's red-rimmed eyes. "What happened?"

Paula shrugged again and looked away.

"Did Evelyn say something to upset you?"

Paula squeezed her eyes shut. "No."

"Then why did you leave?"

"Because." Paula wriggled her shoulders and stepped out of reach. "Don't talk about it, Dani."

Dani glanced at Jake in silent appeal. Maybe he could get somewhere.

"We have to talk about it," Jake said. "Dani arranged that job for you, and you left before it was done. That's not good for you or Dani."

Paula's lower lip trembled.

"Come on," Jake coaxed. "Something must have happened. You're the kind of person who lives up to her obligations. You're not a quitter."

"I can't do it!" Paula wailed, and threw herself facedown on the bed. "I can't!" Her body heaved with each noisy sob.

"Oh, Paula." Dani sat on the bed and rubbed her hand across the young woman's quivering shoulders. "You *can* do it. The Indian patterns you've done so far are magnificent. When it's finished, it will be—"

"No. Never finished."

Jake sat beside Dani. His voice was calm. "Of course it will be finished, Paula. You couldn't leave something half-done. Maybe you needed a day off. We all do sometimes. But I'll bet by tomorrow—"

"No!"

The bedroom door banged open and Ed Jordan stormed into the room. "That's enough. You're upsetting my girl."

Jake stood up and faced him. "Look, Jordan, I think maybe—"

"Don't you two get it?" Regret laced his words, making them almost a plea. "Busing tables is all Paula is ever going to do."

Dani gasped. Under her friend's comforting hand, Paula stiffened and buried her head deeper under the pillow.

Dani rose to stand beside Jake, whose expression was like granite. "Paula is bursting with talent," she said, glaring at Ed. "She proved she could do outside jobs with Jake's truck and my car. Something unusual happened at The Silver Coyote, and we're trying to find out what it was."

"Unusual for you. You haven't lived with Paula all her life. Look at her. She can't take all this stress. You're expecting too much of her."

"And you're expecting too little!" Dani said vehemently.

Ed looked old and beaten. "That's not for you to judge. Why don't both of you head on home? I don't appreciate being called off the golf course for this kind of thing. I moved here to relax, not hassle with people telling me how to handle my daughter."

"But—"

"Dani." Jake took her arm. "This is Jordan's territory and like it or not, we have to play by his rules."

"Good thinking, Clayborn."

Dani glanced back at the figure huddled on the bed. "Hang in there, Paula. I'll see you at work."

Ed shook his finger at Dani. "Don't think you can brainwash her at work, either. Madge's luncheon group will be there today. She'll have instructions from me to keep a close eye on both of you."

Jake's grip tightened on Dani's arm, but his tone remained casual. "Well, Jordan, that's where you go a little far. The restaurant is not your territory."

"It's my daughter!"

"It's also a free country," Jake said. "You can be a dictator here at home, but that's about the extent of your power. Come on, Dani." He guided her through the door and down the hall. Madge was nowhere around. Apparently, she'd called her husband and then hidden in the depths of the house somewhere until the furor died down.

Dani blinked in the sunlight. The hazy clouds had drifted away and the sky was blue and clear once again. She wanted to pick up a rock and throw it at something breakable, like one of the Jordans' plate-glass windows. Jake opened the truck door and she climbed in. Then he walked around the truck and swung up to his seat.

"Do you think Paula really is too unstable to be self-employed?" Dani asked.

"No." Jake started the truck. "But if she lives with Ed and Madge Jordan much longer, she will be."

Dani clenched her hands around her purse. "I wish I knew what happened."

"Ask Evelyn."

Dani glanced at him. "You think she said something mean to Paula, don't you?"

"Don't you?"

Dani didn't answer. Evelyn had said nothing happened, that Paula simply decided not to finish. If Evelyn had lied about that, then Dani faced a whole new set of problems.

THERE WAS barely enough time for Dani and Jake to go home and change for work, then for Jake to drop Dani at the garage. She drove her own car to the country club. Paula avoided both of them all day, and Dani didn't have the heart to question her further during working hours and jeopardize the young woman's one remaining link to the outside world.

That night, Dani walked out to the parking lot half expecting to find her tires flat again, but they weren't. She walked all around the car, checking for any damage.

"Looks like everything's fine tonight," Jake said.

She jumped. She hadn't heard him come out the back door of the restaurant. "What are you doing here? Don't you have another two hours before you go home?"

"My shift's changed. Now I get off when you do."

How convenient, she thought, and remembered Evelyn's warning about Jake. "Okay, Jake. Just why did you move here?" she asked.

"Me? Where did that question come from?"

"I just wondered if you could give me a straight answer."

"Oh, I see. You want to know if I came to Tubac because I'm stalking you and I have plans to do away with you in some gruesome way. Is that it?"

Her jaw tightened. "Exactly."

"Well, it's all true." His voice dripped with bitterness. "I'm just waiting for the right moment to chop you into little pieces. Are you satisfied?"

Dani jerked open her car door and got behind the wheel. "Perfectly satisfied. Catch me if you can." She started the car and peeled out of the parking lot. Jake followed her, but kept a reasonable distance between them. When they arrived at her house, he cruised on past and parked in his own spot. He went inside his house without a word.

Dani gazed at the mesquite tree with its few straggling blossoms still clinging to the vining cactus plant. The peacocks were perched in the branches fast asleep.

Inside, she put on hot water for tea, then barely touched it once it was brewed. She tried to get interested in a book, but the writing seemed insipid so she threw it down. Finally, she went to bed, only to stare into the darkness and wish for the night to be over. She couldn't remember ever feeling so alone in her life.

Maybe this was the kind of deep loneliness her mother experienced every day, as if no one cared, no one was truly on her side. Dani admitted to herself that she hadn't really understood what that loneliness was like for her mother until now.

THE FOLLOWING MORNING at The Silver Coyote, Dani sat across the desk from Evelyn and questioned her as thoroughly as she dared about the incident with Paula. Evelyn maintained that Paula had started acting strangely and that she'd seemed to miss Dani not being there. Then she'd run off, as if she couldn't bear to work on the pinstriping another moment.

Evelyn drained her disposable cup of coffee and set it on the desk. "Last night I unearthed some psychology books I'd packed away. I brushed up on Paula's type of mental retardation. It's a frustrating condition because low I.Q. like this often has no identifiable cause. You don't get the kind of social understanding of say, Down's syndrome, which makes the adjustment rough for everyone concerned—parents, friends, employers."

Dani was touched that Evelyn had taken time to research the subject. "I'd just like to see her develop her potential."

"Maybe she already has." Evelyn stood and tossed the cup in the trash. "Maybe busing tables at Canada Verde and pinstriping a car for friends now and then are all she's capable of achieving."

"I have trouble accepting that."

Evelyn came around the desk and put a hand on Dani's shoulder. "It's admirable that you want to help her, but don't let Paula's troubles drag you down. You have a brilliant career ahead of you. Let's concentrate on that." She glanced at her watch. "The painter's due any minute to put another coat of white enamel on the display case, and you haven't finished those peacock earrings yet. I figure if we both work our heads off all day tomorrow, we can open Tuesday for business."

"All right." A new coat of paint on the display case, Dani thought. Once Paula's work was covered up, she'd never come back.

"You sound decidedly underwhelmed at the prospect," Evelyn said. "Don't tell me you have another engagement tomorrow and you can't work here all day. I planned on your coming, because I remembered you had Monday off."

"I can work here Monday." Dani's thoughts turned back to a week ago, and the company picnic with Jake and Paula. Paula had been so happy then.

"I thought you'd be pleased we're opening the shop. You can't sell your jewelry until we do."

"I am pleased. I just..."

"Forget Paula! She couldn't cut it. You've lived in L.A. You know it's not just talent that counts, but whether or not you can stand up under pressure." Evelyn leaned down and took Dani's face in her hands. Her many-ringed fingers felt cold against Dani's cheeks. "If we play our cards right, you and I could be world-famous, Dani. We're going to put Tubac on the map."

Dani had never noticed Evelyn's eyes before, maybe because Evelyn wasn't in the habit of looking directly into her face like this. Evelyn's eyes reminded Dani of topaz; they were quite unusual, really—gold with flecks that looked almost silver in the light.

A part of Dani responded to Evelyn's ambition. Evelyn had the money and the dream; Dani had the talent and the product. She'd be lying to herself if she pretended not to like the idea of people coming from around the country, around the world, to buy an original piece from Dani Goodwin. Evelyn was the sort of person who could help make that happen, because Evelyn was impatient for results.

Dani tended to become engrossed in her work and forget the marketing side of the business. Her mother was like that, too, which was why she had an agent. And Paula was like that. Paula existed only to weave magic with her delicate lines of paint. The word *career* would frighten her to death. Maybe Dani *had* frightened her, pushed her too hard.

Evelyn patted Dani's cheeks. "You think too much. Let's get to work. Those peacock earrings will be our featured piece on Tuesday."

DANI FINISHED the earrings before she left the shop that morning. They were the finest she'd ever made, and Evelyn's elaborate praise had helped ease Dani's heartache over Paula. Both display cases had been painted stark white, though a few of the shelves Paula had completed still gave evidence to her presence. She concluded that she'd tried to give Paula too many responsibilities too fast.

When she arrived at the restaurant for the noon shift, Dani met Paula coming out of the small office occupied by John Slattery, the restaurant manager.

Dani decided now was as good a time as any to start rebuilding the relationship that had been so damaged.

"Hi, Paula!" She tried to sound cheerful.

Paula wouldn't meet her gaze. "Hi, Dani."

"Ready for another exciting day at Canada Verde?"

"I'm going home."

Dani's stomach lurched. "Aren't you feeling well?"

"I'm okay."

"Then why— Listen, if you forgot something, I'll drive you home, to save time."

"Job's over."

"Over?" Dani's stomach churned in earnest. "What do you mean?"

Paula glanced up at last, her eyes glazed, her expression bleak. "Bye, Dani." Then she started down the hall toward the kitchen.

"Paula, wait! What's going on here?" She grabbed Paula by the arm.

"Dani . . ." Now Paula's look was pleading. "Have to go. Please." Tears welled up in her blue eyes. "Please."

"Okay." Dani patted her shoulder. "Okay. We'll talk later." She knew how much Paula would hate breaking down in front of the rest of the staff. "Come by the house tomorrow morning, okay?"

When Paula didn't answer, Dani knew she wouldn't come to see her. After Paula went into the kitchen, Dani turned and rapped on John Slattery's door.

"Come in," John called in a booming voice. Dani knew by now that just as Paula had said, the hearty tone was a coverup for John's insecurities. He looked wary when she opened the door. "Hi, Dani," he said a little less forcefully. "Have a seat."

Dani remained standing. She wanted fast answers, not a leisurely little chat. "What's the deal with Paula?"

John's gaze shifted. "Well, you know how it is with someone like Paula."

"No, I don't."

John took a paper clip from a sheaf of papers and began unbending it. "She has to really concentrate to do a good job around here, and frankly, that concentration has been missing the past few days."

"She's having an off time. We're all prone to that."

"You're right, but yesterday a customer phoned in and complained that she'd been rude to them."

"Paula? I can't believe it."

"Well, the person described Paula perfectly, so it had to be her." John had the paper clip straightened out, and he was drawing invisible lines on his blotter with the tip of it.

"Who was this customer?"

"That's confidential information, Dani."

"So you fired her? Is that it? On the basis of a couple of bad days and one lousy complaint, which might have been—"

"No, I didn't fire her. She quit."

Dani groaned. "Probably because you told her that her work was inferior."

"I tried to be gentle. Believe me, I tried. I just mentioned that she'd have to concentrate harder on the job, and make sure she didn't say anything unpleasant to any of the customers."

"She admitted she'd been unpleasant?"

"No. She just sort of . . . stood there. Then she quit. Her parents warned me about this sort of thing when she applied for the job, but Paula was so eager that I took a chance, and for a year she's been just fine.''

"I see." Dani felt as if John had stuck the paper clip he was holding right through her heart. Paula had been fine until Dani showed up and started pushing her to be more, to do more. Now Paula had nothing. "Listen, John, this could be all my fault."

"Yours?"

Dani explained about Paula's pinstriping, and the job at a new jewelry shop in town. "So I've upset her, and now I have to come up with some way to make things right again for Paula."

"I wish you luck."

"If I can get her to reapply for the job here, would you consider taking her back?"

John seemed glad to finally have some good news to deliver. "Sure," he said, and smiled. "Glad to give her a second chance. Glad to."

"Good. Now I'd better get to work before I lose *my* job."

JAKE FIGURED the only time he could catch Evelyn without Dani around was during his lunch break at Canada Verde. He didn't feel like eating, anyway. He didn't have much time, but he had to try to get to the bottom of this.

Evelyn appeared from the back room when he walked through the jingle-bell door she'd constructed. "We're not open," she said.

"I know." He noticed her earrings, a delicate pair of silver-and-turquoise peacocks that didn't match the heavy gold necklace and bracelet she wore. "Did Dani make those?"

Evelyn's hand went to one earring. "Yes. I was just trying them on, to see how they look. I think we'll get quite a lot of money for these."

"No doubt. But I'm not here to discuss that. I'm hoping that maybe without Dani around, you'll be willing to talk about what happened with Paula. Maybe it was something you didn't want Dani to hear..."

"Like what?"

He shrugged. "I don't know. Maybe you and Paula had some argument concerning Dani. I know Paula can be a bit of a bulldog where Dani's concerned. Or maybe you thought Paula's work *was* substandard. We all have different tastes."

Evelyn's laugh had an unpleasant sound. "You are a pair, you and Dani. Did it ever occur to you that Paula simply has a little problem relating to the rest of the world?"

"No. That hasn't occurred to me. She's always been easy to work with."

"That's because you're blind to her problems."

Jake felt his temper slipping. "I think you're the one with the problem."

"And I think you'd better leave. You're standing here uninvited in a shop that's not open for business. I have a security system now, although I don't have it activated at the moment. But I'm sure I could turn it on and get some assistance."

"Evelyn, for heaven's sake, be a little compassionate, would you? Paula's so upset about what happened here that she bungled her job at the restaurant, too. When the manager tried to talk with her about it, she quit, or so he said. Do you see how your remarks, whatever they were, even if you didn't mean them to be critical, have affected Paula's whole life?''

"But Jake, I said nothing to her."

"Okay, you said nothing. But if you'd call her and tell her how much you need her back, then maybe we can salvage something of —''

"I don't need her back." Evelyn waved a hand around the shop. "We're finished with that part. Tomorrow, Dani and I will stock the shelves and make the final preparations for opening on Tuesday. It's too late for Paula to be of any help to me."

Jake closed his hands into fists. He'd always considered it beneath him to hit a woman, but he was sorely tempted at this moment.

"Thanks for stopping by, Jake. Now, if you'll excuse me, I have a lot of work to do if Dani and I are going to have a successful day on Tuesday. You wouldn't want to interfere with that, I'm sure."

"No, of course not." He turned and stalked out of the shop, all the while resisting the urge to rip the little jangling bells from the door before he left.

CHAPTER SEVENTEEN

DANI HAD MADE UP her mind to talk with Jake at lunchtime and ask him for suggestions on repairing Paula's life. Somehow they—and she included Jake in her plans—would have to work around Paula's parents. She could see no other way to proceed than by working with Jake, whatever her personal problems with him might be. Dani was ready to resurrect the Three Musketeers, if that would convince Paula to come back to the restaurant. Along with all her other regrets, Dani included her decision to end that little custom.

But Jake wasn't around during the lunch break. She even went outside looking for his truck, and found it wasn't parked in the usual place. She couldn't imagine where he'd gone, except perhaps to Paula's house to check on her. Dani decided to take what was left of her lunch hour to drive past Paula's house and look for his truck. It wasn't there, either.

Feeling completely abandoned, Dani returned to work. If the evening shift wasn't too busy, maybe she'd have a chance to talk with Jake then.

As it turned out, the evening shift was one of the most frantic they'd had since she'd begun working at the country club. Once, when she raced into the bar to fill a drink order, Jake was leaning toward Cindy, the cocktail waitress, and smiling.

The tableau changed the minute Dani arrived, but the sight of Jake smiling like that, looking into another woman's eyes, haunted Dani for the rest of the evening. She'd heard rumors that Cindy had recently broken up with her boyfriend, Steve. Dani hadn't thought much about it, until now.

Before Dani left for the night, she stopped by the bar again, in case Jake might be free. This time Cindy was leaning against the bar and Jake was laughing at something she'd said. Dani wasn't about to break up that sort of moment to ask Jake about Paula, so she walked out of the room and headed out through the kitchen to the parking lot. Still carrying the picture of Jake and Cindy in her mind, she drove away from the country club.

Surprisingly, the headlights of Jake's truck appeared in her rearview mirror on the way home. He must not have lingered with Cindy long. The thought gave Dani comfort. He acted as if he *had* to see her home safely each night. Apparently, he was taking the threatening notes seriously, although after the tire-slashing incident, no other sinister events had occurred.

Dani decided to catch Jake before he got into his house and ask how he thought they could persuade Paula to ask for her job back. Dani assumed Jake was worried about Paula's future, too. Except when he was engrossed with Cindy, of course. Dani discovered she was clenching her jaw and she deliberately relaxed it. It was a free country, as Jake had pointed out to Ed Jordan yesterday.

As Dani parked the Mustang, Jake swung over to his side of the clearing. In her haste to get out and catch his attention before he went inside, she snagged the hem of her skirt on the floor shift and took extra time to untangle it. By the time she extricated herself from the car, Jake had gone inside and closed the door.

Dani hesitated. Maybe the next morning would be better. Yet she knew tomorrow wasn't as good a time to hash out Paula's situation. Dani had promised Evelyn she'd be at the shop very early so they'd be sure to finish everything in time for Tuesday's opening day.

No, now was the best time. Just because she'd feel funny being in Jake's house after what had happened between them there on Thursday night was no reason not to go over. Paula's happiness could well depend on what actions she and Jake took now, and she couldn't be cowardly.

After taking a deep breath to calm herself, she started across the clearing. Just before she reached his door, the lights went out inside the house. He'd already gone to bed. She started to head back home, but an image of a thoroughly defeated Paula in the hall outside the manager's office stopped her.

She turned back and rapped on Jake's door.

After a few moments, the living-room light came on and the door opened. Jake stood there wearing jeans and no shirt or shoes. He gazed at Dani while she tried to remember what it was she wanted to talk to him about. All she could think of was the feel of his chest hair beneath her fingers.

"Would you like to come in?" he asked.

"I . . ." She struggled with her jumbled thoughts. "I thought we should talk about Paula."

"Okay." He stepped back from the door and she walked past him into the house. He gestured toward the sofa and she crossed the room and sat down. He shoved both hands into his pockets and looked at her. "Can I get you anything? Coffee? Wine?"

She shook her head. "Just a shirt."

"A—" He threw back his head and laughed.

His laughter tugged at her, making her smile.

His chuckles subsided and he came over to sit beside her on the couch. "The sight of my hairy chest bothers you?"

Heat stole up to her cheeks. "Well, it's just that, well, you know..."

"No, tell me."

She swallowed. "Could you just do it?"

"You sound like a commercial." Light danced in his dark eyes.

"You look like one."

"I'll take that as a compliment."

"Jake, would you please put on a shirt before we start talking?"

"Absolutely not."

She started to get up. "Then maybe I'd better—"

"Don't go." He grasped her wrist and drew her gently back to the sofa.

Her heart thumped and she grew dizzy gazing into his eyes. "You and Cindy seemed to be having a good time together tonight." She hadn't meant to say that. Some devil had hold of her tongue.

Jake didn't flinch. "She asked me out," he said, keeping his hold on Dani's wrist.

"That should be fun." She tried to twist away, but he held her fast.

"Not if I'm in love with someone else."

She stopped struggling and stared at him.

Slowly he nodded.

Her voice was reduced to a whisper. "I ... don't believe you."

"That's because you won't let yourself believe me. If you listened to your heart and not that hard head of yours, you'd know it's true."

She drank in the words as if dying of emotional thirst. She wanted them to be real, yet still she had questions, reservations. "But Jake, you—"

"I know. I haven't told you all about myself, haven't let you in on all the secrets. If I really loved you, I'd do that, wouldn't I?"

"Yes." The look in his eyes left her breathless. "Yes, you would."

"Not this time." He touched a finger to her lips, tracing the shape. "Life doesn't always work that way, Dani. And let me tell you, I didn't mean to fall in love with you. I fought against it."

Dani was transfixed by the whisper of his finger over her mouth. His light touch sensitized her lips and teased them apart.

He continued to talk in a low, soft voice. "It was a losing battle, trying not to love you. Every time I turned around, you destroyed another piece of my willpower with a smile, a laugh, a movement so much like you. Thursday night I gave up the fight. Gladly." He captured her chin between his thumb and forefinger. "I think it's time for you to give up, too," he murmured.

Her words of protest sounded weak. "I came ... to talk about Paula."

"We'll talk about Paula." His mouth drifted toward hers. "Later."

She wanted to believe in this moment, in him. When his lips touched hers, when he gathered her close, she did. With a sigh, she relaxed against him and allowed the heavy heat of passion to seep into her. His kisses silenced the warnings that there was danger in his arms.

She no longer cared about danger when he stroked her breasts and whispered words of love. Cradling her in his arms, he lifted her from the sofa and carried her into the bedroom filled with moonlight. She lost her shoes somewhere along the way. After laying her down on the rumpled bed, he stretched out beside her.

He took the net from her hair and combed his fingers through the loosened strands. "At first, I told myself to be satisfied with one night," he murmured. "But within hours, I knew one night wasn't enough."

She caressed his cheek, enjoying the texture of his skin, the slight roughness where his beard grew. "When I saw you with Cindy, I went a little crazy."

He caught her hand and kissed her fingertips. "Tell me how crazy."

"I wanted to dump a tray of drinks on her."

"That's a good sign." He kissed her palm, and the inside of her wrist. She shivered as he ran his tongue along her skin to the hollow of her elbow. His breath was warm, tickling. "Does that mean you want me all to yourself?"

"I guess it does."

He eased her blouse from the waistband of her skirt and placed a kiss on her belly. "Glad to hear it." Reaching behind her back, he unfastened her bra. Then he pushed the loosened garments up and cupped his hand under her breast. "I can feel your heart pounding."

"Yes," she whispered.

"Because of this?" He took her nipple in his mouth.

She moaned and raked her fingers through his hair. "Yes. Oh, yes." Warm trickles of desire grew to coursing streams as he sucked gently and kneaded her breast. When he stopped in order to strip away her blouse, she helped him. Then she offered herself again, loving the feel of his hungry mouth.

He kissed his way back up to her throat and recaptured her lips. After making her dizzy with the sensuous thrust of his tongue, he drew back. "Do you like this?"

She could barely speak. "You know I..."

"I know you want sex." He reached beneath her petticoats and stroked the damp silk of her panties. "Your body tells me that, but I want more. Commit to me, Dani." He slipped his fingers beneath the silk and touched her. His voice grew hoarse. "Commit to me, my love. Tell me."

"Oh, Jake." She shuddered in response to his caress. "I've never felt like this... with anyone."

"Tell me."

She felt the climax building, knew he wouldn't stop. "Jake..."

"Tell me!"

The room seemed to spin and the pressure mounted. Yes, this was the man she loved. This man. Now. "I love you!" she cried as the convulsions racked her with delirious pleasure.

His lips covered hers, absorbing her cries as his touch gentled, slowed. Then he gazed into her eyes, the silvery light casting his own into shadow. With one quick wrench, he tore the silk aside. A zipper rasped and denim brushed her thighs as he slipped inside her, heavy and full. Skin against skin.

Her pulse quickened as she realized what he was doing.

"If you don't want children, tell me now."

"Jake…" Ah, but he felt so good, filling her. It was madness, but it was wonderful madness.

"I love you, Dani. I want it all."

She reached up and held his face in her hands. There would never be another Jake. Her heart had made its choice long ago. His features became blurry as tears welled up in her eyes. "I want it all, too."

"Then that's what you'll get," he said, his words choked with emotion. Slowly, he began to move within her, but his gaze remained on her face.

She hadn't thought she could be aroused again after the shattering release he'd given her, but she was wrong. A deeper response awoke within her and grew with each deft stroke. She wrapped her arms around him and his rhythm became hers, his breathing hers. Their bodies seemed less angular, more fluid and sinuous. Slick with perspiration, they melded together, striving with each thrust to form a union like none they'd ever found before.

His words were a gasp. "Now, Dani!"

Now. Release rumbled up from the depths of her being. She held tight as they were sucked into the vortex of the whirlpool they'd created. Down, down they spun, with Jake's moans marking their descent.

Then gradually, the tension eased. Dani grew aware of the sound of crickets outside the window, a clock ticking on the bedside table and Jake's ragged breathing. She was dazed by the power of what they'd just shared. She stroked his back with trembling hands.

"Incredible," Jake murmured into her ear.

She nodded.

"Stay with me tonight."

She nodded again.

There was silence as he lay, not moving, still joined to her amid a tangle of petticoats. "I meant every word," he said at last.

She smiled in the darkness. "I hope so. It's a little late to change your mind."

He supported his cheek on his fist and looked down at her. "I could never change my mind. I'd be thrilled if you were pregnant. I hope you are."

"Jake!" she protested, but she felt the same way. It was amazing, how right it seemed.

He eased away from her and found the button of her skirt. "Let's get rid of all this. It's in my way."

Dani chuckled. "Not so's you'd notice." But she lifted her hips obligingly so he could pull the skirt and petticoats away.

"There." He splayed his hand across her stomach. "Maybe, at this very moment..." He leaned down and kissed her stomach. "I knew you were the one for me, from the first second Paula dragged you into the bar."

"I knew, too." She paused. "Jake, we need to talk about Paula. She—" Dani stopped as he kissed her navel and ran his tongue around the indentation. "That tickles."

"Good tickle or bad?"

Dani was almost embarrassed to admit what was happening to her as he toyed with her navel. "It's making me want you again," she murmured.

"Oh, really?" He bent to his task with more enthusiasm.

"Jake, now stop." She propped herself up on her elbows. "We need to talk about Paula."

"Paula won't be a problem." He slid his hand over the curve of her hip.

"But—"

"We're together now." He tunneled his fingers through the mat of hair at the apex of her thighs. "You know how much Paula wanted us to be together."

"Yes." Dani's breathing quickened as Jake's hand moved lower. She forced herself to concentrate on the subject. "But what about her job?"

"We'll take care of it. Don't you realize that together we can take care of anything?" He coaxed her thighs apart.

"Jake."

"Quiet, now. I've found the woman I plan to spend my life with, and I want to get to know her better."

By that time, Dani was in no position to argue.

ONCE OR TWICE during the night, Dani wondered if she should try to sleep. After all, she'd planned a full day tomorrow with Evelyn, and there was the matter of Paula. But loving Jake was too new, and she couldn't bear to waste precious time in sleep. Neither could he.

They left the bed at three in the morning and raided the refrigerator, where they found a few cans of beer and the makings for bologna sandwiches. They carried everything back to bed and got half of the sandwiches eaten before they tumbled together in renewed desire.

They made love with the light on, and Dani discovered the scars on his right thigh, left by an opponent's cleats. He learned that her second toe was longer than her first, and that she painted her toenails bright red. He counted her freckles and kissed each one, especially the one on her left breast. She found out Jake had the remains of a bruise on his knee from when he'd tackled Paula a week ago.

They talked some, about their families and their childhoods, but they kissed more than they talked. Dani abandoned herself to sensuality when at four-thirty in the morning they showered together and tried to make love on the shower floor with the water splashing in their faces.

When that didn't work very well, they returned to bed to finish what they'd started. Dani had just settled herself on top of Jake when the train rumbled through, shaking the bed.

He laughed. "Is it just me, or did the earth move?"

She smiled down at him. "I guess that means it's time for the day to start."

Jake anchored her hips more firmly to him. "Let it start a little late today."

"Okay." Dani didn't want the night to end, either, and as the sound of the train died away, she took up the steady rhythm. Closing her eyes against the encroaching sunlight, she gave herself up to loving Jake.

JAKE OFFERED to go over and feed the peacocks. Dani countered by saying she'd make him breakfast. He left with a smile and a blown kiss.

Clad in Jake's bathrobe, Dani puttered around, taking stock of the breakfast supplies and the kitchen utensils. She started the coffee and found bacon and a frying pan. When the bacon was sizzling, she looked for a spatula, which she finally found in a cupboard. She expected it to be in a drawer.

"Men," she said softly to herself, and smiled. Weren't they wonderful? Or at least one of them was. One by the name of Jake Clayborn. He'd asked her to trust him, and perhaps she was a fool, but she was going to do it. When he'd made love to her, she knew she'd trust him with her life.

But she didn't believe there was anything to fear from Jake. She'd looked into his eyes so often in the past few hours, and all she'd found there was love and passion. And such passion. Her body reminded her with small twinges here and there of the night she'd shared with Jake. Mm. She stretched and glanced around for paper towels for draining the bacon.

A complete search of the kitchen revealed nothing, not even a paper napkin. She reasoned that he might store paper towels anywhere, judging from the spatula episode, so she rummaged through every conceivable nook, ending up in the living room. Her search led her to a drawer in the end table next to the sofa. She opened it and gasped.

A buzzing sound filled her head. Slowly, she picked up a well-thumbed copy of *The Unvanquished*. She tried to tell herself that Jake had been curious about her mother's writing and had bought himself the latest book. After all, the book was set in Tubac, and he lived here now. It was all perfectly logical.

Except she didn't believe her own logic. Instinct told her there was more to it than that. Her hand shook as she tried to thumb through the pages. Then she saw something, and flipped back to it. Oh, Lord. A passage was marked. She knew that passage. It had appeared in one of the notes.

"Find something interesting?"

She turned. Jake stood in the doorway, silhouetted by the light coming from outside. He held something in his hand. It looked like a knife.

CHAPTER EIGHTEEN

BLOOD POUNDED in Dani's ears as she backed away. There was nowhere to go. Jake stood between her and escape.

"You found the book." His voice was toneless.

"What do you want from me?" She forced the words past her constricted throat, and they rasped in the early-morning silence.

He put down what she'd thought was a knife; she could see he'd held clippers. From behind his back, he produced a pink rose. It had to be the first one from the bush outside. "I want exactly what I wanted last night. To love you, to marry you, to raise our children."

She realized he might possibly be completely crazy. "Did you send the notes?"

"No, but I can understand why seeing the book freaked you out. Please, Dani, don't doubt me now. I bought the book because that's where the notes were coming from. I thought I might be able to find some pattern. I underlined all the passages I could find involving daughters, or those referring to Tubac as a dangerous place to be."

"Why didn't you tell me that? And why should I believe you?"

"I didn't tell you because there was no point in scaring you by dwelling on it. Your mother's done a good enough job of that. And you should believe me because last night I turned my soul inside out for you. If you can't trust what passed between us, and build your faith on that, then..." He shrugged. "Then I guess I can do no more."

Dani tore her gaze away from him and focused on the page in front of her with its underscored passage. Then she glanced back at Jake. She felt sick with uncertainty. "I hate these secrets that are between us. I never know what I'm going to turn up next."

"I hate them, too."

"Then do something about it!"

"I can't. Not yet."

The smell of burning bacon reached them. "I think your secrets have something to do with me."

He didn't answer.

"The bacon's burning," she said. "You'd better tend to it before you have a grease fire."

He gave up his position by the door with an air of resignation, as if he knew what would happen when he did. Once he moved into the kitchen, she fled out the door and across the yard. She looked back once to see if he was coming after her. He wasn't.

She'd left her keys dangling from the ignition of the Mustang. She grabbed them and opened the door to her house. Once inside, she closed and locked it. Then she leaned against the door, breathing hard. Who was Jake Clayborn?

On one level, she knew him as well as she knew herself. They'd formed a physical bond that might never be broken. She doubted another man would ever succeed in creating the kind of intimacy she'd experienced with Jake. Dammit, she loved him! Why was he forcing her to doubt him?

He'd said he wouldn't harm her. She had to believe that or go stark raving mad. Even her mother hadn't thought he was dangerous. If he'd wanted to kill her, he'd had countless chances. She'd have to see him again. She'd left her work clothes there, and there was the problem of Paula. And Lord help her, she wanted his loving again.

Nevertheless, she needed time away from him, time to ease the tension. She'd dress and go to the shop, where she and Evelyn would have a busy day. Concentrating on her work would help. Evelyn and the shop would help take her mind off Jake.

SHE WORKED side by side with Evelyn throughout the morning. The day was chilly, and dark clouds threatened rain, which gave the shop a cozy feel. Dani drank strong coffee all morning to keep herself awake.

Finally, around noon, Evelyn threw down her duster. "We need some new scenery. I'll take you to lunch at a little restaurant I've discovered. It's across from the Tumacacori Mission."

"Sure, why not." Dani hadn't eaten any breakfast. The smell of burned bacon had stayed in her nostrils while she dressed, robbing her of an appetite. Now she was starving, and jittery from too much caffeine.

The restaurant served both Mexican and American food, so Dani ordered a turkey sandwich for a change from Canada Verde's fare.

Evelyn ordered a bowl of onion soup. "Since I won't be kissing anyone," she added with a laugh.

Dani glanced down at her lap. She'd pushed thoughts of Jake away pretty successfully during the morning's work, but they came flooding back with Evelyn's chance remark about kissing.

"I could swear that's a little beard rash on your cheek," Evelyn said. "Who've you been kissing?"

Dani glanced up, fumbling for a reply. Nothing suitable occurred to her.

"Aha. I thought so. He came to see me yesterday, you know."

"No, I didn't know." Another of Jake's secrets. Would they never end?

"He wanted to know what I said to drive Paula away. He just won't believe that Paula left on her own account, simply because she couldn't take the pressure."

"I'm beginning to believe it," Dani said, remembering the incident at the country club.

"Well, thank you, dear. Your lover obviously doesn't."

Dani couldn't contradict Evelyn's label for Jake. He was her lover.

"But enough of that," Evelyn said with a wave of her hand. "We have other matters to discuss. How would you like to take a sample of your work to a gem and mineral show in Tucson next weekend? We've missed the big show they have there each February, but this small one will do for a start."

"Next weekend?" Dani was taken aback. Evelyn certainly didn't let any grass grow under her feet. "I don't know. I'm not sure I can get time off from work."

"If I were you, I'd quit my job to go."

"I'm not quite ready to quit, Evelyn. I have to pay my rent and eat."

"Then try to get some time off, because this would be a terrific way to broadcast our presence here and bring some people down to see us. We'll take the peacock earrings, of course, and anything else along those lines you make between now and then. And of course the trip will be on me. I wouldn't expect you to pay for accommodations or food." She laughed. "At least not until you become world-famous."

"Evelyn, I really appreciate all you're doing for me."

"For *us*, dear, for *us*. I intend to ride on your coattails."

"You're certainly welcome. I hope I won't let you down."

"Not a chance." Evelyn paid for the lunch and glanced at her watch. "That didn't take long. Let's go over to the mission and walk around. I love that place. Ever been there?"

"Once, when I was a kid. I thought it was kind of spooky."

"I find it wonderfully relaxing, myself. The rain will keep most of the tourists away, so we should have the place to ourselves."

The prospect didn't sound very inviting to Dani.

"Come on," Evelyn urged. "Maybe you'll get some inspiration for a jewelry design."

They left the Jeep parked in front of the restaurant and walked across the two-lane road. As Dani approached the National Parks building that served as an entrance to the mission grounds, she thought about touring the place with her parents years ago. Her dad had read every word of explanation posted in the small museum, while her mother had flitted quickly around the room, absorbing impressions of early mission life. Helen had been most intrigued with Tumacacori Mission itself, a structure that had reminded Dani of a war ruin.

Evelyn and Dani stepped out of the chilly breeze into the lobby of the museum, and Dani fished in her purse for the admission charge.

"Never mind." Evelyn put her hand on Dani's purse. "I have a pass that's good all year."

"Oh."

"Do you want to see the museum?"

"Well . . ." Dani wasn't in the mood for looking at dioramas and ancient weapons. She knew the history of the mission was violent, and violence wasn't her favorite topic at the moment.

"Let's just go to the mission. It's so evocative."

Dani trailed after her as they hurried through a portion of the museum and out a door that led to the mission about a hundred yards away. Under a lowering sky, they walked down a paved path lined with tiny yellow flowers. A young couple passed them going back to the museum, but otherwise they were alone.

The facade of the mission was a patchwork of white stucco and bare adobe where the stucco had eroded. The top to the bell tower was missing. Dani squinted at the building and tried to imagine it in its glory days, gleaming white, the columns decorating the entrance unpitted by time, the bell in the tower tolling the hour for prayer. Maybe it was just the weather, but the image wouldn't hold.

"The place needs a little work," she said to Evelyn.

"They've decided not to do much more restoration. They've stabilized what's here, and now they'll maintain it. I think that helps preserve the authenticity."

Dani glanced at her. "You're really into this, aren't you?"

"I love it. I've become friends with the caretaker and his wife. Last Thursday they gave me a tour of the mission by the light of a full moon. You should come with me next time. It's spectacular."

"No, thanks. Since you know my mother's books, you probably remember the scene she set in this place."

"Oh, I do! That was a fabulous scene."

They came to the cavernous entrance and Dani hesitated.

"Go ahead. You first."

The interior smelled of cool mud and old wood, which made sense when Dani remembered that the building had been constructed two centuries earlier with adobe blocks and heavy wooden beams fashioned from trees harvested in the Santa Ritas. The inside of the mission was pretty much as Dani recalled—a hollow shell that had been ransacked by thieves and time. Ragged niches in the walls testified to what had once been the Twelve Stations of the Cross, and the altar was nothing more than a crumbling rectangle of adobe about the size of a coffin.

Dani touched the rough surface of an exposed adobe wall and thought of the hours of labor that had created this place of worship. Above the altar, a few faint rust-colored designs were all that remained of the elaborate frescoes that had decorated the walls. Perhaps Evelyn was right. Books were the only enduring art form, because they could be reproduced.

To the right of the altar was a small room that a sign designated as the sacristy. Iron gates barred the openings to the outside, making Dani feel imprisoned by the thick, musty walls. She'd had about enough of this place.

"Can't you hear the ghosts whispering in here?" Evelyn said.

"Unfortunately." Dani shivered. "Let's go."

"You don't like it?" Evelyn's voice echoed off the bare walls.

"I told you before—I think it's spooky."

"But we haven't even gone out back to the graveyard."

"Fine with me."

Evelyn laughed, and the sound careened around the dim interior. "I can see why you're not a writer like your mother. She obviously loved this place the same way I do. It gets my writer's juices flowing."

"Not me. Some of the scenes she creates, like that one in here where the guy almost kills the heroine, would have me peeking in all the closets for the ax murderer."

"But that's half the fun, scaring yourself like that!"

"I'd rather work with silver and beautiful stones, if you don't mind."

"Okay, spoilsport. Let's go back to the shop." Linking her arm through Dani's, Evelyn led them out into the brisk air again. "I want to warn you about something," she said as they walked back across the street to the Jeep.

"What's that?"

"I'll bet your friend Jake will object to the gem show."

"Why would he do that?"

"He's the most possessive man I've ever met. You said you were trying to get out from under your mother's thumb, but if you'll excuse a little amateur analysis, I think you've picked a man who's just like her."

Dani fell silent as she climbed into Evelyn's Jeep. Could that be true? She remembered the time Jake followed her down the road when she'd walked into town, how he'd rearranged his work schedule so he could accompany her home each night. He'd said he was concerned about her safety, but was that all of it? No, she had to admit to herself. There was the lovemaking. He'd mastered her completely, and she'd found it thrilling, but perhaps that was because of a flaw in her character.

Evelyn backed the Jeep onto the road and started toward Tubac. "You'd better stand up to him one of these days, or you'll be completely dominated in no time."

"But why would he object to a gem show?"

"Because frankly, I don't think he wants you to succeed in this business. He's been bucking me from the beginning. With your potential, you could be rich and famous. He's a washed-up baseball player turned bartender. He'll want to keep you down at his level, if you allow it."

"I'd hate to think that's true." But what about his desire to make her pregnant? She'd thought it was a sign of his deep commitment, and hers as well. Viewed another way, however, it could be part of a plan to bury her under a mountain of diapers and formula so she wouldn't have time for her jewelry.

Evelyn combed her dark hair back with her fingers. "Maybe I'm wrong. Maybe he'll love the idea of your going off with me for the weekend. But I doubt it."

Dani lifted her chin. "It doesn't matter what he thinks of the idea. I'm going."

"That's my girl."

THEY WORKED until six that night. Evelyn offered to make dinner for the two of them, but Dani wanted to get home. Having had no sleep the night before, she was tired. She was also anxious to find out how things stood with Jake. Maybe he'd given some thought to Paula, or perhaps he'd taken some action while she'd been at the shop. And weak though she might be, according to Evelyn, she missed him.

When she arrived home in the deepening twilight, she found her clothes washed and folded neatly on one of the wooden porch chairs. The rose he'd picked that morning sat in a bud vase on the table beside the chair, and a note was underneath. Like Jake himself, the handwriting was bold yet somewhat hard to read. She realized she'd never seen his handwriting before. She held the note up to the waning light and puzzled out the words.

Dearest love,
The future is ours, if you will trust that I love you and want only your happiness and well-being. (Well, I want a few other things, which aren't appropriate for a note on a porch that anyone might read.)

Dani smiled and continued reading.

Breakfast was a disaster. Let's try dinner. I'll be waiting for you.

All my love,
Jake

P.S. I fed the peacocks.

Dani noticed that the peacocks were already dozing contentedly in the branches of the mesquite tree. She glanced over at Jake's house where a light was glowing from the kitchen, and the scent of browning hamburger drifted toward her. How she yearned for him. Maybe this yearning wasn't good for her, but she couldn't deny its force. And maybe Evelyn was wrong about his possessiveness.

She picked up the pile of clothes along with the bud vase containing the rose and carried everything inside. Apparently, he'd taken her clothes into town to wash them. She was touched by the gesture. Then she saw a small package tucked in with the clothes, and she unwrapped the tissue to find a dainty new pair of panties inside. The ripped ones weren't there. Had he kept them? She guessed that he had.

Desire tickled her insides as she remembered the way they'd made love the night before. Her tiredness slipped away as she imagined spending another night in Jake's bed. He obviously wanted her there. The choice was hers. Or at least, she liked to believe it was. But as she crossed the yard toward Jake's house, she wondered if she'd abandoned her will along with her body when it came to Jake Clayborn.

He opened the door before she knocked. "I saw you come home." He held open the screen and she stepped inside. Before she could say a word, he folded her in his arms and kissed her until she was breathless. At last he lifted his head. "I was so afraid you wouldn't come."

"I can't seem to help myself."

His gaze searched hers. "I love you."

"And I love you, although I wonder if I'm crazy."

"Then be crazy with me. Are you hungry?"

Desire pounded through her now, unleashed from the restraint she'd kept on it all day. When she didn't answer, he smiled and led her to the bedroom.

They undressed each other with frantic movements, each protesting when buttons wouldn't give and sleeves got stuck. Finally, they threw the last of their garments to the floor and tumbled onto the bed. Dani opened her thighs and urged him forward.

"Wait, I've barely kissed you at all," he said, holding back.

"I don't care. I need you inside me."

With a groan, he fulfilled her wish. Their ascent was rapid and thorough. Dani reveled in his cry of completion on the waves of her own satisfying climax.

As their breathing returned to normal, he nibbled on her ear. "Ready for dinner, now?"

Dani sighed and wiggled against him. She loved the feel of his skin against hers, his weight on her. She loved the woodsy scent of him and the way his chest hair brushed against her breasts. "You know, people are always talking about having happy hour before dinner. Maybe someone should consider starting a new kind of happy hour?"

"I think you're on to something."

Dani hugged him closer. "I'm getting hungry. Did I smell hamburger cooking earlier?"

"I turned the stove off when you came across the yard. Just in case."

"Smart man. What are we having?"

"Spaghetti. It's the only thing I know how to cook."

"I love spaghetti." Dani knew she'd have loved boiled weeds if Jake cooked it for her. She was in love as she'd never been before in her life.

Later, they sat at Jake's battered kitchen table. He'd created a centerpiece from a few carnations he'd bought in town and a couple of candles and candlesticks.

Dani eyed the setting. "I'm impressed."

"Paula kept bugging me to get you flowers, so I'm doing my best. Although the rose backfired."

"I saw those clippers and thought you were coming after me with a knife."

"Oh, Dani." He reached across the table and slid his fingers through hers. "I'd die before I let anything happen to you, and you thought..."

She gazed into his eyes. "I listened to my head again, instead of my heart."

"And then you ran away. That about broke me."

"I needed some time to recover. But I knew, even minutes after I left, that I'd be back."

His smile was crooked. "Wish you'd given me a call to tell me so. I spent one hell of a day wondering if I'd lost you again."

"And washing my clothes. Thank you. And thank you for replacing my..." She hesitated, embarrassed.

"I don't sew." His eyes sparkled. "Plus I kind of liked the modifications I made in your other ones."

"You kept them, didn't you?"

Now it was his turn to flush. "Yeah. Call me deviant if you want, but I—"

"I think it's kind of exciting that you did."

"It's my private souvenir. I promise not to get them out to show our grandchildren."

Dani squeezed his hand. Grandchildren. She could imagine having grandchildren with this man, and the idea made her warm all over.

"How was your day with Evelyn?"

"Fine. The shop's ready to open. At lunch she took me to Tumacacori Mission. She loves that old place."

"Oh, yeah? I've never been there."

"It's interesting, but kind of eerie, in a way. Anyway, Evelyn asked me something today."

"What's that?"

Dani's heartbeat quickened. Surely Evelyn would be wrong. "She thinks we should go to a gem show in Tucson this weekend. It would be good publicity for The Silver Coyote and for me, too."

"What about work?"

"I'll try to convince John to give me time off."

Jake frowned. "I don't think it's a good idea."

Dani's dinner turned to stone in her stomach. "Why not?"

"You very well could have some nut on your trail. Tucson's a big city. In the crush of people coming to this show, anything could happen. It would be the perfect opportunity for someone to—"

"It would also be an opportunity for me," she said quietly.

"I know that, but there will be other times. Let's not rush things."

Dani withdrew her hand from his. A lump grew in her throat. "It's too bad you can't support me in my work, Jake."

"Wait a minute. Of course I support you."

"Not really. You've tried to drive a wedge between me and the person who's ready to launch my career in Tubac. You went to see Evelyn without telling me, to harass her about Paula, didn't you?"

The muscles in his jaw twitched. "I still don't think we're getting the truth on that. I tried to contact Paula today, but her parents have put up a brick wall. They don't want either one of us talking to her."

"Maybe we pushed Paula too fast, Jake. Maybe we just put too much pressure on her."

"That's bull, and you know it! Paula was fine until she ended up alone with that viper-tongued woman."

"Jake, stop talking about Evelyn that way. She's the only one around here who seems to care if I sell my jewelry or not."

"I care! You're a wonderful artist, and I think you deserve tons of money and loads of fame."

"Oh?" Dani pushed back her chair. "Then why are you telling me not to go to the gem show?"

"Because it's not safe, dammit!" He stood, knocking over his chair.

"Or because you want to keep me under your thumb?" She stood slowly and glared at him.

"No. Dani, please don't agree to go to this thing. It's not safe. Evelyn should know that."

"Evelyn's trying to bolster my career. And you, apparently, want to sabotage it."

"That's not true."

Her fingers grew icy and she trembled. "Is that why you want me to get pregnant, Jake? So I'll forget about my career?"

"My Lord." He was around the table in two strides and grabbed her by the arms. "How could you think such a horrible thing?"

"I don't want to! But Evelyn said you'd object to this gem show. She says you're possessive. She—"

"And Evelyn is a fake! Your mother sent her down here!" He blanched and released her.

She stood very still. Her lips felt frozen, but she made them move with great effort. "What did you say?"

CHAPTER NINETEEN

JAKE SIGHED and turned away from her. "Maybe you'd better sit down."

There was a roaring sound in her ears and the room seemed to tilt. She swayed.

He glanced back at her and took her gently by the elbows. "Sit," he said, guiding her back to the chair.

She gripped the edge of the table and gradually her equilibrium returned. Evelyn. Everything about Evelyn, the shop, Dani's future, was a lie concocted by her mother? No! She couldn't accept that. Yet somehow, once Jake said it, she knew it was true. Her mother had sabotaged her bid for independence.

"Okay, now?" Jake inquired cautiously.

She wondered if she'd ever be okay again. She nodded anyway. "So Evelyn is a plant."

Jake paced the length of the kitchen, his hand rubbing the back of his neck. "She's a friend of your mother's, a rich friend, who offered to come down here and keep an eye on you. She chose a jewelry shop as the perfect vehicle. The irony is, I think the two of you could probably succeed at this business."

Dani laughed mirthlessly. "And I thought my talent won me this chance."

Jake returned to the table and braced his hands on it. He gazed intently into her face. "You are immensely talented, and you will succeed, with or without Evelyn Ross. You don't need her. You never did."

Dani returned his gaze. Slowly, another thought pushed out the first shocking revelation. She spoke softly, as if doing so would make the answer soft, too. "Tell me, Jake, how do you happen to know who Evelyn is?"

His eyes closed and his head dropped forward. The muscles in his shoulders tensed. Gradually, he raised his head, and his expression was bleak. "Because your mother hired me. I'm your bodyguard."

"No!" The shriek erupted from deep within her as she leaped up from the table and flew at him. "No!" she cried again, flailing at him with both hands. "No, no, no!"

"Dani!" He grabbed her wrists. "That doesn't change anything between us. I still—"

"That changes everything," she said, sobbing, gazing at his blurry image. "She's paying you. Paying you! You bastard!"

His tone was pleading. "The money means nothing to me. I came here because I was paid to, but as soon as I met you, the money became unimportant. I love you, Dani."

"I trusted you. I thought you were my friend, and all this time you were working for *her*. Why didn't you tell me?"

"Because I'm afraid for you. I knew this would happen, that you'd go crazy. We thought you might run, leave without a trace. You've told me how you feel about your mother interfering in your life."

We thought you might run. The idea of him scheming with her mother made her physically ill. "So now I have three of you interfering in my life.'' She twisted in his grasp. "Let me go."

"What are you going to do?"

She sniffed and straightened her back. "Call my mother."

Jake sighed and released her. "Okay."

"I'd like to use your phone."

He gestured toward the wall phone in the kitchen. "Incidentally, she's the one who called me late on Thursday night. When you thought I was some gigolo, or something."

Dani picked up the receiver. "I almost wish you had been, Jake."

He glanced at her, pain in his eyes. Then he walked over to the counter and braced his hands against it, with his back to her and his head lowered.

Dani took a shaky breath and punched in her mother's number. Her mother answered after two rings, as she normally did these days, as if she were snatching up the phone. Dani didn't bother with a greeting. "I just found out who Jake is," she said.

"Oh." Her mother didn't try to make any excuses, for which Dani was grateful.

"Fire him."

"Dani, you need someone down there to protect you. I know you don't appreciate what I've done, but—"

"Fire him now if you expect to have any sort of relationship with me again."

"Is he there with you now?"

Dani glanced at the tense figure across the room. *Jake, how could you do this to me?* "Yes."

Her mother sighed. "Let me talk to him."

Dani took the receiver from her ear. "Jake."

He turned, his face unreadable. She held out the receiver and he walked over and took it from her. "Hello, Helen," he said quietly.

Dani wrapped her arms around herself and moved away from Jake, away from this person who was more dangerous than she had ever dreamed.

"She and Evelyn are planning a trip into Tucson for a gem show. I think it's foolish. When Dani insisted on going I...lost it. I told her about Evelyn and then about me." He paused. "No, but I might as well. This couldn't get any worse."

The sound of his voice rasped against her raw nerves, but she had to stay until she was convinced he was no longer working for her mother.

"I realize that," Jake said. "No, you don't owe me a cent. For one thing, I haven't adequately done the job. She's still at risk."

At risk? What a laugh. Her life was in shambles because of how they'd tried to protect her from risk.

"Yes, I'll be in touch. Right." He hung up the phone.

"Did she fire you?"

"Yes. But there's something else you might as well know. She's a close friend of John Slattery's."

Dani's stomach twisted. "She set me up for the job?"

"And me."

Hysterical laughter bubbled in her throat. "Is there *anything* I accomplished on my own down here?"

"You found this place."

She stared at him, remembering. "You paid Ron and Liane to move, didn't you? With my mother's money."

She read the answer in his bleak gaze. "Lord! What a fool I was! Running over to the bar in the rain, to save you another night in your camper, and you had it all *planned*. How about that first kiss? Did you mastermind that, too?"

"Dani—"

"Did you figure I'd be easier to control if you seduced me?"

"Stop it! Don't destroy everything we shared!"

"Destroy? Me? You just dropped a nuclear bomb on what we've *shared*, as you so quaintly put it. You and my mother." She gripped the back of a chair for support. "I want you out of my life, Jake. I don't want to see you or talk to you ever again."

His eyes reflected his agony, but his voice was hard. "I'd hoped for more maturity from you. Apparently, I won't get it."

"You'll get nothing from me ever again. So you might as well move on, Jake."

"Now you're sounding like Ed Jordan. You can't order me out of town, Dani. Turns out I like Tubac, and the job's not bad. I even kind of like this house."

"That's ridiculous. You probably have a house in L.A., and a whole life there, too. So if you're thinking of staying down here as some grand chivalrous gesture, forget it. I don't want you here."

"Too bad. I called a real estate agent today and put my house in L.A. on the market."

Panic rose in her. She'd thought she could make him go away. "Jake, that's idiotic! You're not going to spend the rest of your life as a bartender, and you just lost the only bodyguard job you'll ever find in Tubac."

"You're right, but you see, I began rearranging my life today. I made a few calls and found out they needed a baseball coach for the next school year at Sahuarita. I'm set up for an interview."

Her chest was tight with unshed tears. She was the one who'd planted that idea and he was following her advice, but it was too late. She ached with regret. "You betrayed me." She threw the words at him like rocks and felt the pain as he winced. "If I'd known you were in league with my mother, I would never have made love to you. Never."

"I know."

"So you admit that you lied to me, just to get me into bed with you!"

"I concealed the truth."

"Same thing." She needed to get out of there before she hurled the chair at him or broke down. Losing control would be a kind of defeat. She turned and walked toward the door.

"What are you going to do?"

She opened the door and glanced over her shoulder. "My mother's not paying you anymore. You have no reason to ask."

"The hell I don't. I love you. I—"

"Goodbye, Jake."

WHEN HE WAS SURE she was gone, Jake picked up the phone and dialed Helen Goodwin's number. "All right, you fired me like you were told."

"I had no choice."

"I know. I'm still on the job, but I meant what I said about the money. I'm also repaying the advance. This isn't about money anymore. In fact, it hasn't been for some time."

"You're really in love with her."

Jake closed his eyes. Everything was so screwed up.

"I should have thought of it. I never—"

"Never imagined your little daughter would be powerful enough to make a man like me beg to marry her? No, I guess you wouldn't. You still see her as a child. She's not, although she's acting a little like one now. She's so furious at both of us that she's vulnerable, and I have to take responsibility for that. What I want from you is any information, any more notes, anything that will help me."

"There have been no more notes so far."

Jake paced the length of the telephone cord. "Why do you think Evelyn's pushing this gem show thing?"

"I don't know. Maybe she's been humoring me about the notes and doesn't believe there's a threat. She's obviously having a great time with her jewelry shop."

Jake still couldn't swear the notes were real, but he had to act as if they were. "I've read *The Unvanquished* and found all the sections the notes came from. I've tried to anticipate if something in the book would tell us where or how an attempt might be made against Dani. It's a long shot, but I want you to think of scenes when the heroine is threatened."

"I'll go through the book again. I'll call you back."

"Good. I have to go. I'm keeping her house under surveillance, in case she goes anywhere. Call me with anything you've got." He hung up, his attention already focused on the little house across the clearing. It would take all his concentration, all his skill and cunning to do what had to be done. The next few days would be the most important ones of his entire life.

DANI SHOWERED and changed clothes before making the drive to Evelyn's house. She thought of throwing away the clothes she'd had on before, the ones Jake had touched, but settled for stuffing them in a far corner of her closet.

She'd called Evelyn and asked to see her without explaining why, wanting to confront her face-to-face with this latest revelation. At least Evelyn had been acting out of concern and friendship, she thought. *She* wasn't a paid stool pigeon like Jake.

Dani shuddered to think of how naively she'd confided in Jake about the problem with her mother, and all the time he'd known the whole story. He'd played her for a fool, and she hated him for it. If by some chance she'd become pregnant...she didn't know what she'd do.

Evelyn lived in a rented house in the hilly country just north of Tubac. It was typical of many of the better homes in the area—a low-slung adobe with arched windows and a red-tiled roof.

Evelyn opened the door as soon as Dani knocked. She had a margarita in her hand. "Come in and have a drink! What a great surprise. I thought you were exhausted and ready for bed."

"I need to talk to you." Dani glanced around at the comfortable house. "Did this come furnished?"

"Yes, fortunately. Come on out to the Arizona room. It's where I like to relax."

Dani followed Evelyn through the house. It wasn't as plush as Paula's home, but authentic Indian blankets hung on the walls and attractive southwestern-style furniture filled both the living and dining rooms. The Arizona room was a long enclosed porch at the back of the house. Evelyn settled into a chair made of wooden latticework and pigskin. She motioned Dani to a companion chair on the other side of a low pigskin-covered table. "Equipale furniture," she explained. "From Nogales. When I get my own house here, I think I'll buy some."

Dani thought of all the money Evelyn had spent. She'd rented this house and a shop in town. She'd redecorated the shop and bought inventory. Although Dani's work was to be offered on consignment, the gift items had been purchased. "You don't have to keep up the charade anymore, Evelyn. I know this is temporary, for as long as you decide to spy on me for my mother."

Dani had expected to shock Evelyn, which she did. Evelyn's eyes widened and her hand went to her throat. But Dani was taken aback by the spark of anger that followed, briefly lighting Evelyn's topaz eyes. Then it was gone. Maybe she'd imagined it.

Evelyn set down her margarita glass. "Oh, dear. She's told you, then."

"Actually, she didn't. Jake did."

"Jake? What the hell does he know about this?"

It was Dani's turn to be surprised. She'd thought all three of them had been in cahoots. This shed a whole new light on the situation. "You don't know about Jake?"

Evelyn gazed steadily at her. "What about him?" she asked carefully.

"That my mother hired him as my bodyguard?"

This time Dani was sure about the anger. It blazed for several seconds before Evelyn got up and paced the room.

"I thought my mother would have told you."

"Well, she didn't." Evelyn stared out the large windows at the shadowy peaks of the Santa Ritas, just visible in the moonlight. "I always knew there was something fishy about him, though. Helen should have told me." She stayed there a moment longer before turning back to Dani with a sad smile. "You must be devastated. Here he was paid to watch you and I'm guessing he seduced you in the process. Does your mother know about that?"

"No." Dani's cheeks grew hot, but she couldn't deny that was exactly what had happened. Of course, she'd been a willing accomplice.

"Well, I won't tell her."

"Thanks."

"I think your mother and Jake have duped us both."

"I just feel duped, period. And exhausted." She stood. "Well, Evelyn, I'll come by tomorrow and clear my equipment out of the shop."

"What?"

"I'd do it tonight, but I'm so tired that—"

"I plan to open that shop for business tomorrow, as planned."

Dani stared at her. "But it's all a lie."

Evelyn walked back to her chair and sat down. "This is how I feel about things, Dani. I came down here as a favor to your mother. That much I admit. But I've loved every minute of our venture together. I was a bored rich lady looking for something to do with herself, and you've provided the perfect outlet. I know you're probably upset that I haven't been candid about my identity, but I have been about your work. It's magnificent.''

Dani pressed her fingers to her throbbing temples.

"In fact," Evelyn continued, "I think it would be a great joke on your mother and Jake if we made a screaming success of The Silver Coyote, don't you?''

"I don't know what I think, Evelyn.''

Evelyn rose and put her arm around Dani. "Go home." She started Dani toward the front door. "Get some rest. Come by the shop in the morning. We'll talk.''

"All right.''

Dani drove home in a daze. A message from her mother was on the answering machine when she arrived. She chose to ignore it.

WHEN DANI REACHED The Silver Coyote the next morning at nine, she'd made her decision. Evelyn was alone, adjusting baskets on the shelves. The shop wasn't to open officially until nine-thirty.

Evelyn turned when Dani opened the door. "Well?''
"I'm in.''

Evelyn crowed with delight and ran forward to embrace her. "I knew it! I knew I could count on you.'' She stepped back and surveyed Dani as if the young woman had just won a beauty contest. "Congratulations.''

Dani managed a smile. "Are we still going to the gem show this weekend?''

"Can you get off work?''

"I should think so. I also found out my mother got me that job. I guess John Slattery will do anything I ask."

"Then use it to your advantage. We'll leave about two in the afternoon on Friday and be back on Sunday."

"You don't agree with my mother and Jake that it's too dangerous?"

Evelyn ran her fingers through her hair. "Now that I know who Jake is, I'm wondering about the whole note-writing business. I thought maybe he was the bad guy, but if your mother hired him, then it begins to look as if she did cook this up, doesn't it?"

"After finding out that Jake is a hired bodyguard, I'm willing to believe just about anything. I wonder why she didn't tell you about Jake?"

"That's easy. She knew I wouldn't have come. If she'd told me about Jake, I wouldn't have offered because it wouldn't have seemed necessary. This way, she could really monitor your life."

Dani looked down at her hands. She was embarrassed for her mother—her sad, manipulative mother. "I'm sorry, Evelyn."

"Don't be. I'm glad it all happened this way, and I didn't know about Jake. It gave me a chance to meet you and open the shop. By the way, is Jake leaving town?"

Dani grimaced. "Don't I wish. He's being very stubborn, even though my mother fired him. I forced her to. But he says he likes Tubac and wants to stay."

"Probably some macho pride thing. My advice is to stay away from him if you want that career. He's out to keep you down."

"He disapproved of the gem show, the way you said he would. That's what brought all this out in the open. He told me about you to keep me from going." The initial sharp pain of Jake's betrayal had subsided to a dull ache that felt like the kind that would stay with her for a while.

"I think he'd do anything to keep you in line. Stick with me, Dani, and we'll be famous."

Famous. Dani believed Evelyn could help make it happen. She wondered if being famous would heal the gaping hole in her heart.

JAKE DIDN'T THINK Dani realized how closely he was following her. He was thankful that Tubac was a small town and he could do much of it on foot. He'd tailed her to Evelyn's house and tried to listen to the conversation, but the house was too well insulated to hear much through cracks in doors and windows. Still, because Dani was at the opening of The Silver Coyote on Tuesday morning, he assumed that Evelyn had been more successful than he had in soothing Dani's outrage. He understood that. His betrayal had been far worse.

If Dani was still working with Evelyn, they were probably going to the gem show. And if they went, so would he. He arranged for the Friday through Sunday off after explaining the problem to Slattery. Jake had also been surprised and pleased that Dani hadn't quit her waitressing job. Apparently, she wasn't going to run as he'd been afraid she might. Working with Dani that day had been hellish, but he'd gotten through it. He was sure it was no picnic for her, either, judging from her pallor and the set line of her jaw. Lord but he hated this.

Helen Goodwin called him back Tuesday night. "I wanted to make sure I did a thorough job of this, and I think I've covered every possibility in the book," she began. "There are three passages where Sarah's life is in danger," she said. "One's up in the Santa Rita Mountains, one's in Tumacacori Mission, and one's when she almost drowns in the Santa Cruz."

"Nothing in the area of Tucson, or that could be construed that way?"

"No."

Jake felt slightly relieved. Maybe the gem show wasn't the danger he anticipated. "I didn't think so, either, but I wanted to be sure I wasn't missing something. I doubt Dani's going up in the mountains any time soon, but I sure wish we didn't live so close to the river." He tried to remember what had come up recently about Tumacacori. Oh, yeah. "You know, Evelyn took Dani over to the mission the other day."

"Well, of course she'd go over there. She loves the place. I knew that."

"Have you talked to Evelyn since all this hit the fan?"

"No. I've left messages, but she hasn't returned them. I guess she's upset because I didn't tell her about you."

"Well, if you talk to her, ask her to keep Dani the hell away from that mission."

"I'll tell her."

After Jake finished talking to Helen, he paced the kitchen trying to decide what avenue to explore next. Maybe looking for some mysterious assailant was a wild-goose chase, but something in his gut said it wasn't. All he could do was watch and wait.

PAULA HAD a bad feeling in her tummy. She wanted to talk to somebody about it. But she didn't want Dani to get in trouble. Dani's jewelry was so beautiful. Paula could sit and stare at it for hours. Dani was going to make lots of money. Evelyn said so.

But there was this bad feeling in Paula's tummy. She couldn't tell her parents. They never listened to anything she said. They didn't want her to talk to anybody, either. But Paula thought if she could just talk to somebody, the bad feeling would go away.

She'd talk to Jake, but she didn't work at the restaurant anymore. She wasn't supposed to talk to Jake, either. Or Dani. Her parents said if she did, they would take away her paints. She couldn't get new ones. She didn't have money.

Paula thought and thought how she could see Jake and not have her parents know. Then she remembered about Fridays. Fridays her father played golf. Fridays her mother ate lunch at the restaurant. If Paula was very careful, she could try to see Jake on Friday. She could stay in the kitchen so her mother wouldn't know, and make Jake come there. Everything would be better if she could just see him at the restaurant on Friday.

CHAPTER TWENTY

JAKE WANTED DANI to think he was going to work as usual on Friday morning, so he drove out at the normal time, turned off on a side road and parked beneath some overhanging cottonwoods. Then he hiked back to Dani's house and crouched behind a clump of pampas grass on the river side of the property.

The sun beat down, hinting of the summer heat to come, and the water gurgled pleasantly behind him. The soft buzz of bees seeking pollen in the purple lupine made him long to stretch out and take a nap.

He hadn't had much sleep recently. The sleep he'd had was tortured with dreams of Dani being chased by maniacs. Many times each night, he'd crossed the clearing to check on her. He had a favorite spot where he could watch through her window. He'd squint in the darkness until he made out the rise and fall of her breasts under the light coverlet. Watching her like that was sweet agony. He thought he deserved a medal for self-control. Each night as he hunched in the darkness fighting his desires, he promised himself that someday he'd hold her again. It was the only way he kept his sanity.

PAULA WAITED until she was sure her mother would be inside the restaurant with the rest of the ladies. Then she rode her bike to the country club. She wheeled around to the kitchen door and tapped on it.

Enrique, one of the busboys, came to the door. "Hey, there, Paula! What's up?"

"Could you tell Jake to come here?"

"I would, but I think he's off today. Yep, I'm sure I saw Jeff come in."

Paula's ears buzzed. Gone. He was gone. "Where?" she asked.

"I don't know."

She had to talk to somebody. Had to. "Can you get Dani?"

"Well, Paula, you're striking out. Dani's off today, too."

"Together?"

"I don't know. Dani's going to that gem show in Tucson. You know, for that jewelry place, The Silver Coyote."

Paula's mouth dried up like when she ate too many potato chips. She turned and headed back for her bike. She had to find Jake.

"Paula?" Enrique called after her. "Can anyone else help you?"

She didn't take time to answer. She had to find Jake.

As Jake waited for Dani to come out and drive away in the Mustang, the peacocks grew curious and pranced over to check him out. Apparently, they remembered he'd fed them a couple of times. He shooed them away. He wondered if Dani had contacted the landlord about feeding the darn birds over the weekend. She sure hadn't asked him about it. Knowing Dani, she'd asked the landlord. She wouldn't want anything or anyone to suffer. Except him, of course.

At last she walked out onto the porch. She had her purse slung over her arm, a sign she was ready to leave. She gazed around the yard, and the peacocks picked that moment to strut over in his direction again. He held his breath. Heaven knew what would happen if she discovered him hiding in the bushes. She'd probably call the cops and have him arrested for harassing her. That could make matters sticky.

She seemed to stare straight at him, but her expression didn't change, so apparently she couldn't see him. He loved looking at her. She wore a white knit top with a lacy collar that crossed over her breasts, leaving a sexy V in front, and a pastel print skirt that reached to midcalf. A glint of silver shone at her ears and at her wrist, but he wasn't close enough to see the design. Her hair was down, the sides pulled away from her face with some clip affair in the back. He remembered how she smelled, how she felt, and longing shot through him. He kept very still.

A bee buzzed in front of his face and landed on his ear. The peacocks came closer. He held his breath and waited.

Then, for some unknown reason, the male peacock swung his plumage around and headed back across the yard. The two females followed, and Jake slowly released air from his lungs.

Dani got into the Mustang and Jake brushed the bee away. Once she was out of sight, he started walking down the driveway and onto the road. He turned off at the place where he'd parked the truck. He'd wait there a few minutes, to give her time to get into town. He knew Dani was going to The Silver Coyote. He'd managed to overhear her telephone conversation with Evelyn the night before. They were meeting there, picking up the cases of jewelry and taking Evelyn's Jeep to Tucson. He'd also found out the name of the hotel where the gem show would be held.

After checking his watch, Jake climbed into the truck and started the engine. Then he pulled onto the road and nearly ran into Paula speeding along on her bike. He slammed on his brakes.

Paula threw down the bike and ran to his truck. "Jake!"

"What are you doing here?"

"Looking for you."

Jake stifled a groan. Her timing was terrible. He couldn't afford to talk to her now. "Do your parents know you rode over?"

She shook her head, sending her blond hair flying. "But I have to see you, Jake."

He got out of the truck. "Let's put your bike in the back and you can ride with me. I'm going into town. We can talk on the way."

"Can we go to your house?"

"No." He picked up her bike, swung up the back window of the camper and heaved the bike over the tailgate. "I'm worried about Dani. She's going to Tucson with Evelyn, and I don't think it's a good idea." He latched the window.

"Will you stop her?"

"No. I probably couldn't stop her. I'm just planning to tag along, out of sight, to make sure she's okay."

"Do you think she's bad?"

Jake looked at Paula. Her blue eyes were wide with fear. He could only think of one person who would inspire that sort of emotion in Paula. "Who do you mean? Evelyn?"

Paula nodded.

"Do you?"

Paula nodded again.

His gut tightened. "Get in the truck. You can tell me about it on the way." Paula ran around to her side as he swung into the driver's seat and started the engine. "Okay, what happened at Evelyn's that day you left?"

"She said not to tell."

"But that's why you're here, isn't it?" He swerved the truck onto the road toward town. From the corner of his eye, he saw Paula nod. "It's okay. You're safe with me."

"She'll be mad at Dani. Not sell her jewelry."

"Listen, I think you'd better tell me. Don't worry. Dani's going to sell lots of jewelry. What happened with Evelyn, Paula?" He was grateful traffic was light. He gripped the wheel to keep his hands from shaking.

Paula let out a long sigh. "She went for coffee."

"That's what she said. Then what?"

"My nose dripped. I looked for something to wipe with. In a drawer I found a book."

Jake told himself not to panic. It could be any book.

"It had a name on it like Dani's mother."

This is perfectly natural, Jake thought. Evelyn had said she liked Helen Goodwin's books.

"Evelyn came back. She got real mad. Started screaming. I didn't hurt the book, Jake."

"I'm sure you didn't."

"Besides, she didn't take care of it."

His heart hammered in his chest. "What do you mean?"

"She had lines on some pages. Heavy lines."

"Oh, Lord." He pushed his foot to the floor. He couldn't let them leave, after all. It was Evelyn. All this time. He didn't know why, and he wasn't even sure how, but Evelyn planned to harm Dani.

He tore down Tubac Road sending dust billowing. People strolling the street raised their fists at him, but he didn't care. Before they reached The Silver Coyote, he could see the Jeep was already gone. How far a head start did they have? He'd spent more time than he'd meant to because of Paula, but if he hadn't talked to Paula, he wouldn't be so sure of what he had to do. He barreled out onto the frontage road leading to the highway.

He thought of the police, but discarded the idea as soon as it came. Evelyn wasn't dumb. She'd destroyed the book by now and it would be her word against that of Paula's. So far, Evelyn had done nothing wrong, nothing that could be proved. The notes were untraceable. But why was she doing such a thing? Why?

"Jake? Where are they?"

He jumped. He'd forgotten Paula was in the truck with him. And he had no time to take her back.

DANI FELT BETTER with every mile they put between the Jeep and Tubac, although she wished Evelyn would drive a little slower. She kept the speedometer at eighty unless her radar detector beeped and she was forced to slow to the speed limit.

"Do you know how many exhibitors are expected to be at this show?" Dani asked.

"I'm not sure of the number, but there should be some heavy hitters there as far as buyers go. Someone will undoubtedly try to woo you away from me and suggest you move your operation to Phoenix or Tucson."

"But I would never do that, Evelyn."

"If I thought it would further your career, I'd tell you to go ahead, but I believe you'll create more mystique if you stay in Tubac and make the customers come to you. Just watch. In a few months, a year at most, the Tubac Chamber of Commerce will be wanting to give you a plaque for all the tourist business you bring to the town."

Dani laughed. This kind of praise felt good, if a little overstated. "I'd be happy with enough business to quit my restaurant job." *And get away from seeing Jake six days a week.*

"Who knows? Maybe you'll make so many sales this weekend, you'll decide to quit right away. In fact, I predict you won't put on that stupid little outfit ever again."

"That would be nice." Dani thought of Paula, who had once worn "that stupid little outfit," too. Dani had called the Jordans several times, but they wouldn't let her talk to Paula. Dani pleaded with them to let Paula reapply for her old job at the restaurant, but they wouldn't consider it.

Dani had hoped that Paula might rebel and contact her, but she hadn't. Maybe Paula didn't want the job or her friendship anymore. Dani feared she'd been too aggressive with Paula; she didn't want to repeat the mistake.

So without Paula at Canada Verde, and with Jake behind the bar, his eyes tormenting her every time she had to fill a drink order, Dani dreamed of the day she could leave the restaurant. She thought of all the jewelry stacked in the cases behind her seat in the Jeep, and started calculating how much she'd need to sell in order to quit.

JAKE PUSHED the truck as hard as he dared. The damned thing wasn't built for highway chases. "I didn't mean to drag you into this, Paula. I'm sorry."

"I'm not."

"Your parents will have my hide. Anyway, we'll call them the first chance we get so they won't worry too long."

"I don't care. What about Dani? Will she be okay?"

"That's what we're racing down the road dodging speed traps for, to make sure she is."

"Evelyn said Dani would be in trouble if I told."

Jake reached over and patted Paula's knee. "You did the right thing. Dani would have been in big trouble if you *hadn't* told."

"Will Evelyn hurt Dani?"

Jake's stomach churned. "Why? Did she tell you she would?"

"No. But something else was there. In the drawer. Something I don't like."

"What?"

"A gun."

DANI AND EVELYN checked into the Ramada Inn a little after three in the afternoon. A bellhop helped them carry their luggage and the jewelry cases up to the room.

"We'll get settled in and then we'll register for the gem show," Evelyn said, handing the bellhop a generous tip. "The exhibition hall won't open until seven tonight, anyway, so we'll even have time for dinner."

Dani spread the jewelry cases on her bed and opened each one to check that nothing had been damaged during the trip. "I feel like a leech not paying my share. If some of the jewelry sells, I'll chip in for all of this, I promise."

"Don't worry about it." Evelyn peered over her shoulder. "Everything okay?"

"Looks like it."

"How about the peacock earrings? I spoke to a dealer the other day who's just about promised to buy them."

"Really?" Dani turned to her with a smile. "Is that a surprise you've been saving?"

"In a way."

"Well, let me find them and make sure everything's in order." She opened the last two cases and then glanced through the others again. She opened a small metal box containing some emergency tools—glue, tweezers and a teasing rod in case a stone came loose. Maybe the earrings had somehow ended up in there. She picked up the teasing rod and looked under the polishing cloth. Nothing. A hollow place developed in her stomach. "Evelyn, I can't find them."

"Can't find them? I— Oh, no!"

Dani turned. "What?"

"I've done something terrible. I think I left them in Tubac."

Dani felt a wave of panic. She'd worked so hard on those earrings. "But didn't you pack everything in the cases this morning? How could you have left them?"

"I'm too embarrassed to even tell you, but I think I know exactly where they are."

"You *think* you know?" Dani remembered the hours of painstaking, delicate positioning of silver wire, the endless grinding and regrinding of turquoise and abalone shell.

"I'm sure. I'm going back."

"I'll go with you."

"No. Stay here and enjoy the nice room. Order up room service for dinner. I'll be here in time for the opening of the exhibition."

"No. I want to find them as much as you do." Dani started out of the room. "Come on. We're wasting time arguing about it."

"Okay."

As they hurried down the hall and out through the lobby to the parking lot, Dani realized she still held the teasing rod in one hand. She stuck it in her pocket.

"Good thing this Jeep gets good mileage." Evelyn unlocked Dani's side and went around to her own. "Dani, I feel like an idiot."

"As long as we get the earrings back, there's no harm done."

"That's true. Well—on the road again, as they say."

JAKE STOOD in the lobby of the Ramada with the courtesy phone to his ear. No one answered in Evelyn Ross's room. She hadn't registered at the gem show. More than that, no one had a record of her as an exhibitor. The hair on the back of Jake's neck prickled.

With Paula in tow, he walked through the parking lot. No doubt about it; the Jeep wasn't there. They'd checked in, but they weren't at the hotel anymore. Where had they gone? He thought of *The Unvanquished*. The heroine had been in danger once at the river, once in the mountains and once at the mission. He'd read the mission scene again last night. It was by far the scariest. *And Evelyn had taken Dani there the day she'd first proposed going to the gem show.*

Jake grabbed Paula's hand. "Come on. Run. We're going back to the truck."

"Why, Jake?"

"We have to get back to Tubac. Fast."

ON THE WAY BACK Evelyn explained how she'd misplaced the earrings. "The caretaker at Tumacacori wanted to see the earrings, so I took them there. I was sure he couldn't afford something like that for his wife, but I didn't want to insult the man by saying so. To keep the whole thing a secret from his wife, we walked over to the mission. I must have left them there."

"Where?" Dani pictured the hollowed-out interior. The crumbling structure could swallow up something as small as a pair of earrings.

"On the altar, as I remember. After I showed him the earrings, I got involved in giving him back a set of keys I'd borrowed the day before because I'd wanted some moonlight pictures of the mission. He and his wife had had a bingo game or something and couldn't be there to let me in. Anyway, I must have set the earring box down and walked off without it. I'm such a dummy."

"I hope no one picked them up." Dani swallowed a lump of nervousness. Traffic was heavier now than when they'd traveled the road earlier. It was already past five, and the setting sun lit the flanks of the Santa Ritas. Evelyn's carelessness shocked her. She had to face the possibility of losing the earrings. With all the tourists in and out of the mission, someone could easily have taken the earring box. Then she thought of something else. "Won't the place be closed?"

"That won't matter. The caretaker suggested I make a set of keys, since I love going to the mission so much. I guess that's one of the perks I get for being such a generous contributor to the restoration fund."

Dani glanced at her in surprise. "They gave you keys?"

"Don't let it get around. It's a special arrangement between the caretaker and me. He might get in trouble if anyone knew, but he and I have an understanding. He doesn't meet many people who truly appreciate this mission."

Something didn't feel right, Dani thought. She didn't want to go to the spooky old mission, especially not at dusk. But at this point, she didn't seem to have any choice. What had begun as a wonderful weekend, was fast turning into a nightmare. She'd have to play this Evelyn's way or not at all. Without Evelyn there was no shop, no gem show, no way to display her work. "I hope we find the earrings."

"I'm sure we will."

JAKE DECIDED to tell Paula the whole story of Dani's mother, the notes and his job as Dani's bodyguard. If she was going into this with him, she deserved to have all the facts. Paula listened, her eyes getting wider with each revelation.

"Does Dani know you're a bodyguard?"

"She found out Monday night." As he drove, he searched the highway ahead of them for a Jeep.

"How?"

"I told her." He couldn't see the Jeep ahead, but dusk was making visibility more difficult.

"Oh, boy. She was mad, I bet."

"Yes, she was."

"She might get mad at me, too."

"She wouldn't ever be mad at you, Paula."

"I poked her tires."

He gave her a startled glance. "You? Why?"

"It was a full moon, Jake. You had to ride together."

He laughed incredulously. "Good Lord. You're something else. Why hers and not mine?"

"It's better if the man drives. The books say so."

"Wow." He shook his head. "It's hard keeping all this straight."

"So Dani might get mad at me, too."

"I hope she treats your confession better than she treated mine. She never wants to see me again."

Paula chewed on her fingernail. "We have to fix that, Jake."

"I know." But first he had to find her. He prayed he was wrong about this. Maybe Evelyn and Dani went out for a bite to eat away from the hotel. But his instincts screamed at him that wasn't what they'd done. They were on their way to Tumacacori.

"Do you have a gun?"

"Yes."

"Now?"

"In the glove compartment."

Paula chewed her fingernail some more. "I don't like guns."

"Neither do I. But—dammit, why is traffic backing up?" Reluctantly, Jake put his foot on the brake.

"What in the hell is going on?" Both lanes had slowed to a crawl.

Panic twisted through his muscles, making his stomach clench and his fingers tighten on the wheel. Finally, he could make out an overturned utility trailer up ahead, with the contents of someone's household strewn all over the road. If he stayed behind the slow-moving traffic edging past the mess, he'd add another ten minutes to the trip. He couldn't afford another ten minutes. If he'd guessed right, ten minutes could end Dani's chances.

CHAPTER TWENTY-ONE

THE MUSEUM WAS indeed closed when Evelyn drove the Jeep into the narrow parking lot in front of the mission grounds. "Good thing I have my keys," she said as they got out of the Jeep. "Here, you hold the flashlight."

Dani glanced across the street. The little restaurant where they'd eaten lunch was closed and dark. "Isn't that place over there open for dinner?"

"Nope, just breakfast and lunch. You hungry?"

Dani wasn't hungry, but she was uneasy. A restaurant full of people across the street from the deserted mission would have made her feel a lot better. "No, I'm not really hungry," she said. "Let's go find the earrings."

"I'm sure they're still right where I left them." Evelyn led the way through the darkened museum and unlocked the door to the outside. Dani flicked on the flashlight as they walked down the path to the mission. In the gathering darkness, it loomed menacingly in front of them. Dani had been spooked being there in daylight. This was not going to be fun. But she wanted the earrings back.

"You have the flashlight. You go first," Evelyn said.

Dani stepped into the chilly interior. She swept the floor with the shaft of light and walked forward. "You think you put the box on the altar?"

"That's right. Do you see it yet?" Evelyn's voice echoed in the darkness.

Something fluttered and whisked past Dani's ear. Bats. Then, from outside the church came an eerie cry. "That sounded like a peacock."

"Probably was. I understand the caretaker just got a couple of them. They do so well in this area."

Dani shivered and wished she'd brought a jacket. She moved the flashlight beam over the altar at the end of the church but could see no small box. She mounted the steps to get a closer look. "I don't see anything, Evelyn. I hope to heaven the caretaker picked them up."

"I doubt that." Her voice resonated with quiet excitement.

Startled, Dani turned, swinging the flashlight in Evelyn's direction. Evelyn stood three feet away. The peacock earrings dangled from her earlobes. And she held a gun.

Dani gasped.

"You never guessed, did you?"

The flashlight beam wiggled as Dani's hands shook. Cold sweat trickled from her armpits. Her mouth tasted rusty and dry.

"I'll take that flashlight. And don't try to throw it. I'll shoot you down right there if you do."

Dani held out the flashlight. Evelyn took it, and for a moment it shone upward, transforming her face into a skull-like mask. Then Evelyn directed the flashlight at Dani's eyes, nearly blinding her. Dani raised her arm to block out some of the light.

"You really didn't guess, did you?" came the voice from behind the glare of light. "You believed all that nonsense about leaving the earrings here by mistake. They've been in my pocket all the time. And no caretaker worth his salt would encourage someone to make an extra set of keys. The poor man has no idea I did that.''

"You…" Dani was hoarse. "You wrote the notes."

"Of course. And then befriended your mother. She was so vulnerable right after you left. She needed someone to talk to, so I listened, and found out where you were. The rest was child's play, really.''

Dani's heart raced and she felt sick to her stomach. "But why?"

Evelyn's cackle ricocheted off the crumbling walls. "I told you we'd be famous, didn't I? I intend to keep my word. The famous murderer and her victim.''

Light-headedness nearly claimed her, but she fought it. Evelyn would kill her. Not kidnap or hold for ransom. Kill her. "You *want* people to know?"

"Eventually. I'll be hiding out in Mexico by the time they discover your body, but the police will know I did it soon enough and arrange to extradite me. I just need time to finish my manuscript and send it to a publisher. True crime, as told by the criminal. What an angle!''

"You're insane."

"Good for you!" She praised Dani as if she were a star pupil. "That's my defense. And I expect to get off, but in the meantime, what publisher would turn down an account of this bizarre plot to murder a famous writer's daughter? In the very spot where Helen Goodwin almost did in the heroine of her bestseller?''

Dani struggled to draw a breath. "I can't believe this."

"You don't really understand, because you're not a writer, but I knew Helen Goodwin when she was nothing." Evelyn's voice rasped in the darkness. "She's no more talented than I am, but she got the breaks and I didn't."

Dani tried to think. Evelyn wanted to be published. *That was all.* It would be funny, except that Evelyn was willing to kill to get there. "Maybe I could help. The right agent—"

"It's too late for that. I'm tired of waiting. I want a shortcut to immortality. I deserve it. I told your mother years ago that Tubac would be a good setting for a book. She doesn't remember that it was me, of course. But she took my idea! She made all that money, and now *The Unvanquished* is going to be a movie. All that with my idea! While I collect rejection slips. But not anymore. They won't reject this story."

"You can't do this. I'll scream. The caretaker and his wife will hear me."

"Go ahead. By the way, I appreciate your solving that problem for me. When I heard your peacock cry, I knew the mission grounds needed a couple of them, to confuse anyone who might hear a woman scream some night. I made a donation of two birds."

There had to be a way out. "Someone will hear the gun."

"People don't respond to gunshots out here, where nearly everyone has some sort of shotgun or rifle. They'll think it's someone scaring off a coyote. Besides, I hadn't planned to use a gun unless absolutely necessary. It's not dramatic enough." Evelyn tucked the flashlight under her gun arm and reached in her shoulder bag for a long, wicked-looking knife. "This will be the murder weapon."

Seeing the knife brought Dani out of her frozen state. The gun was almost an impersonal method, but not that knife. No one was going to stab her. No one. Obviously talk wouldn't get her out of this. She'd have to distract Evelyn somehow without getting herself shot or stabbed. She evaluated her resources. She was younger than Evelyn and probably stronger, and she had the will to survive.

"Climb up and stretch out on the altar, Dani."

"What?"

"For drama. It'll make a good ending to the book. A sacrifice to the goddess of art."

Chilling as the idea was, Dani recognized that this might be a chance for her to regroup. She turned, and as she did, the teasing rod shifted in her skirt pocket. It was about the size of a letter opener, with a wooden handle and a metal shaft something like an icepick. It wasn't much against a gun, but it might be a match for a knife.

"Go on, get up there."

The adobe altar had been frosted with a gritty plaster top that scraped against her hands and knees as she climbed onto it.

"Lie down on your back."

She did. While arranging herself, she slipped her right hand into her pocket and grasped the handle of the teasing rod. Then she lay with her heart pounding as she stared up into the shadowed dome above her.

"That's good." Keeping the gun trained on Dani, Evelyn deposited her knife and purse on the floor. "Now for some atmosphere." She took four votive candles from her purse and set them along the base of the altar. Tucking the flashlight under one arm, she flicked a cigarette lighter over each one. The flames cast a surprising amount of light and created dancing shadows on the walls and ceilings.

Dani grew clammy with sweat and she shuddered with the urge to leap from the altar and run. But then Evelyn would shoot her. Her only chance was to wait until Evelyn came close enough, and then strike with the teasing rod.

"Now then, Dani, any last words?" Still pointing the gun at Dani, Evelyn picked up the knife and approached the altar. "I'll be glad to put them in the book."

"Yes." Her heart was pounding with rage now more than fear. How dare Evelyn do this! Dani had lived with a writer. She knew Evelyn's worst nightmare. "I hope your book is rejected by every publishing house in New York. I hope as you rot in prison, you keep getting rejections, until you run out of places to send it."

"You bitch!" Evelyn dropped the gun and lunged at her with the knife.

Dani's reflexes were faster. She stabbed at Evelyn's descending hand with the teasing rod and felt the tip sink into the woman's wrist. Blood spurted from the wound and the knife clattered to the floor. Dani leaped from the altar but Evelyn had retrieved the gun.

She held her bloody wrist and pointed the gun at Dani. "So this won't be quite as poetic a way to die, but so what?"

Jake's voice boomed into the church from the entrance. "Evelyn! Drop it!"

Evelyn whirled and shot into the shadows at the entrance, and Dani lunged at her. Evelyn was stronger than Dani imagined. She got an arm around Dani's throat and pointed the gun at her temple. "Okay, Jake! Any false move and your lover's dead."

JAKE WAS HALFWAY up the aisle leading to the altar when Dani leaped to his defense. He couldn't shoot for fear of hitting her, and before he could reach the steps, Evelyn had the gun to Dani's head. He'd told Paula to call the sheriff from the visitors' center and then stay in the truck until the patrol cars arrived.

"Back off, Jake," Evelyn ordered.

He moved back a few steps. He worked on slowing his racing pulse, maintaining his balance. He'd get Dani out of here alive. Somehow.

"Put the gun on the floor."

He did. He couldn't look in Dani's eyes or he'd go crazy. He concentrated on Evelyn.

"Kick it toward me, nice and easy."

He slid the gun forward. "You won't get away with this. Everyone will find out that you're the one who wrote the notes."

"That's just fine. As Dani could tell you if I didn't have my arm tight against her throat, I planned for everyone to know. I'll be famous, Jake. And so will the book I'm writing about this."

A chill passed over him. If all Evelyn wanted was fame, she couldn't lose, no matter what happened. That made her very dangerous.

He could tell her he'd called the police, but she still wouldn't care. She might shoot Dani sooner if she knew that. "Maybe we could make a deal." His voice echoed in the cavernous church. "So far, I'm the only one who's figured out your scheme. You let Dani go, and I let you go. I have some connections in L.A. Turn your book into a screenplay and I'll swing a movie deal for you."

"You must think I'm stupid, Jake. I know how tough it is to make it in Hollywood. I want something surefire. This is it."

"I tell you, I could make you a deal." Jake bargained for time while he tried to figure a way out of this. The candles at the foot of the altar cast giant shadows on the walls. Whenever Evelyn moved, the peacock earrings she wore flashed. If he had his gun, he might be able to aim right at that spot. But his gun was three yards in front of him, on the ground.

He continued his monologue. "I know some big movie producers. Don't forget I'm a professional bodyguard."

Evelyn laughed. "Have you ever lost a client, Jake? Or will this be a first?"

Dani. He clamped down on the rush of emotion. Emotion would only slow his reaction time. He had to keep Evelyn talking.

"You were the customer who ratted on Paula at the restaurant, weren't you?"

"Had to. She was a meddlesome little thing. Couldn't take chances she'd tell what she knew. Incidentally, I see you brought her along."

Jake heard the footsteps behind him. "Paula! Get back in the truck."

Paula's voice was small but determined. "No way, José."

"Let her stay, Jake. The poor girl leads a sheltered life."

Jake gritted his teeth. "Out, Paula. Now."

Instead, she came up behind him and touched the small of his back.

"I mean it, Paula. Go."

She shoved against him again, and he realized she had something hard in her hand. It felt like... "You're pretty smart, Evelyn," Jake said, dropping his right hand slowly to his side.

"Why, thank you, Jake."

He uncurled his fingers and Paula gently placed the rock in his hand. "You had us all fooled."

"Well, Jake, this conversation has been fascinating, but I want you and Paula to leave now. Dani and I have business to transact. You can close the door on your way out."

"I don't feel like leaving."

"Then I guess you can stay here while I shoot her. Either way."

Jake's fingers closed over the rock. It wasn't very big, not even as large as a baseball. He was counting on the element of surprise. And what used to be a golden arm.

"Maybe I'll do this like in the movies. On the count of three. Does that sound dramatic, Jake?"

"If that's the way you want it." He focused on the gleam of the peacock earring.

"One."

Jake brought his arm back.

"Two."

The rock sailed through the shadows.

"Thr—"

In the pocket. Her cry as she went down sounded like... the cry of a peacock.

DANI SAT with Paula in Jake's truck while Jake stood outside with Evelyn. She'd come to with the help of some cold water from a drinking fountain, and he'd tied her up with rope he had in his camper. He continued to train his gun on her, for which Dani was grateful.

Dani kept her gaze on Jake. Every once in a while he rotated his shoulder and grimaced. "He's hurt his shoulder again," she murmured.

"He pitched hard," Paula said.

"Yes."

"He drove wild, too. Passed a bunch of cars. On the dirt."

Dani shivered. "And if he hadn't...oh, Paula." She turned in the seat and the two women put their arms around each other and held on tight until they both stopped shaking. Three patrol cars from the Santa Cruz County Sheriff's Department arrived, sirens and lights going. They took charge of Evelyn and hustled her into the back of one of the cars. Then they talked to Jake for a moment. He nodded and walked back to the truck.

"We have to follow them to the station in Nogales," he said as he climbed into the cab. "They'll need signed statements from all of us."

Dani was sitting in the middle. She turned to Paula. "Are you okay with that?"

Paula nodded.

Jake glanced across at Paula. "Of course she's okay. You can handle anything, can't you, Paula?"

Paula beamed at him. "Damn straight."

JAKE CALLED Paula's parents from the station, and they arrived in record time. Judging from the way Ed Jordan clamped down on his pipe as Jake told them what had happened, he longed to punch Jake in the nose. Dani was glad they were in a police station and Ed couldn't act on his impulses.

Seemingly impervious to Ed's rage, Jake put his arm around Paula. "The bottom line is, Paula's proved beyond a shadow of a doubt that she's capable of running her own pinstriping business."

Dani jumped to support his stand. "You can't keep her locked up in that house. She needs so much more in her life."

Ed glared at them without speaking.

Paula gazed at him, and finally eased herself out from under Jake's protective arm. When she spoke, her tone held a new maturity. "I want a business, Dad. I want Jake and Dani to help me. But I can do most of it myself."

Jake glanced at Dani in silent triumph. She smiled back. This was the Paula they'd been looking for.

Ed's jaw went slack and he almost dropped his pipe.

Paula continued to gaze at him steadily. "I can do it," she said again.

"But, baby—"

"I'm not a baby."

Ed stared at her. Then he glanced at Jake and Dani. "We'll talk about it," he said, all belligerence gone from his expression.

Paula nodded. "Damn straight."

Dani bit her lip to keep from laughing.

Ed shook his head in wonder. "I think…maybe it's time for everybody to go home and get some rest."

"Good idea," Jake said. He stuck out his hand. "Thanks, Jordan."

"Yeah." Ed still seemed dazed as he walked away with his wife and Paula. At the door of the station, Paula turned and gave Dani and Jake a thumbs-up sign.

When the Jordans had left, Jake turned to Dani. "Paula was the one who slashed your tires that night, to force us to ride home together."

Dani stared at him. "Really?"

"Really."

"I'm glad you didn't tell *that* to the Jordans."

"Are you glad she slashed the tires?" He was watching her closely.

She glanced away from the intensity in his gaze. He'd betrayed her, then saved her life. She owed him everything, yet he'd willfully deceived her. "I'm not ready for that question, Jake."

He sighed. "Then let's go home."

As they started down the nearly deserted highway for Tubac, the silence was full of things unsaid. Finally, she could stand the tension no longer. "You saved my life. I'm grateful for that."

"How polite of you."

"Dammit, Jake! What do you expect from me?"

"How about some understanding for my position? How about something like 'Gosh, Jake, there really was someone after me. I guess it's a good thing my mother hired you, after all.' How about that?"

"Maybe it was a good thing, but you still lied to me, Jake."

"No, I didn't. And I sure as hell could have. I didn't tell you everything, but I didn't make up lies, either."

Her insides twisted. "Doesn't it come to the same thing? You concealed the truth. You made love to me under false pretenses."

"Wrong. I made love to you because I fell in love. Nothing false about that. I also had an obligation not to tell you the complete truth. If you want to crucify me for that, I can't stop you."

Dani stared out the window at the dark slopes of hills rolling toward the mountains dimly outlined in the moonlight. She'd been manipulated by her mother and by Jake. The bitterest part to swallow was the realization that if they hadn't stepped in to protect her, she might be dead. It was hard to sort out. Very hard. "I don't know what I want," she said quietly.

Jake didn't respond. Finally, when he did, his voice was gravelly from strain and fatigue. "Too bad, Dani."

CHAPTER TWENTY-TWO

HELEN GOODWIN ARRIVED in town the following day. When Dani called her that night, she'd announced she was coming, and Dani hadn't objected. Much as she hated to admit it, she wanted to see her mother. Besides, it made the sheriff happy; he could take Helen's statement in person.

Dani still had the weekend off, so she was able to pick her mother up at the Tucson airport, retrieve her cases of jewelry from the Ramada Inn and drive Helen down to Nogales to give her statement. After they were finished there, Helen wanted to see The Silver Coyote.

As Dani unlocked the door, she wondered if Evelyn's former presence there would bother her. After an initial moment of adjustment, it didn't. She enjoyed showing her mother the worktable in the back and the striking decor of the shop with its turquoise walls and the shelves Paula had pinstriped. Sun poured in through the windows as if to clean out any shadows Evelyn had left there.

Dani stood in the doorway to the back room and looked out at the main area of the shop. The craft items were still on the shelves, and only the display cases were empty because Dani's jewelry had been packed into the portable cases for the gem show. Dani thought of all that had happened since she'd left the shop yesterday afternoon. "Mom, do you think Evelyn will actually get her book published, just because of what she did?"

"You never know, but I doubt it." Helen moved around the shop touching the shelves and the display cases. "Her grand plan failed, and I don't think anyone's interested in that sort of botched attempt." She faced Dani. "But I can't believe how stupid I was, to send her down here. I'll never forgive myself for that."

Dani walked over and took her mother by the shoulders. "It was perfectly understandable. You were lonely and scared. She was clever. Please don't blame yourself."

Her mother's smile was tremulous. "I'll work on it." She sighed and glanced around the shop. "I like it. Evelyn is a horrible person, but she's smart. This is a good location."

"Yes." Dani took her hands from her mother's shoulders and turned to survey the place where she'd hoped to gain fame and fortune. "Jake said the irony was we could have been successful."

"Jake. I need to talk with him."

Dani pretended to study a section of Paula's work on the shelves. "Okay. I . . . didn't tell him you were coming."

"You haven't talked with him since you called me?"

"Well, no, actually. You see—"

"Dani! Are you aware the man's head over heels in love with you?"

Dani's stomach started fluttering. "I—"

"And you're interested in him, too. I could tell from the careful way you didn't mention him when you first moved down here. The man saved your life, and you haven't talked to him since last night?''

The fluttering grew worse. "It's complicated. I mean, when I discovered you'd hired him, that the two of you were treating me like some child..."

"I didn't know what else to do, Dani. You wouldn't listen when I said you were in danger."

Dani looked away. "I know. And I was in danger. But to have the two of you in league against me was...demeaning. Jake should have told me sooner what was going on."

"You're probably right."

Dani glanced at her mother in surprise. "I am?"

"Yes. He should have ignored my instructions. I pleaded with him not to reveal his identity unless absolutely necessary. I said his doing so could destroy your relationship with me. I told him you were all I had left in the world, and I couldn't bear it if you turned your back on me. He honored that obligation for far too long. Now I see how important the relationship he was building with you was."

Dani listened with her mouth open. "I thought you'd do anything to hold on to me."

Helen smiled gently. "I thought so, too. But believe it or not, you made your point by moving away. We do each need our own lives...although I may be a bit hesitant about befriending widow ladies after this."

"Oh, Mom!" Dani ran over and hugged her.

Helen hugged back. "Let me do one last thing. Let me buy this shop for you and give you some operating capital for a few months."

"Oh, no." Dani released her and stepped back. "I don't think so." Her independent streak resurfaced immediately.

"What will you do, instead?"

Dani shrugged. "Work at the restaurant, keep looking for places to sell my jewelry. Someday I'd like my own shop, but I'll earn it."

"You'll earn it this way, too. You can pay me back eventually, if that would make you feel better. Dani, you've always been stubborn, and my dependence on you has made you worse."

"Thanks a lot."

"There are some things only a mother will tell you. And here's another argument. Didn't you say your friend Paula will be starting a pinstriping business? What if you had her headquartered here?"

Dani had to admit the location would be perfect for Paula. As it was, Paula would have to work under the eye of Madge and Ed. Despite their behavior the night before, Dani didn't trust them not to backslide.

"And think about this," Helen continued. "When I first started writing, how did I support myself?"

"Well, um, I guess Dad supported you."

"Exactly. He was my angel. Most creative people need one. Let me be yours."

Dani gazed at her mother. The sparkle was back in Helen's eyes and her shoulders were straighter. She no longer looked defeated. "Let me think about it," Dani said.

"That's a start. And now let's go see Jake."

THEY FOUND HIM down the slope of the riverbank with a fishing pole. He was sprawled on a grassy ledge, his shirt unbuttoned, his elbows supporting him while he kept an eye on his pole with half-closed eyes. The sun burnished the hair on his chest to a rich auburn. He hadn't shaved, and the bristle of his beard made him look careless and sensual, exactly the way he'd looked the morning after they'd made love all night.

Dani stayed at the top of the bank, but Helen scrambled down to Jake. He stuck the pole securely into the ground before rising to shake Helen's hand.

She ignored his hand and hugged him. "Words aren't enough," she said, stepping back with a smile. "And money damn sure isn't enough. You're my hero, Jake."

Dani was amazed that Jake seemed to lose his cool. He all but shuffled his feet in his desire to shake off the praise. "You hired me to do a job," he said.

"Ah, but you went beyond that, didn't you?"

Jake glanced up the bank at Dani. He looked more uncomfortable still. "Helen, about that—"

"Never mind, never mind. Try to give Dani some time, and I think she'll come around. She's as stubborn as her father was, but I have a feeling you have a stubborn streak, too." Helen glanced at her watch. "Well, Dani, we have to leave for the airport if I'm going to catch my plane."

"You're not staying?" Dani hadn't thought to ask her mother when the return flight was. She discovered to her chagrin that she was disappointed Helen was flying out again so soon.

"Oh, I'll be back in a few weeks. They're filming the movie here, you know, and I've been asked to hang around and give advice." Her eyes twinkled. "I think I can do that, don't you?"

"But, Mom, I thought we'd at least have dinner. And I have a double bed. You can sleep there, and leave tomorrow, or maybe even the next day."

"Goodness, Dani, do you actually *want* me to stay with you?"

"Yes. Yes, I do. I've missed you."

Helen chuckled. "Music to my ears. And that's just the time to leave. Besides, I'll bet you can put that double bed to better use than having your *mother* sleep in it with you."

Dani flushed and glanced away from the two of them, her mother and Jake, standing there as if allied against her. Well, they had been before, hadn't they?

Helen looked at her daughter and sighed. "Oh, Jake, I've said the wrong thing once again. I'll just count on you to repair the damage."

"I'll walk you to the car." He climbed the slope, assisting Helen with a hand at her elbow.

As they reached the top of the bank, Dani glanced at him. "I didn't know you fished," she said, almost in an accusatory way, as if he should have told her that about himself, too.

"Didn't have the time before. Didn't have time to do a lot of things I like to do." His gaze was steady.

Dani had a flash of a different kind of Jake than the person she'd known—someone who coached baseball and took his kids fishing, someone who enjoyed walking lazily along a dirt road to admire the wildflowers, someone who liked to make love after a morning of reading the Sunday paper.

Helen touched Dani's arm. "The sooner we leave, the sooner you can get back."

Dani flushed but kept her gaze locked with Jake's. She wanted to come back. She wanted...this man. "Will you...will you be here? I think we need to talk."

Helen chuckled and shook her head. "Talk. I don't know what this younger generation has come to."

"I'll be here."

DANI LONGED for Evelyn's radar detector on the return trip to Tubac. By the time she pulled into the driveway leading to the two houses, the sun hung low on the horizon, gilding the emerging leaves of the mesquite tree and bathing the clearing in a golden light. Jake stood there scattering seed for the peacocks. He turned as she pulled into her parking spot. His hand stilled.

She got out of the car. What could she say to him? They'd hurt each other so much in the past few days. Was there anything left to build on? She wouldn't insult him or herself by suggesting they start over. There was really no such thing. If they wanted a shot at happiness, they would have to acknowledge the good and bad they'd created up to this moment.

She walked toward him. He had on a different shirt, and it was buttoned. He'd shaved, too. He watched her with an intensity that made her tremble. She sensed that she had to say exactly the right thing, or they'd be at each other's throats again, unraveling an argument that had no end.

She stopped when they were a yard or so apart. His apparent stillness was belied by his rapid breathing. Her heart beat faster. She could ruin this.

And then she looked into his eyes. They glowed with an inner fire that reached out to her, reminding her of the strength of his arms, the gentleness and the hunger of his kiss, the wonder of lying with him in the moonlight. Suddenly, everything was simple. She couldn't live without him.

"I love you," she whispered.

He groaned, and she hurled herself into his arms. Words were lost in a breathless exchange of kisses. And then he cradled her head for a deep, probing kiss that weakened her limbs and stirred the molten fire within her. As she strained against him in mindless abandon, the peacock cried.

The sound made Dani shiver as she remembered the last time she'd heard it.

Jake lifted his head and gazed down at her. "Don't worry." His lips curved in a soft smile. "It sounds like a call for help, but it's really a call for love."

She smiled back. "Are you sure?"

His lips hovered close to hers once more. "Trust me."

"Forever," she murmured, and gave herself up to his kiss.